The Profiler's Mask

Margaret Savoy

Book Cover Design by: @ivalivanillustrates

ISBN: 979-8-9882631-2-8 (Paperback)
ISBN: 979-8-9882631-3-5 (ebook)

Your courage, strength, and nature
bring out the best in me.
I will follow you into hell and
bring you back into the light every time.
Ben Walker to Zelda Alexander

CHAPTER ONE

The Poker World Series

A bead of sweat dripped down from my opponent's temple. His confidence was shaken while mine was soaring. A quick tug to his collar meant he had a good hand but was not confident enough to beat me. A blink lasted a moment too long. My opponent was uncomfortable fighting the impression of defeat I had planted. I had him.

My favorite part of the seductive dance of game theory, probability, and profiling is the moments before my prey realizes I am about to finish them. A little luck floated my way this tournament, not that I would ever admit the phenomenon. Many of the best players in the event had already been eliminated in previous rounds.

Hundreds of entrants began event #2 two days prior. The final round contained eight players. Snatching their confidence was easy. Pouncing opportunities shook their self-belief while I displayed the ultimate discipline hand after hand with unwavering stoic patience. My training at Quantico had only improved my inherent skills.

Self-assured and goal-driven, my brain worked more cognitively than emotionally. My personality embraced self-efficacy. Even at the Poker World Series, my opponents were so predictable. Tics and tells became readable antecedents I read like a ticker tape, constantly giving me information about their cards. Body and eye movements were a roadmap to deception. No one could bluff in my presence.

Sneaking a glance toward Rowan, I knew the decision was upon me. Win and receive the coveted World Series Poker Bracelet and a huge payout, or lose and escape the wrath of the Italian mob. Rowan nodded to me as if he knew I would make the correct decision. I was not in Vegas to make good decisions. I was here to self-destruct.

The last woman standing in Event #2: $25,000 High Roller Six-Handed No-limit Hold'em, how could I refuse?

"All bets in." The dealer called.

"I raise all." Steeling my eyes at my opponent, daring him to call. He had a good hand, but not as good as mine.

"I call." My opponent rubbed his knuckles. Subconsciously, he knew he had lost. The brain has a way of protecting us against the degrading emotions of failure.

"Ma'am?"

"Flush Queen-eight-diamonds."

"Sir?"

A beat before he spoke, his eyes met mine in acceptance of his loss. "Full house-Queens-eights."

"The lady wins." I nodded to my opponent. As magnanimously as a predator would to their prey. This was a competition, not a tea party.

My chip count was considerable, earning me a place at the champions' table in the final event. The goal for this tournament had been reached. Well, one of them. Rowan had left during my applause, but my appointed guard was ever-present. When I arrived at the Horseshoe Casino several days ago, Rowan placed a tail on me. This was not my first Vegas trip. In the past three years, this was my tenth. Rowan counted my trips in lost revenue.

Rowan was one of the bosses of the gambling underworld in Vegas. He was also chairman of the Nevada Gaming Commission. A government agency appointed by the governor. A conflict of interest, in my view, as owner of one of the most prestigious casinos in Las Vegas. In this century, casinos were properly legitimized by being bought out by corporations. Now, the mob ran the corporations. Illegal gambling and racketeering were alive and well on the Vegas strip.

My goal had not been to subdue the mafia. My goal had been to possess the most coveted non-monetary prize a poker player can win and a symbol of accomplishment and respect in the gaming world. The presentation of the WSOP bracelet for Event #2 was a big deal because it was a High Roller event. Only those with considerable experience and bankroll could enter. Plus, only 5% of the entrants in the World Series of Poker were women. I was named the last woman standing as well as the winner and earned a space at the final table of the concluding event.

Traditionally, Rowan, as the owner of the Horseshoe and representative from the Gaming Commission, would have presented me with the prize. Even mafia bosses sulked. His nephew Luca stood sentry to the winners' platform, waiting impatiently for me. Luca was preverbally tall, dark, and handsome with a powerfully cut physique made for sin. The stern look of disdain and contempt only magnified his prince of darkness vibe. The confines of a well-tailored black suit contained his fitness and power. Luca stared at me as I approached. A mixture of malice and desire flitted over his harsh Italian features.

"You owe us body and blood." Luca spat. I ignored him, taking my place. I was not afraid of Luca. With any beast, you have to know how to tame them. I had played with Luca before.

A master of ceremonies monologued information that bored me. Luca's intense stare continued close to me. He smelled of black pepper, cedar, and amber wood. His musky scent captured my full attention. We had to be told twice what to do. The tension between us unnerved those in attendance, and onlookers gave us a wide radius. Luca took the bracelet from his breast pocket and ceremoniously attached it to my wrist. His fingers lingered, pressing into my skin, taking my pulse. Every move Luca made was methodical and sexy.

The artistic piece of jewelry had about three thousand gemstones in the elaborate design. The piece contained over two thousand diamonds, both white and black. One hundred blood red rubies added to the total carat weight in gems close to sixty. The gold bracelet had a diamond backdrop and the four card suit motifs, one in each corner. The front plate gold lettering spelled out WSOP world champion and was flanked by similarly gem-encrusted links on either side that repeated the suits motif. A removable, solid-gold poker chip was delicately hidden. The bracelet this year was stunning.

Luca leaned into my ear, where I was expecting a word of congratulations, "I will take your body. Rowan will have your blood." His threat made me smile. "We expect payment for your insolence."

"Insolence? You just bet on the wrong man." I sneered back. We continued to lock eyes, continuing to make everyone else uncomfortable. My fingers roamed the bracelet's surface, ensuring it was real. A silent prayer was sent to my father as our dream had come to fruition.

Luca leaned in further, pulling me from my benediction. I licked the side of his neck while he was close enough to my face. His eyes went black.

"You are expected at the House Party tonight. Don't be late." Luca growled and sped away. *What a baby.*

When I returned to my room, a large gold box draped in a red velvet bow was on my bed. Dress, heels, lingerie, and a Macallan Reflection single malt whiskey bottle. *Classy.* The sleeveless dress was royal blue with intricate beading and sequins on the tight bodice. A sharp v-neck line showed my lingerie underneath. The dress was couture-well-made and extremely sexy. Matching Manolo Blahnik shoes completed the exquisite look.

Unknowingly, Luca was giving me additional power to defend against his bullying. I was ready for battle and began toasting my success.

* * *

Four days earlier....

"The reservation is under Alexander, Zelda Alexander. I'll be here for at least a week."

"Welcome to the Horseshoe Las Vegas. Yes, here it is, Ms. Alexander. You'll be with us for seven days in one room, king bed, strip view, and nonsmoking. Are you here for the World Series?"

"In part." The rooms at the Horseshoe evoked nostalgia and belonging in me. I had come here with my father. It was a time when we had each other all to ourselves, talking, playing poker, and making great memories. My escape from the real world would always lead me back here.

"Here are your room cards. You'll need them to access the elevator as well. Good luck. Let me know if you need anything."

The hotel clerk's face told me my name had already been flagged. I expected a visit from Rowan or one of his goons soon. Tomorrow, I will register for the tournament. Tonight, I needed to get out some angst.

After a quick shower and changing clothes, I headed to the Lobby Bar to wait for my companion. Rowan was predictable. He would never let me wonder his casino on my own. Feeling amicable, I would have my assigned stalker join in my adventure tonight rather than ditch him.

My tail was handsome, fit, and new since he was ridiculously easy to identify. I always liked to play with my prey, but this guy was no challenge. "Please send a Manhattan over to the handsome man at the end of the bar. Tell him I saved him a seat." The bartender obliged.

"Ms. Alexander." Rowan's goon was not what I expected.

"Mr...?" His surfer boy's good looks were emphasized by a good black suit and a crisp maroon shirt that opened enough to see his hairless, taunt chest.

"Chase Eklind." He bowed rather than shake my hand. I liked the respect.

"Ah, Swedish. What are you doing working for the Italian mob?"

"Rowan said I wouldn't last a night trailing you. I think they are even betting on me." Shame replaced sadness as he spoke.

"I'll behave tonight. Tomorrow, not so much." I took pity but was not sugarcoating my goal here. "Your job will be easier as companions rather than a handicapped stalker.

"Why am I tailing you?" He looked generally at a loss as his eyes trailed up and down my body.

"What did Rowan say about the job?" I sipped my drink as nonchalant curiosity made him divulge information effortlessly.

"Protection. From others but mostly from yourself. Information. He wants to know where you are and what you are doing at all times. Rowan thinks you are here to ruin his series. You don't seem that threatening." Ah, Chase will be fun. Underestimating a woman always is.

"Rowan and I had a few run-ins the past few years," I said modestly. Chase and I had a couple more drinks. He was a simple man with a pretty face. The mob offered him the hope of a better life. It's too bad that his only skill set is his complicity and prowess with women. I took advantage of both skills in my room for the rest of the night.

My specialty was in high-stakes poker. I had played enough over the years to have an impressive bankroll. I keep my gaming money completely separate from my regular life. Trained at Quantico in the FBI Behavior Science Unit, profiling is my interest and career. I rely on classic psychology and my ability to read others based on observations, patterns, and evidence. I know what you are thinking, why you are thinking it, and how you will react to varying situations. I can read about your current divorce, the disappointing morning coffee, or the embezzlement of company funds, all while observing your current state. A running catalog of behavioral characteristics rotates like a carousel constantly in my head.

The FBI assumed that I would use my skills to track killers or undermine terrorist organizations. The one-dimensional application of the skill set was not attractive for my career. The motives and modus operandi of serial killers became rote. The patterns were all the same, and I got bored. My brain needed challenges. I was a systems thinker. I would instead apply the profiling skill set to a major corporation by flushing out weaknesses and inefficiency to increase productivity, management, and profitability. I like to find the flaws in a multidimensional system and expose the weak or immoral. A game I always win.

My added knowledge of game theory and statistics added another facet to my success at the casino. Poker is as much of an art as game theory is mathematical. The pragmatic strategy interacts with the rational parts of the play and independent behavior. My only issue is when irrationality enters the formula, which is uncommon. Each player has a series of decisions to make based on a set number of cards in a deck. Where most players play the odds, I consider many variables to make an informed decision.

My brain naturally maps patterns and outcomes based on a mixture of information. The balance of probability, norms, and human behavior dictates that there is no such thing as chance or coincidence. Asymmetry adds a layer of individualization from each player, adding to the variables to keep track of. You employ different strategies against each player at the table. I am never bored.

My approach is to engage the players' common knowledge and understanding. When conflict arises, tells and mannerisms are magnified and easily discovered. My play is almost unexploitable by my opponents. My poker face is severe. I love the constant readjustment of my analysis based on the new information as each hand is played. Each game is unique, like a battle to win.

The next night, I went to the registration table with my companion in tow. The Poker World Series was held at the Horseshoe most years, probably due to Rowan's influence. I liked the feeling of the home-court advantage.

"Zelda Alexander preregistering for Event #2: $25,000 High Roller Six-Handed No-limit Hold'em." The woman behind the table thought I was joking at my request. *Commoners.*

"Ah, Ms. Alexander. You look well." Rowan emerged from the shadows behind the registration desk.

"Rowan. Thank you for my companion. He is a delicious distraction." I licked my lips to annoy him.

"You have cash?" Rowan hated being bested. "$10,000 series entry fee and $25,000 for the event."

He knew my bankroll was significant. He was throwing down a challenge. "Fine. I'll be back tonight."

"Better make it before registration closes." Rowan taunted.

"It's open twenty-four hours…"

"Not for you." *Fucker.*

"Come on, Chase. We have some houses to beat. Let's go to the Cromwell." Chase followed after me like the submissive I already trained him to be.

We were back several hours later. "Zelda Alexander preregistering, again, for Event #2: $25,000 High Roller Six-Handed No-limit Hold'em." Rowan was waiting for me. "I have cash per your request."

"Luca said you left Cromwell with 100k." I rolled my eyes but was annoyed I didn't see my additional tail. Rowan was more clever than I gave him credit for.

"Listen, I want in, Event 2. I'm playing for a bracelet. I got it from a different casino…"

"One event, Zelda. You lose. You're done." *Whatever.*

"Fine. A three-day event will give me lots of playtime with my prey." An evil snicker left my lips. "Speaking of prey. Where is my toy? You should give him a raise, Rowan. He is working overtime meeting my needs."

"That is not part of his job." Rowan barked.

"You're lucky he is amicable and obedient. His ability to distract me is saving you thousands." Rowan's eyes bore into mine as he tried to intimidate me. My resolve and nonchalance would probably get a bullet in my head someday. As Rowan handed me my event ticket, a ghost of a smile passed over his face. *Men.*

CHAPTER TWO

Self Destruction

Chase had changed and came to escort me to Rowan's House Party. My presence was not a request. I'm sure Luca had gone through a lot of trouble securing a lesser sentence than Rowan wanted to give me. The mafia in Vegas was depravity masked in elegance.

The House Party was in a large suite and invitation only for the series VIPs. Event winners, sponsors, and poker royalty were invited alongside those from the Nevada Gaming Commission and the Mafia. Luca drew my attention the moment I arrived. I ditched Chase instantly as Luca's gaze pulled me to him.

Malice and dominance vibrated from Luca as his eyes bore into mine. He was the temptation of the ultimate bad boy. Ruthless, cunning, and sexy. My body shivered with desire toward the prince of darkness, secretly hoping he would devour me.

"You're late, princess." Luca gripped my arm, drawing me in closer. His other hand threaded my hair, pulling it back, opening my face toward his. A long finger traced my jawline and down my neck. His lips hovered over mine as he spoke. "Let's see if fucking you is worth the 3 million you cost us today." My eyes closed in agreement. I wanted what was forbidden and perverse—an event to eradicate any light and cause my ruin. Be ruled by the devil and live in hell where I belonged. Luca was designed to feed my demons, allowing my darkness to consume me. It was no coincidence we were so drawn to each other.

My lips pulled his to me. His kiss was strong, forceful, consuming, and fulfilling all that was promised. His hand traveled down my torso, landing on my inner thigh. Luca gripped the flesh with his fingers, drawing my legs apart. His hand slid towards my core. He broke from the kiss and whispered in my ear. "So wet for me, princess." Fingers dance on the fabric, torturing, fueling my need.

Luca disengaged his seduction, leaving me panting with desire. I knowingly gave him the control he wanted. Sex with Luca was epic. He kept me off balance and pushed my boundaries satisfying something deep in me.

He walked to the bar, taking his time to choose a bottle of whiskey. Rowan had taken up court in the grand room. As Luca whispered in his ear, a bag of coke appeared in his hand. Luca knew my drug of choice.

My predator stalked back towards me, inclining his head for me to follow. I went willingly to my ruin. The third door to our right was a suite designed for a king. Bold red and purple fabric swirled around the four-poster bed. A sitting area was around a fireplace and a large white marble ensuite bathroom. The room was barely lit, and the thick black-out curtains were drawn. *Perfect.*

Luca unzipped the back of my dress, allowing it to fall to the floor. Long fingers began to trace the lingerie he picked out. "Perfection." The slow movements increased my heart rate. "So few women have real breasts anymore." He cupped them one at a time, weighing their heaviness. "Lie down, princess." Compliance was my only option.

"Arms above your head." My body was on display for his pleasure. He took his time burning me with his black eyes. "You are so beautiful. No one would know you had so many secrets." Luca lay beside me with the bag of coke in one hand and a long razor in the other. "Stay still, princess, or I will make you bleed."

A thrill shot through my nerves to my core. Danger, drugs, and sex. Luca placed a small pile of powder on my stomach. A long razor scraped close to my skin as he molded the powder into a line. Pressing his face lightly on my skin, he snorted it up one side of his nose and then licked the leftover traces. My body was taut with need. He pulled down the bra cup over my breast, folding it underneath. The same movements were done close to my nipple. Two fingers snaked between my legs, sliding easily into me. He pumped them against my tightening walls while his lips covered mine.

"You need to come, princess?" His voice was almost threatening.

"Yes. Luca. Please." I pleaded. He kissed his way down my body until his mouth met my aching nub. The moment he latched on, I came.

Luca rode out the rest of my tremors. "Baby, you are strung too tight." He took off his shirt and belt, only undoing the button to his pants. "Blow me." I knew it meant drugs first, penis second. I mirrored the same act he did with me. Snorting a line from his stomach and another by his nipple to which I stayed to suck and pinch until his body was tight with need.

"Off," I commanded, pointing to his pants. I got off the bed and poured a glass of whiskey. Taking a sip, I warmed the liquid in my mouth. Hovering over his erection, my mouth drizzled a light stream onto the head. Luca's whole body bounded off the bed. "Do I have to tie you down?" I purred. He nodded in agreement, releasing dominance to me.

"Top drawer."His voice was ragged as he trembled with desire.

A long scarf reinforced with bands lay in wait in the bedside table drawer. I secured his wrists to the bed posts and began again. Warm whiskey drizzled over his penis as he cried out. "Fuck, please." He whimpered. I licked up all the spilled alcohol, only stopping to snort another line against his shaft.

"Does my dark knight want to come?" The table was now turned.

"Yes." He hissed. I licked, stroked, and sucked him until he came violently. I untied him, and we returned to devouring each other's mouths. Need built quickly again. Luca had me on all fours with the scarf wrapped around my neck. He tied it like reins and pulled as he entered me from behind. He fucked me while keeping the scarf tight. As my airways were being compromised, I welcomed the flight close to death.

Peace was close before Luca released the scarf, pulling my body upright against his. "Come with me, Zelda." His fingers rubbed between my legs as he continued to his own release.

Whiskey was drunk, and more lines were done as we rested. He laid me down again, playing with my body and kissing me while stroking my neck. "I need you." I nodded approval to what I was not sure of.

Luca took off his ring and unfolded two prongs from the platinum head. His lips devoured mine again as his hand caressed my body. Lips went to my jaw, then down my neck, where he bit. I imagined two long, sharp canines sinking into my neck deep enough to draw steady blood flow. One hole he sucked and drank from. The other hole was filling a small vial with my blood. The vampire fantasy was real. I gave myself to him willingly. As he sucked on my neck, I began to hope he would drain me dry.

My wetness covered his hand as he rubbed between my folds. His tongue continued to lick my neck. "Princess, come for me." He looked into my eyes as my blood dripped from his mouth while his hand moved faster between my legs, making me come again. Gloriously. Luca gave me no reprieve and rolled on top of me, entering me. The feel of blood dripping down my neck played again with my mortality. Luca rolled his hips to go deeper inside me while his mouth covered mine. Death would give me no regret. We climaxed again just as the darkness came.

* * *

"Come on, princess." Luca was trying to wake me. "Rowan will think I killed you." He placed soft kisses across my face, trying to rouse me. My tongue licked him as he got too close, and we were making out again. "Fuck, Zelda. You are insatiable. But we need to get some fluids in you." He sat me up. I noticed he was already dressed.

"How long was I out?" There were no traces of blood anywhere but the soaked sheets underneath me. "What is this?" A three-jeweled choker was fastened around my neck, hiding a large flesh-colored bandaid underneath.

"Not long." He answered and pointed to my neck. "The choker has to stay on until your blood fully coagulates around the wound." He lifted me off the bed and helped me get dressed. A comment didn't even form thinking about what we did. Luca towed me back outside and ordered orange juice for me. "Drink these the rest of the night." He kissed my forehead and left to talk to Rowan.

Chase was patiently waiting for me. "Are you okay?" His look was of genuine concern.

"Fine." I walked back to the bar, downing the orange juice. The rest of the night, I added vodka to the mix. Chase and I continued the party in my room for the rest of the night. We interrupted sex with drinking and drugs until the morning light began to filter into the room. He closed the blackout blinds before collapsing next to me. My warrior was satisfied for the moment. A drug-induced peace consumed me.

* * *

Chase and I needed until the afternoon to recover. He was a great companion even though he was a spy for Rowan. Expecting that Rowan wanted me away from the poker tables for the rest of the tournament, I waited patiently for the plan to be revealed. I qualified for the championship round, but the event held little interest since I already reached my goal. My father would have been thrilled. I hoped. Fulfilling one of his dreams ended up filling me with more sorrow than accomplishment.

"Babe, let's go off-site today. My friend has a pool we can lounge by and is having a party tonight. We'll grab food and cocktails on the way there. He always has good drugs to sell."

Chase rolled towards me, leaning on his elbow as he spoke. He did not have the muscle mass Luca did, but he was still delicious to look at. His chin-length hair had a tousled, just fucked look, and his blue eyes sparkled, ready for more fun.

"Who'll be at this party?" I mirrored his position, letting the sheet drop below my breasts. Chase's knuckles absently began to make circles around my nipples.

"Just some friends. Guys, I grew up with. They live just outside the strip. Come on. We'll have fun. You need some fresh air." He began to inch closer as his hand traveled down my torso.

"Fine. Does Rowan know?" My lips began to suck on his neck, nipping down his jaw.

Chase laughed. "He suggested it." No interrogation was needed for this honest spy. He hooked my left leg over his hip, opening me for him.

"How much are you getting paid to babysit me?" He began rubbing between my legs. My wetness coated his hand immediately.

"This is hardly babysitting. I would hang with you for free." Two fingers entered my canal as his thumb circled my aching nub. My breasts arched to his mouth, and he latched on.

"What are you getting paid for exactly?" Moans, more than words, came out of my mouth.

"Rowan said I just had to follow you and send him texts of everything you did." He said as he switched to my other nipple. "You're the one who wanted non-stop sex, drugs, and rock n roll. He said to stay away from Luca. I guess he has a thing for you. That guy scares the shit out of me."

Chase kept my attention all morning. He was a generous lover, giving me multiple orgasms. We never made it to the pool but went out for dinner and were ready to party again by nighttime.

Chase didn't have fuck like Luca, but he satisfied my urges, and I loved having sex while high. He learned what I liked and was ready to service me anytime. What was he getting paid for

A shiny red Mustang GT was parked in the semicircle, waiting for us. His pride was apparent as he tucked me in. Rowan must be paying him well and keeping him busy. I didn't want to think too hard about his usual job responsibilities.

He took my hand in his as we walked up the stone pathway to the back of the small ranch house. "My friends will tease us. I never bring a girl around." Chase kissed my forehead before opening the gate. I think my companion was becoming too attached.

The backyard was set up for regular parties. Lanterns were strung around the fence's perimeter, and tiki torches were lit around the pool. Several small bars were strategically placed, keeping the flow of guests spread out.

"Chase, who is this exquisite woman?" One of his friends sauntered over to us immediately. "There's no way he could catch a beauty like you. You must be paying her, or maybe she lost a bet?"

"Are you calling me a hooker or insinuating I would lose a bet?" I looked at the cocky adolescent in disdain. "I'm not sure which is worse."

"Zelda, this is Jim. We have known each other since grade school. He's a dick. Ignore him." Jim was unremarkable. I'm not sure which pissed me off more, his overconfidence or his low IQ.

"Zelda. Princess Zelda. Yummm." He actually licked his lips. "Is that your real name?" Low IQ wins.

"You are a dick. I'm getting a drink." I left the group in search of a drink. Tolerance of stupidity and common people was not an asset I possessed. I was arrogant. I know my gifts and understand my deficits. Patience, sympathy, and empathy were absent from my emotional palate. Only those who reached my high standards of ability or intelligence would deserve my attention. Usually.

Tending the nearest bar was a massive hulk of a man with rope-like muscles surrounding his regular muscles. A tattoo sprouted up from his back, climbed his neck, and ended up swirling around his bald head. The pattern was intricate and sexy.

"You want to lick it, don't you?" His gravelly voice sent shivers up my spine while my eyes were still focused on the design.

"Yes." I hissed as my eyes finally met his. We stared at each other, assessing. A slight grin rose on one side of his face.

"What can I get you to drink?"

"Vodka splash of something fruity."

"Mason."

"Zelda."

"Here you go, Zelda. I'm sure I'll catch up with you later." He winked as he gave me my drink. I couldn't tear my eyes from his.

Luckily, Chase helped me out of my trance.

"Mason! You met my girl Zelda. We have been hanging out at the Poker World Series. She won event #2. I know you follow that shit." Chase put his arm around my shoulders and kissed my cheek in pride.

"You won $25,000 High Roller Six-Handed No-limit Hold'em? There were 500 players in that event." Mason stared at me in astonishment.

"I wanted a pretty bracelet." I batted my eyelashes and shrugged before walking away. I'll definitely be seeing Mason later.

This was Mason's house. He had regular parties to sell drugs. Some customers came and went, but most stayed for the atmosphere. Mason threw a great party. I gave Chase a thousand dollars to get us a large bag of the good stuff. We snuck off for a couple of hours to do body blows in private.

The party raged on all night. Thumping techno music kept people dancing around the pool. Chase was playing beer pong with his friends when I went in search of Mason.

"Darlin', I've been waiting all night for you?" Mason was sitting in an oversized winged back chair in his living room with a few people milling around. "Leave us." He ordered, and everyone scurried out. "What can I do for you, Zelda?" He purred my name.

"I've had hamburg all week. I need steak." Licking my lips, I was wet just looking at him.

"You think I am steak?" A full smile lit up his face. I wanted to climb him like the oak tree he was.

"You are definitely steak. Steak with a bearnaise sauce." I moved closer, and he began to undo his belt, sliding it out of the loops of his pants but keeping it within reach. My heart beat faster as he pulled me onto his lap. Mason was going to be extraordinary.

"If I'm steak, you are Godiva." He licked me from my sternum to my lips. Moaning and growling as he went. His lips sucked mine while he cradled my face in his large hands. My body shamelessly began to rub up and down his as we continued to make out. "Fuck, Zelda. I need some privacy with you." He took out his phone and made a call. "Mike, I need you to mind the store. Maybe hours." He winked at me, making me wetter.

Mason scooped me up as Mike arrived. I clung to the front of him as he moved us to his bedroom, barely breaking our kiss. Mason was steak. Delicious corn-fed Nebraska Agnus steak. Gold foil Magnum XL steak. He filled me, so full pleasure erupted from me instantly. The hulk of a man was a generous lover who could suspend me in unique positions, testing my limits. He fuck me so hard for so long that I hoped I would be sore for days.

"I'm spent, Zelda. I'm never spent." His breaths were labored as we dressed. Mason gathered me in his arms and flung me on his back like I was a baby ape. My face rubbed the tattoo of dragonfire on the sexiest muscular neck I had ever had the pleasure of fondling.

The party had ended by the time we emerged. Only Mike and a few others sat outside by the pool. "Babe, you need something?"

"Gatorade or water, whiskey, and blow."

"You got it, darlin'." Mason retrieved the items while I was still clinging to his back. He gently placed me in a chair by the others and kissed me. "How long are you in town?"

My eyes danced at the thought of more hulk steak. Mason chuckled. "I'll see you tomorrow night then." He gestured to Mike and went back into the house. Business called.

"Rowan's not happy with you." Chase sat down next to me. He looked deflated.

"With me or you?"

"Both of us. He wants us back at the hotel. I guess you were supposed to see Luca tonight?"

"We didn't have plans. Well, any that I'm aware of." The insinuation pissed me off. "Fuck them both. Let's go, hot stuff. Our evening has just begun." I held up the bag and bottle.

"About that. I said my friends could come back with us if they stayed with me. I wasn't sure how long you were going to be. Mike was creeping me out." Chase tried to look sheepish, but I needed to cut the guy a break. Babysitting me was not easy.

"They have to bring their own supplies." I kissed Chase and led him to his car. Two of his friends followed along, carrying bottles of booze and a couple of small bags of drugs. I was down for ruling over additional escorts. Thwarting Rowan and Luca fed the darkness to a wicked level. Three boys and one villainess depravity abound.

CHAPTER THREE

Psychological Warfare

Theo Alexander knocked on my door, a welcome break from the multiple data screens displayed on the monitors on my desk. "Ben, great to see you again. Hope I'm not disturbing you. Your secretary said to go through." He made it to my desk in the time it took me to stand.

"Not at all. Come on in, Theo." We shook hands before he continued.

"Just making sure you're all set for this weekend. Marilyn has been preparing for weeks. She is delighted you'll be joining us." His words seemed sincere, but it was odd that he made the effort in person when he could have called.

"I appreciate the invite …" My pleasantry was interrupted by an alarm sounding from Theo's phone tucked away in his jacket. His hands shook as he opened the screen.

"I have to take this. Excuse me a minute." Instead of taking a call, he opened an app that was tracking something or someone. I could see a map with a red dot marking a location out west. "Jesus Christ. Fuck, Zelda." Theo sounded exasperated. Under the map was a list of health data that seemed to be streaming live. He looked at his watch and signed. He ran a hand through his hair, making it stand uncharacteristically straight up.

"I'm sorry, Ben. Family emergency. I have to go." Theo walked into my office elated and left deflated. His shoulders were slumped, and worry lines predominated his face.

"Theo, can I help? Is there anything I can do?" I liked Theo. A good man in finance was hard to find. He made millions, but his philanthropy was his main focus. Learning from Theo excited my rather dull existence.

"No. But I'm even more glad now you are coming this weekend. I have to catch a flight. I'll see you in a couple of days. He stopped and turned to me, laying a hand on my shoulder. "Thank you. No one ever offers to help with Zelda." The poor man aged considerably since the alarm went off.

The afternoon was not productive as my mind kept perseverating on Theo's change in demeanor. He hadn't talked with anyone but urgently had to fly out west based on health data and a red dot named Zelda. Princess Zelda, I mused. The Legend of Zelda was one of my favorite video games growing up. Link was the hero of the story. Saving Princess Zelda, guardian of the Triforce artifact from the evil Ganon. My old Nintendo and I defeated over ten games in the series. More games have been released in the last decade, but adulting has made me forget the joy.

The Alexanders were good people, which was rare in the society I revolved around. Power and money dominated agendas here in high finance. I was thrilled to be invited to the Gentleman's Retreat. A handful of friends met every year to update each other on their respective industries and share ideas for the future. Theo and I met at a fundraiser a few months ago. He and his wife Marilyn insisted I sat at their table when the Robert's Group overbooked theirs.

So who was Zelda? I searched Zelda Alexander, and a myriad of contractionary articles popped up on Google. Most recently, Zelda Alexander, 25, won the $25,000 High Roller Six-Handed No-limit Hold'em. She won a World Series bracelet for her win and earned a seat at the champions' table for this coming weekend. That's interesting. Something must have happened to her in Las Vegas.

As I scrolled to the next article, The Wall Street Journal mentioned Zelda Alexander was the primary reason The Lormas Corporation's balance sheet was in the black again. Her restructuring ideas streamlined manufacturing processes, unearthed inconsistencies in financial distribution, and terminated dead-weight positions. Inconsistencies? That is code for someone caught embezzling. The articles continued highlighting other major companies Zelda had worked with over the last few years. The article used a signature name, calling her the Black Diamond.

Towards the bottom of the screen, local papers had articles about her arrests, disorderly conduct, public intoxication, and other misdemeanor offenses. One drug possession arrest led to incarceration for sixty days. Under the last of the criminal charges were articles from the society pages. Grayson & Rose Alexander died in a plane crash three years ago, leaving behind their only daughter. Alice Alexander, wife of financial advisor Theodore Alexander, was also on the chartered plane. *Holy shit.*

A degree in psychology was not needed to figure out the path of Zelda's life over the last couple of years. The poker success was an interesting twist into a fascinating story. I selected images in the Google search to find a picture of the woman I was already enthralled with. A selection of images as diverse as the articles flooded my screen. Zelda in a beautiful shimmering forest green gown flanked by her parents at the same fundraiser I met Theo at but years prior. She was laughing as her father whispered something in her ear. Her mother's smile looked happy and proud. They looked like a family you would want to know. Other pictures weren't so kind. Luckily, in most of them, large black Aubrey Hepburn sunglasses covered her face.

As I continued to scroll, one picture froze my hand on the keyboard. The most beautiful woman I had ever seen with piercing green eyes stared directly into my soul. Her long, wavy, auburn hair flowed gently over her shoulders and down her back, framing her lovely face elegantly. Full, wide red lips begged me to reach out and touch them. A firm jaw and a flawless porcelain complexion completed her sultry look. The two-dimensional picture held me captive for an indeterminant amount of time. Nothing was more important than memorizing the details of Zelda Alexander. My afternoon was lost. Researching into the night, I learned everything I could about her.

As if the world now made sense, I was compelled to know this woman. *Link had to save Princess Zelda.* Protect her, keep her, and love her. As odd as it sounded, I was already in love with Zelda Alexander. I knew it in my heart and would only admit it in my head. The hope of seeing her this weekend bloomed inside me. I hadn't been excited about anything in such a long time. The feeling was unnerving. A mere picture of Zelda brought me back to life.

* * *

The do not disturb sign on my hotel door was defective. My coma was being interrupted. The door opened, and the light from the hallway flooded in. Overindulgence wreaked havoc on my body. I lay there listlessly, listening to the intruders.

"Shit, Zelda." Uncle Theo stood mesmerized at my destruction. Bottles of whiskey littered the small room, unused drugs were dumped on the nightstand, packets of condoms were lying around, and a naked male lay beside me. My uncle's intolerance filled me with glee. He deserved to have to pick up the pieces of my episodes.

A woman from housekeeping followed him in, waiting for further directions. I was not moving in my current state. The two of them could stare at me all they wanted. "Honey, let's get you up." Uncle Theo was always kind but disappointed at my impertinence.

"No, thank you," I mumbled into the sheets. Face down, my body wasn't responding.

"Who's this?" He acted like this was the first time his niece had been caught having sex.

"My tail. Rowan had security on me from day one." One eye opened to confirm Theo's shock. "Seemed efficient to fuck him. Less likely to betray me."

The events of last night were so foggy. Chase and I brought a small party back from Mason's, but the details eluded me. We partied hard with two of Chase's friends. My brain stopped me from pursuing any more details. "There should be more than one naked man here," I said breathlessly. Probably not that far from the truth, but I really just wanted to push Uncle Theo.

"Zelda, let's get you out of here." His voice shook, unsure how much trouble I caused and was in.

"No." My warrior was exhausted, keeping me immobile. Theo placed his fingers on my pulse and then ran his hands on the back of my neck.

"Fuck, Zelda." A needle was jabbed into my ass. Naloxone. My body was out of duress instantly. Not that I approved. My uncle dutifully carried Narcan with him at all times.

"You had too much again." *Duh.* Theo thought his miracle shot was going to motivate me. He tried to get me to move, not wanting to stay in my cell of corruption for another minute.

"Not happening, Uncle. My body is wasted." He went around the bed to try to wake Chase. "Leave him alone. He earned some rest. Apparently, I'm insatiable."

"Zelda, don't be crude. It's not ladylike." Theo tried to admonish me.

"What part of any of this is ladylike?" An evil cackle slipped from my lips that sent my body convulsing to throw up. "Fuck. Uncle?" I pleaded.

He scooped me up and had me kneeling over the toilet before the first round began. Theo ignored my nakedness and held me as sickness purged from my body. Days of abuse tried to escape like I was keeping it prisoner. As the rounds went on, Theo barked orders to the maid. He ordered a new room and all my belongings to be transferred. He gave her a list of supplies to collect, including new clothes for each of us and specific food and drinks.

I must have passed out on the floor since the next thing I woke to was two maids holding me under the shower. They weren't gentle, not that I deserved it. I was scrubbed from head to toe and wrapped in a giant towel. They called Theo to transport me to the new room. Being swaddled like a baby released a trigger in me, and I sobbed like one.

Theo held me tight. For a moment, I felt regret and empathy for my poor guardian. I'm sure he had better things to do than rescue me after an overdose. He sat me in his lap at the end of the bed as I released demons differently. Soft words of love and support were whispered in my ear while tears dropped on his shirt. "Uncle, I'm in so much pain." Emotional pain crippled me.

"I know, baby girl. I'm sorry." The maid had turned down the bed so Theo could lay me under the covers. I passed out again immediately.

CHAPTER FOUR

Insolence & Obediance

A new morning in a clean environment made me feel a degree less vial. My body was thrashed, and my head was pounding, but the dominant force pumping through me was anger. I didn't think too hard about what I was angry at. The emotion was all I could focus on.

The impression on the mattress where Uncle Theo had slept was still there. My impudent juvenile modality was in full force. Gratefulness and humility were not on my emotional palate. Theo had interrupted my self-destruction. Again.

The bucket I used during the night had been removed. Gatorade and aspirin sat on the night table. I could hear Theo talking on the phone, pacing outside our room in the hallway. As prior protocol dictated, I needed to be ready for battle.

Inclining my head, I took a sip of Gatorade but wasn't ready to swallow anything else. Annoyingly, Theo could sense the moment I moved. "Zelda, honey, let me help you." He ignored my growling as he pulled me into a sitting position.

"Marilyn found a five-star facility in Providence that has an opening."

"I'm not going to rehab."

"Zelda honey…."

"Rehab is for addicts who want to stop using drugs, Uncle."

"Zelda, this is the ninth time in three years …"

"More than nine." I snickered, and Theo's shoulder slumped so easily defeated. "Uncle, just let me go. I don't understand how you even find me. My phone is never with me."

"Zelda, I love you. As your guardian…"

"I don't need a guardian. I'm twenty-five years old. I'm not a …"

"Then stop acting like one. You're not the only person to ever endure great loss. Most people deal with their grief and move on with their lives."

"I'm not 'most people 'and my parents…" Rage was boiling the tears welled in my eyes, keeping them from falling.

"Yes, Zelda, you have a brilliant mind but are seated so deeply in your elitist superior attitude. Your indifference to others has isolated you. Your parents would be furious at you for wasting your gifts."

"Don't talk to me about my parents or my aunt. You dishonor them daily." Misery loves company. In a matter of minutes, I turned a dutiful, kind man into facing his demons. His face crumbled in agony. The rush of self-loathing flooded my system, and I bathed in guilt and recrimination. Theo left the room. I turned over and fell into a fitful sleep with haunted dreams.

A gentle hand rubbed circles on my back, recalling me from despair. "Zelda, honey, we have to catch a flight." Theo's kindness was back. I was undeserving but needed it. I rewarded him with my silence and my obedience.

He helped my shaking, weak body shower and dress. My things were packed, and all arrangements had been made. He even had a wheelchair ready for me at the airport. We spoke little, maneuvering through the paces until we were seated on the plane.

Theo took my hand in his as the door to the plane closed. Tears streamed down my face as my own imagination made me relive my parent's last flight. I was adrift in a sea of loss, with Theo as my only anchor. He was extraordinary to endure me. Not that I would ever tell him so.

My head leaned on his shoulder, and I allowed him to kiss my head. His head rested on mine in a solemn embrace for the remainder of the flight.

* * *

My large dark sunglasses held no reprieve from the bright daylight. After every episode, Theo took me back home with him. Usually, we went to his apartment in the city, but time during the summer months was spent in Newport. His first wife had inherited Land's End, a Newport Mansion on the ten-mile drive in Rhode Island. His second wife restored it with his first wife's money. I was not a fan of his second wife.

"Zelda, honey, this weekend is the Gentleman's Retreat at Land's End. We have invited about fifteen people for the holiday weekend."

As we pulled up to the entrance, several vehicles were already parked. "Marilyn has been entertaining them today, but I'll have to play host. You understand?"

"Yes, Uncle. You could've just dropped me off in the city?"

"You know I can't do that. I promised your father." At the mention of my father, all communication was consequently shut down. Anger seeped back in.

Theo helped me from the car just as another guest pulled in. He linked his arm around mine, stalling my movement. "Let me greet Ben. He's new to our group."

I drew my hood closer to my face, avoiding all contact with others. Between my sunglasses and the fallen whisps of hair from my bun tucked under the terrycloth jacket, I felt safe from anyone's gaze.

"Ben Walker, glad you could make it this weekend. Come meet my niece, Zelda." Ben and Theo shook hands, but I remained immobile.

"Zelda, say hello to Ben. He is the CFO of the Robert's Group. We are happy to have you aboard." Theo was the chairman of a self-imposed elitist club for Fortune 100 company heads in NYC.

"A pleasure to meet you, Ms. Alexander." Ben nodded. He earned a nod in return since he was wise enough not to offer his hand. A gust of wind blew off the ocean, swirling around us. The scent of bergamot, sandalwood, and jasmine mixed with sweat and sun wafted off Ben. *Fuck.*

"Uncle." My body was already reacting to the new stranger. I needed to flee.

"Yes, of course, honey. Let's get you settled." I hated how Theo had to help me in front of Ben Walker. I assuredly hated how wife #2 was fast approaching up the pathway.

"Zelda, darling. I'm so glad you could join us." She looked at Ben as she spoke. She came in for a hug, but I shut her down immediately.

"No." I snapped at Marilyn. Uncle's grip increased as Marilyn looked deflated.

"Marilyn, this is Benjamin Walker. This is his first retreat. Can you show him in, and I'll get Zelda settled."

"Oh, I can help Zelda, darling." Marilyn was probably earnest in her request, but I was not buying into it.

"No, thank you," I tried to pull away, but Theo's grip tightened even further.

"Behave." He whispered loudly.

"No," I whispered back and heard Ben chuckle.

After an embarrassingly shaky walk to my room, Theo tucked me in, kissed me on the forehead, and left me in peace for the rest of the night.

CHAPTER FIVE

Intolerance & Civility

The next day I didn't wake until the afternoon. My escapades in Vegas had taken their toll on my body. Fortunately, my uncle wasn't using my room for any of his guests. The closet and drawers were full of my belongings. Most of them had been bought by Marilyn in vain in the hope of fostering a relationship.

Dressed in a black bikini and a sheer white eyelet coverup, I hoped to relax in the sun undisturbed for the afternoon. I placed my coveted WSOP bracelet on the nightstand, proud of my personal victory. Grabbing a bag, I filled it with sunblock and a book I had started the last time I was at Land's End.

The kitchen was filled with ladies just finishing lunch. They all stopped and stared as I ignored them and walked through the room.

"Zelda, darling, nice to see you. Let me introduce you.." Marilyn, the perfect perky little hostess, popped up from the table.

"No, thank you." I stayed hidden beneath my large sunglasses as I made a huge espresso. The ladies continued to watch me as if I was an anomaly. I exited without a word, taking some leftover croissants with me. Ignoring the world seemed like all the energy I had today.

"Please excuse my niece. She is...difficult." Marilyn was being gracious. The ladies stared as I left to tuck myself away on the patio.

A light breeze wafted off the ocean, keeping my body cool enough in the sun. Although I could hear people milling around, no one bothered me. I finished my book and went in search of another. The library at Land's End was well-stocked with classic novels, primarily due to my parents' library being sent here after their death.

The room was constructed with mahogany wood panels and exquisite moldings. Large brown leather couches squared off a section while a long library table took up the other half. Dark red velvet highback chairs made working at the table comfortable. Several landscape pictures added serenity to the pensive room. Marilyn had thankfully left this room alone in the redecoration.

Sneaking in was impossible when Theo was having a meeting there. Not that I cared. I breezed through the stacks already with a book in mind while continuing to ignore humans.

"Zelda, honey. I'm glad you are about, but we are having a meeting. Can this wait?" Theo made the mistake of talking to me like a delicate flower. I looked around the room, and seven men were staring at my assets in a bikini.

"I'll escort her, Theo." Tanner, one of the members' sons, hopped up at the opportunity.

"Great idea, Tanner." Theo tried to move me towards the door. I ignored him, continuing to search for my book. Zelda, if you behave, I'll let you play tonight." We locked eyes for a moment, sternness replacing tentative kindness.

I reached around him, taking a book off the shelf, "Fine." I huffed. "You," I turned to Tanner, who was about to take my arm. "Are not to touch me." I turned and left, hearing Ben chuckle to himself. I couldn't quite remember what Ben looked like. But his laugh reminded me of the playfulness of my father.

"Come on, Zelda. This is like old times. You look hotter than ever, and I hear you are a bad girl now." Tanner followed in my wake, clearly still too dumb to get the hint. He was a boy in a man's body. "Zelda..." He placed an arm around my waist, squeezing me toward him. I turned and abruptly kneed him in the balls. Tanner yelled in pain as he crashed to the floor, cupping between his legs. The men came out of the library to his rescue as I continued on my way.

"She did warn him." Ben chuckled to himself again.

* * *

After the cocktail hour, I was already intolerant of the company. Marilyn tried to be attentive and sweet, whereas I wanted to be angry and brooding. My weekend warrior remnants were still pulsing through my system. Everyone else left me alone. I made an impenetrable shield around myself as I looked through the long windows into the vastness of the ocean. Theo tried to keep a close watch. Thankfully, he had many guests to entertain.

Hunger won over my absence from dinner. I entered last so I wouldn't have to hunt for my seat. The large dining room had a table that could seat over twenty. Marilyn had proper social graces and dutifully played her role as hostess. We all had placards dictating our seating arrangement. Ben stood behind the chair next to the only empty one. As I approached, he held out my chair. "So you are the unfortunate one who has to sit next to me?" I tried to be funny as he tucked me in, but it came out snotty. His scent was pissing me off.

"I snuck in here earlier and traded placards with Tanner." I looked at Tanner sitting next to Grace and then back to Ben. His face softened as light danced from his intelligent eyes. I could feel my pupils dilating as I took him in.

Yellow highlights naturally combed through his wavy brown hair. Longer sections on top covered the short sides, giving him a carefree tousled look. Ben was classically handsome. His square jaw, high cheekbones, and full lips defined his rugged good looks. His thin cashmere sweater barely hid muscle definition. Ben worked out—a lot. I didn't want to be interested in a man full of light.

"Why would you do that?" The thought was incredulous. Couldn't he see I exuded darkness?

"Let's just say I'm enamored." His claim didn't make sense. He sat down next to me, coveting his seat. I took a few minutes to study him. Our wine glasses were filled even though most of us still had cocktails. Ben maintained eye contact as if he knew a secret. It was time to send him on his way.

"Being enamored with me is as superficial as your current life choices. You know nothing about me. You, on the other hand, are bored with life. Working out is never a viable substitute for sex. You're bored in a job you hate, completely ignoring your passion in search of power and money. How has operating under diminished capacity been working for you? You can have both with a more fulfilling life, but bravery does not seem to be in your wheelhouse...and ask Marilyn for the name of the mattress in your room. Buy one for yourself immediately."

Ben choked on his cocktail. "How do you know that?"His chin moved sideways. He was trying to escape the discomfort I unearthed.

"Am I wrong?" Ben stayed quiet for a minute as the smoked salmon appetizer was set down in front of us. He took a couple more sips of his cocktail before answering me. The inner dialogue was openly displayed on his face. As he came to terms with the truth, his body relaxed. Confidence pulled his posture upright while his arms and legs crossed at several points naturally.

"No, you're not. But those are private thoughts…"

"Not to me." We slowly nibbled at the food. I was processing what more I should confide in him as he was processing me. Ben's intelligence and demeanor made me feel safe. I took the chance.

"Brooks and Ella Kelly." His eyes were drawn to the couple as I nodded in their direction. "They're hopeful Tanner will take an interest in their daughter, Grace. He's well-connected and a good match for her being in the same sphere." Ben agreed with the match with a nod. "Grace is gay."

His eyes roamed my face for deception. "Have you met them before?"

"No." *Commoner*.

"Then how do you know that?" *Men*. How could a beautiful young woman be gay? His character stock dropped immediately.

"See Leo and Ava Abbott. Leo wanted kids. Ava did not. They're an arranged marriage in these modern times." I rolled my eyes at the ludicrously. Ben's eyes instantly jerked to the floor. *Interesting*. "Leo pretends he works in the Asian financial markets to keep odd hours. He has another family on the side. Ava is fine being ignorant because she's having an affair with Grace."

"Are you just guessing?" I rolled my eyes again, having to defend my gifts.

"Leo had a different, simpler wedding ring on when he arrived. He changed into a fancier one. Who does that? Also, he smells like baby powder and ointment. Leo is the only one who didn't drool at my presence in the library. He's too tired, keeping up the guise of two relationships." Ben looked around the room, confirming my observations. "Pay attention to the looks Ava and Grace have for one another. Women don't flirt with each other."

I gave Ben a few moments to process before I continued. "Lincoln and Evelyn Fisher have a ruse going on as well. They came in separate cars. He arrived earlier in his Aston Martin Vanquish Zagato Speedster. Classic midlife crisis purchase to show off to the younger ladies. No middle-aged woman wants to bend down that far to get into a car." I sipped my drink, aware that Ben's brain was not keeping up. "You realize I'm just giving you the highlights to make you more aware of the people around you." He nodded in agreement but was still not focusing. Maybe I had given him too much credit too soon.

"Evelyn came later in a limo. She's having an affair with the driver. Lincoln is having an affair with someone much younger, probably a receptionist or a nurse. He recently had Botox and frequents a tanning salon. Isn't his black hair just a little too black? They were both disheveled on arrival. Should I go on?" Ben stared into my face and nodded. "Tanner's father, Calvin Harris' company, is about to be taken over by the board. His wife left him recently. He's too embarrassed to tell anyone." Ben and I were in a whispered exchange all through dinner. He absorbed every word I said as fact the more details I continued to give. "A person's secrets can be read easily if you know where to look."

"How do you know where to look?" Ben's simple question was excused. His closeness was making me jittery. I was enjoying his company.

"I'm a profiler. I study the cognitive, emotional, and social processes and behavior by observing how individuals relate to one another and how they act in their environment." This was as simple as I could define my skills.

"Why do companies hire a Quantico profiler?" Ahhh. Ben had googled me. I'm sure he found out more than he bargained for.

"I apply my skills as a Systems Analyst. I consult with companies and point out what does not make sense. I'm very pragmatic."

"No doubt." As our plates were being removed, Ben wanted to continue to play. "You forgot a couple." He nodded down to the end of the table.

"Waylon and Jordan Hughes. Even though there's a significant age difference, this is the first marriage for both of them. She's pregnant but hasn't told anyone yet."

"Not even her husband?"

"Nope, he keeps filling her wine glass. She keeps handing the glass to the servers. They replace it with a fresh, empty one." We snickered as it happened again as we watched.

Ben and I only talked with each other for the rest of the dinner. Uncle Theo stole glances in our direction. The smug smile on his face needed wiping away.

* * *

The women retired to what I call the white room. As you can imagine, everything was white: curtains, walls, furniture, rug, and, oddly enough, paintings. A straightjacket seemed necessary to exist in such a space. I knew I wouldn't be invited. The white room was Marilyn's domain; I would tarnish the light with my darkness.

The men and I made our way to the game room for Poker. Six of us sat at the card table while the others watched. Ben, Waylon, Lincoln, Theo, Tanner, and I began with one thousand dollars in chips. Six-handed no-limit Texas Hold'em was the chosen game by Ben. *Interesting.*

As with their lives, my opponents were easily profiled. The tells and behavior patterns were obvious, except for Ben. Having disclosed my abilities to him created a variable I never had before. Rowan knew I had abilities, but I assumed he limited them to card counting and game theory. Ben was the only one to whom I divulged my other skill set.

Ben rotated the mannerisms that gave me clues or insight into his hand. The more I studied him, the more the data was conflicting. He was behaving irrationally. Behavior with a good hand or bluffing with a bad hand didn't differentiate. His personality tells rotated, as did his physical tics. He was doing this on purpose. My card counting and probability calculations ceased as I studied Ben further. He would smile at me or wink like this was the most fun he had in a lifetime.

Ben and I were the last ones standing in the early morning hours. Most of the men were still watching our showdown. We had an equitable pile of chips, but there needed to be one clear winner with the no-limit betting option.

The final hand was dealt. Ben smiled at me, giving away nothing. He went from being prey to an adversary. Rarely done. After three community cards were turned over, we both bet minimally at the flop. The turn or fourth card was shown, and we matched the bet. Raising at this point was inconsequential since we both knew it was all or nothing in the end. The river card was turned, and we waged our final bet. The five community cards were now turned over. I knew Ben had a winning hand. He had forgotten to mask his tell. His right eyebrow was raised as he held his hole cards tightly. The smile on his face changed to defeat.

"Don't you dare!" I growled. He didn't know I knew. He was going to fold to let me win. No one had let me win since I played slapjack with my father when I was five years old.

Ben froze. Dumbfounded about what to do. "Finish." I barked at him. He called and pushed all his chips into the center of the table. Unable to commit to what was about to go down, his eyes failed to meet mine. His deception infuriated me. He was playing me like an experiment. Ben Walker's genius failed him.

"Turn them." I continued to spit. I was a big girl. I could lose. In theory.

Ben turned over his cards. Full house. Kings over Queens. *How telling*. I turned over mine boring my eyes into Ben's face. "Straight." Still in shock, Ben stayed emotionless.

"You win. Congratulations." My tone was anything but gracious. I stood from the table and said good night, not waiting for a reply. My theory was wrong. I couldn't lose civilly.

CHAPTER SIX

Land's End

Last night, playing cards with Zelda was exceptional. I tossed and turned all night as I replayed the events. Mesmerized by her grace and beauty, I watched her intimately gain insight into her competitors. She memorized every card, every hand. I could watch her make the necessary calculations in her head, balancing the probability of everyone's hand. She was amazing.

The last hand still made me uncomfortable. I wanted her to see me as a worthy opponent above the common player but not hit her pride. I showered and dressed quickly in search of my beautiful girl, curious if she would be full of reproach or see my value.

On the patio, I looked down to the ocean and saw a lone person swimming parallel to the shore. Her stroke was strong, and she looked formidable, unlike the creature I met, having to be supported by her uncle only days prior.

"This is a good sign. She's coming back from the darkness." Theo leaned over the railing next to me. "This episode was a bad one."

"Episode?"

"Since my first wife and her parents passed away three years ago, she has difficulty processing grief. The triggers are happening further apart, but they are still very destructive. I live in fear that one day I won't be able to get to her in time."

"The day in my office?"

"I should have realized the perfect storm was approaching. Her parents died at the end of June. She had just finished a job, which usually keeps her distracted. Then, the World Series Poker tournament was taking place in Vegas. Vegas is her destination of choice. Although I have pulled her out of some clubs in New York and Chicago."

"She was telling me about her analyst job last night. She is talented and brilliant."

"I'm amazed she has connected with you. Tolerance of other people is not her forte. She has a genius IQ and incredible skills. Companies pay huge sums of money for her to flush out their weakness. Their profit margin always increases considerably. As her guardian, I have to keep close tabs on her. I owe it to my brother."

"She is twenty-five. Why does she need a guardian?"

"She had no destructive behaviors before her parent's death. Zelda has gotten in considerable trouble since. We have a deal with the courts to keep her out of jail. Swimming or running is a sign that she is coming out of an episode. She is a beautiful woman inside and out. She's just lost and refuses to accept help."

"Why is poker important to her?"

"Her father taught her. That's how he discovered her ability to read people and her mathematical mind. They won most tournaments together, mostly overseas. Playing makes her feel close to him."

"Winning makes her feel good about herself."

"She won the event #2 bracket last weekend at the World Series. My lawyer is extraditing her winnings. She has no idea she earned about 2.4 million dollars and won a seat at the champions' table with her chip count. She had almost fifty thousand dollars stashed in her room at the hotel."

"That is astonishing." The details of the information I already knew made the story even more amazing.

"Aside from the seven days of nonstop drugs and drinking, yes, the win was amazing." Theo's brows creased in anger. "She has been marked by one of the Vegas syndicates. I'm not sure by whom. Someone connected to Rowan."

"Rowan Morelli? He's a big name in Vegas."

"Yes, and Zelda has caught his attention. I'm sure she has ruined his betting tables with her play."

"How many episodes does she have a year?"

"Too many in the beginning, but this was the first this year. If I had to guess, the next one will be around Christmas. They are when she misses her family the most. She won't come to us because she partially blames me for the accident. She dislikes Marilyn. Zelda believes I remarried too soon."

"What does she blame you for?"

"Zelda and I stayed in the city to finish working. We were taking a different flight the next day to meet up with the others. In her mind, she feels we should have died on the plane with them. I know it's not logical, but that is as far as she can process her grief."

"Is she in danger?"

"Yes, Ben. Always. Especially from herself. In her darkest moments, she wants to join her parents, having difficulty living without them."

Zelda was coming to shore from her swim. Theo held a bag out to me. "Do you mind? Follow the path to the left of the rock wall down to the cove. There's a small beach there. She will hide there for a while. I would like her not to be alone. As I said, she seems to tolerate you the most right now." Theo stopped me as I started toward the path. "Beating her was the best way to earn her respect. She sees you as an equal now. Not many people are given that distinction."

The path was sandy and steep. It led to a beautiful beach tucked away from prying eyes. Zelda was lying on a blanket as I approached. My girl needed unconditional love and support. "Hey, that was some swim. I brought supplies." I gestured to the bag, hoping she wouldn't send me away.

I handed her a Gatorade and a water bottle as she sat up. She immediately drank both. "Thank you."

"Your uncle gave it to me. He really loves you." She looked out to the ocean, ignoring my comment.

"Is there sunscreen in the bag?"

"Yes, of course. Here, let me help you." Zelda lay face down on the blanket. Overzealously, I put too much cream in the middle of her back. She allowed me to work the lotion into her skin for a long time. Her muscles relaxed under my touch. My gut told me that my girl had been devoid of affection for years. We had that in common. *My girl.*

We lay on the beach, relaxing in the sun. Being in her presence was overwhelming. She gave off a formidable aura, and her genius was never masked. Zelda's beauty was immobilizing. Her long auburn hair coiled around her like thick ropes. Depending on her mood, her green eyes changed shades constantly. Men had to be steadily courting her. In a short time, my feelings toward her were already powerful. Theo gave me hope, and I dared to dream how this would play out.

"You don't vacation," Zelda spoke, but I stayed quiet since it was not a question. "Vacations are important. The human body was not meant to stay in one modality."

"What else do you see?"

"You sleep well at Land's End, but last night you were restless. You have a new, exciting venture to think about replacing a problem that has vexed you for a long time. You're apprehensive but hopeful. I wish you well, Ben." Zelda got up and dusted the sand off her body.

"Theo said you knew a lot about the manor. How about lunch and a tour?"

"I'm always hungry. So sure. I have to warn you my tours are prejudiced."

Zelda never ceased to amaze me.

* * *

We sat on the patio having lunch while everyone else ate inside. Zelda's attention to the details around her was incredible. She noticed a person's appearance, dress, mannerisms, and voice inflection. She watched their faces for signs of deception and confirmation. The social cues led her to patterns that most people would miss even if pointed out to them. I never thought about how people behave in such predictable ways or that a pattern gives details and insight into a situation.

Zelda gave me a historical tour of Land's End. Novelist Edith Wharton once owned the house. Although the house changed owners many times, she was the most notable prior owner, according to Zelda. "She loved the view most of all," Zelda explained. "The 'endlessly changing moods of the misty Atlantic' inspired her to add to the house, with most rooms having a vantage point from which to view the ocean. The climate and society eventually caused Edith to move to the Berkshires. She later built The Mount in Lenox, MA. A more appropriate summer home for her tastes."

Zelda continued. "Most of the moldings are original, even though some rooms hide them with paint rather than showcase their beauty with stain. The white stone bench in the entryway dates back to the 1800s. I guess that no one wanted to move it because it was so heavy. Edith remodeled the house and added a large wood-burning fireplace to the great room. Smaller windows were replaced with these long floor-to-ceiling ones that give unobstructed views of the ocean." We moved through each room with Zelda giving more facts than any tour guide could.

"The estate sits on 8.5 acres. Most of Edith's gardens are still intact. Marilyn hires a full-time gardener every summer to return the flora from the winter's toil. Marilyn also redecorated the inside. As you can see, most of the Gilded Era charm has been lost in the update."

"You're not a fan of Marilyn." Zelda looked at me like, 'duh.' The observation was unworthy of a comment.

"This house was designed to be simple yet architecturally beautiful. Marilyn does not have Edith's vision."

We walked down the path through the gardens just as Grace and Ava exited the cottage at the other end. We stilled silently as they romantically embraced before going their separate ways. Another of Zelda's observations proved true. Without saying a word, she continued with my lesson on Edith Wharton. Her insights about the novelist were more important than validating her knowledge of the affair.

"There are eleven bedrooms and nine bathrooms. The guest house is where the gardener stays in the summer. There is also a caretaker who lives there in the winter. The cottage at the end of the garden is another small residence. There are over 12,000 sq ft of living space."

"Why does Edith interest you so much?"

"Edith Wharton was as intriguing as her heroines. Her own life was filled with great success and scandal. She owned the complex facets of who we are rather than excusing them. She believed we are given one true love in a lifetime. The one person who sees you for who you really are and accepts all parts of you. A deep, unwavering connection to another person drives you to be your best self. Edith had that love, but not with her husband. It's rare I can forgive infidelity."

As she finished her statement, we rounded the corner to the back of the house. Evelyn and her driver were having sex behind a large oak tree. Zelda pulled me back the opposite way, and we ran to the front of the house. We were doubled over, laughing so hard we could barely breathe.

"OMG. I hate when my profiles burn my eyes." Zelda continued to laugh as we fell onto the grass near the patio. She was luminous. Her face was relaxed and glowing with a beauty that would stun a god. We continued to snicker, then reverted to a roar each time our eyes met.

"What is that noise?" Marilyn and Theo stood on the patio above us.

"Why, that is the sound of Zelda laughing, darling." They both smiled down at us. Zelda had laid her head on my chest as we calmed down. I felt like the luckiest man on the planet that this woman was allowing me in.

"What a rare and beautiful sound, my dear." Zelda ignored them, but I somehow had to validate our circumstances.

"Zelda was giving me a tour of the house and grounds. We ..." I couldn't account for our sudden laughing fit.

"The fauna seem overly active in the garden." Zelda quipped, sending us into hysterics again. I couldn't remember the last time I had laughed that hard. I loved the enigmatic Zelda Alexander.

CHAPTER SEVEN

Shooting the Moon

Happiness flooded through me as Ben and I sat on the rock wall overlooking the ocean. Ben had an aura around him that filled me with peace. Light and energy radiated out of him. I didn't want the moment to ever end. We sat in silence. Words were replaced with feelings. I could read all I wanted to know from Ben, and I felt he could read me too.

Disdain, intolerance, and arrogance were less burdensome in Ben's presence. The heaviness of oppressing emotions rarely allowed a sense of happiness to flow through me. My brain seemed to ruminate less on my internal struggles. A bridge to normalcy was constructed. In such a short time, my neuroses were forgotten as I embraced the simple pleasures of everyday life.

I was fully aware that an exceptional mind was a gift and a curse. I knew my limits and difficulties. I could read them easily on people's faces. Acceptance of remarkable skills in one area made you lacking in others. Isolation kept me safe from the struggles of routines I failed to remember. Deciphering social expectations had always been difficult. I realized how dependent on my parents I was navigating life. Allowing Ben to lead, a constant strain was lifted. Even sitting on a rock wall pensively with a companion was an unnatural event.

Ben was a white knight. He was caring and considerate, exposing emotional vulnerability. He gave without asking for anything in return. Our instant connection gave me the safety to not work so hard on my shields. Calmness and ease made me forget my angst. My white knight wasn't perfect. He also tended to idealize and ignore my misgivings.

Love was a difficult emotion for me to acknowledge and process.

The love I had for my parents was crippling me since their death. Love was a power as destructive as tender. A power that overwhelmed and scared me.

Unfortunately, Ben chose that moment to lay his hand on mine. He tried to entwine our fingers as I pulled back as if in shock. "Zelda." He leaned in and whispered in my ear. His scent halted my retreat. "My feelings are unconditional. I enjoy being with you."

My body relaxed, but my mind did not. "You are misguided, Ben." He took my hand, holding it firmly with his. My eyes dilated, feeling the heat from his body. The white knight would be my ruin, or I would be his. We were opposite forces drawn to one another. His goodness could save me from perdition. The question was... did I want him too?

* * *

On the last night of the weekend holiday, I felt good about my progress with Zelda. She tolerated me, confided in me, and I positively affected her well-being. I couldn't think too hard about what would happen next. The little bonding I did with the group seemed to be forgiven by all.

After dinner, a pitch tournament was set up in the game room. Four card tables were arranged in the room. A bar was stocked in the corner, and a table of snacks and desserts was laid out in another. The teams were to be decided by drawing names from a fish bowl. Marilyn did the honors as the hostess.

"Calvin, you are with my sister, Gretta. Theo, darling, you are with Evelyn. Lincoln and Jordon." I think Waylon growled at the announcement. "Ella, you are with Waylon—Brooks, ah, a father-daughter team. You are with Grace. Leo is with me. Ava and Tanner. That leaves Ben... oh, Ben. I thought we were in even numbers."

Theo stepped in, conscious of his wife's charade. "Darling, you forgot to put Zelda's name in. Ben, do you mind partnering with Zelda?" Everyone seemed relieved. I was thrilled and thankful.

"Not at all." I smiled at Zelda, but she stuck her tongue out at me before retreating to the bar.

Theo placed our name cards around the table with partners sitting opposite one another. Zelda and I were first paired with Tanner and Ava. We were playing best of three games to 21. Each team would play a winner from another table. In three rounds, there would be a sole winner.

Pitch is a bidding game where you try to win the bid. The bid winner chooses a trump suit, and points are awarded in that suit. A strategy is to defeat your opponent's bid by cleverly winning points for yourself. Four points are available to win each hand, High-Low-Jack-Game. We were playing the *Shooting the Moon* version of the game where, if stated, the bid winner has to win all six tricks to win an additional point.

Tanner and Ava tentatively sat down at our table. Zelda's mere presence was intimidating. When her mind began to work, she was fierce. As Ava started to shuffle the cards, Zelda finally met my eyes. "I've not had a partner since my father." All I could do was nod to show I understood her pain.

At first, Zelda didn't trust me. She tried to win the hands by herself, not even considering she had a partner. Not that we could speak about our strategy, but a good partnership can infer a language through the cards being played. Tanner won the first hand with a three bid and took all four points. Zelda snarled at me. I found it endearing. I winked back at her. The snarl turned into a lopsided grin. She seemed to relax as I shuffled the cards when it was my turn to deal.

Zelda did her thing and tried to regard me as an asset. She paid more attention to me rather than counting the cards. We began to win every hand. The game ended 21-4 and 21-3. We didn't need to play the third game since it was the best two out of three to continue to the next round. The winners of the other groups were Theo and Evelyn, Ella and Waylon, and Lincoln and Jordan. We were to play Theo and Evelyn next.

Our group was done first, only playing two games. Zelda and I had a cocktail out on the patio. The night was warm, but the breeze off the water kept the air cool. Zelda wore a sable brown halter dress that exposed most of her back. Her long hair covered most of her bare skin, teasing admirers. She rarely wore shoes or sandals at Land's End, and tonight was no exception. Blood-red polish adorned her toes more as a warning rather than fashion.

"You played brilliantly, princess." I could feel the shift as she opened her heart to me. Her body bent towards mine, and her eyes were lit with an energy that drew me. My finger reached out and traced her shoulder. As that movement was permitted, my hand traveled toward the back of her neck. I stroked it gently but possessively. Her eyes closed, relishing my touch. My heart was so full it was pounding in my chest. This beautiful, enigmatic woman continued to let me in.

"Your green eyes change shades depending on your mood or

emotions."

"Your deliberate observations are sexy." Zelda's hand reached out and fisted my shirt, pulling me towards her. Arching her neck upwards, our lips met. The first touch zapped us with a jolt, making us fight through it for more. Soft touches quickly pressed into firm kisses as our mouths devoured each other. Zelda was full of passion, drawing out mine with equanimity. My hands cupped the side of her face, keeping her in place as if this moment was unreal.

Her hands snaked under my shirt, feeling the planes of my chest and abdomen. My body was on fire, ready to consume hers. We stayed lip-locked while our tongues danced and roamed. Zelda pulled back slightly before sinking her teeth over my lower lip and sucking.

"Ah, hem. Zelda, Ben, we are playing you next." Theo called to us from a window, but Zelda wasn't ready to let me go.

"Princess," I mumbled into her mouth. "We need to go play the next round."

"No." She continued to kiss me. I started to chuckle as social norms didn't deter her. "Fine." I loved it when she was vexed.

As we took our seats, I peeked at Theo, looking at Zelda. He had a huge grin on his face that made my heart happy. She, of course, refused to look at him. "Uncle, are you going to shuffle or continue to stare at me." Zelda's tone was more joking than her usual disdain. Theo continued to grin as he looked at me instead.

Zelda and I continued to play well. I followed if she led the bid, giving her the support she needed. If she had high, I had low. If I needed game, she gave me a ten. We were ready to put a higher card down when Theo tried to trump a hand. We were unstoppable. All the while, slight touches under the table and heated eye contact fueled our desire for one another.

We won each round easily again. 21-3 and 21-5. Theo couldn't have been happier at our play. Lincoln and Jordan had won their round, too. We moved on to the final match.

Lincoln didn't want to have a break. He was geared up to continue winning, embarrassing Jordan with his boasting. Zelda and I knew that, with our connection, we couldn't lose. Theo gave Jordan the cards to shuffle. Everyone else took a seat to watch.

"So, shall we make this interesting?" Lincoln needed his smarmy smile to be wiped from his face. "What do you want to play for?" He continued.

"I like that Aston Martin Vanquish Zagato Speedster you have in the garage," Zelda added quickly.

"I'm not betting my car."

"Then there is nothing of yours I want. You'll have to earn your pridefulness."

"Something is wrong with you, woman." I was offended, but Zelda laughed.

"You're just figuring out that now?" She chuckled like he was such a funny little man.

The foreplay between us continued as we began to play. The energy around us zapped and burned as we scored point after point. Lincoln became enraged as we easily won the first game.

"You two have signs. You're cheating." He accused.

"You're a poor player and are ignoring your partner." Zelda barked back. "Jordan is trying to help you, but you are blind to her cards." Lincoln's face turned red, and his body puffed up. He was embarrassed. When I confirmed my observation with Zelda, she blew me a kiss.

"Just deal." Lincoln snipped back. I felt he was holding a derogatory remark under his tongue.

The next few hands were back and forth with the point distribution. Lincoln took Zelda's advice and paid attention to Jordan's play. Soon, we were tied at 16-16. Zelda dealt the next hand. Jordan bid 2. I bid 3. Lincoln bid a cocky 4. Zelda could take the bid for 4 as the dealer.

"I'm *shooting the moon*," Zelda claimed, and everyone gasped. She had to not only get all four points but win all six hands. This was a sheer domination play. She led with the Ace of diamonds. I gave her the jack, and Jordan gave her the duce. She made three points on the first trick. Lincoln followed but growled at his partner. Zelda followed with the king of diamonds. Jordan was out of trump. I gave her my ten, then I was out of trump. Lincoln had to follow up with the queen. The man was turning beat red and sweating. The next hand, she led with the nine of diamonds which was the boss card after all that was played previously. No one followed her trump card.

Zelda gave a triumphant smile. "The rest are mine." She had three more trump cards in her hand as she laid them on the table.

"Wow, that was a good hand, princess." I smiled at her, proud as I could be.

"You gave me the jack." She winked at me, which enraged Lincoln. Zelda earned 5 points, which brought us to 21, winning the game.

"You are fucking cheating." Lincoln bellowed. "A cheating fucking addict. You have no business being here this weekend. Theo should have let you overdose to be done with you."

My fist hit Lincoln's nose faster than I could track. I was standing over him without knowledge of how I got there. My other fist was going in for a mirror hit but was stopped midair by two delicate hands. Long fingers unfurled mine and wrapped around them as I shook.

"Ben," Zelda said softly in my ear. I was still panting with anger, "He's just a poor loser. Words only hurt us if we let them." My lovely girl licked the back of my ear and then secretly kissed the same spot before she pulled me away from the bloody man. Now, my focus was all on her.

"Come. You have blood on your shirt. We should soak it right away." Zelda led me from the game room. God, I would follow this woman anywhere.

* * *

Zelda silently towed me to my room. The adrenaline dissipated from my body during the walk. She led, and I followed. The pitch game foreplay had ratcheted my desire for her, leaving me barely in control of myself. She closed and locked the door as soon as we entered. My body began to shake, overwhelmed by her in this intimate moment.

Zelda snaked her hands underneath my shirt as she had on the patio earlier that evening. Her fingertips dragged over my muscles, rubbing them to soothe me. She continued until her hands pushed my arms in the air, taking the shirt over my head. Breathing as she touched me was forgotten.

Her lips hovered over mine, not allowing them to touch. The torture made my panting increase. Her hands glided over my belt buckle, slowly undoing the notch. "My white knight is so hard." The words were breathed into my mouth.

"Princess. I've been hard for you since the moment we met." The belt was pulled from my pant loops, and the top button unbuttoned.

"I know." She ran a finger into the waistband of the boxers. Her seduction would be my undoing. My hands threaded her hair, and I raised her mouth to meet mine. Holding her in place, our lips crashed together almost violently. We unleashed the pent-up emotion and desire that had been brewing for the past few days. Clothes were ripped from our bodies and thrown to the floor as we clawed at each other desperate to unite.

"I'm clean. I haven't had sex for over two years." My admission was desperately said to get inside of her.

"I'm a drug addict and had lots of sex the past week." The truth didn't sway me but rather fueled my need for her more.

"Do you use condoms?" I asked breathlessly while her fingers elongated my erection to incredible lengths.

"I tell all my lovers I have syphilis." She swallowed my chuckle as her tongue fucked my mouth.

"Do you use needles?" My hands shifted between her legs opening her up to me while my lips sucked on her neck.

"No. I just blow it up my nose." Self-preservation took a back seat to the carnal lust driving me. I would take any consequence to take Zelda bare. "I'm on birth control." She yelled as I thrust into her. "Fuck, Ben!"

My pace barely allowed her walls time to accept me. She was so wet and wonton. I wasn't a man but an animal claiming her as mine. We fucked at a furious pace rubbing our bodies over one another. The bed banged against the wall, echoing the sound through the room. Every sense, sight, sound, taste, touch, and smell was feeding my possession. Our kisses turned to bites. Our touches became scratches. We pulled and grasped at each other to become one.

"Ben. Fuck. Ben. Help me." Zelda came so hard that she propelled my release from her contractions. Momentum allowed me to continue to thrust as the rest of my body ceased. She screamed my name each time waves pulsed through her in a litany of pleasure.

The fever began to slow, but our hearts were pounding in our chests. I could feel hers as I planted loving kisses, getting her to make out with me. I wanted to stay inside her. Forever. I rolled her on top of me, pushing myself deep inside her. Sparks flew around us again. She was riding me with zeal. Zelda was strong and sexy. Not needing my help, I let her lead and take what she wanted.

"Fuck, Zelda! I'm coming again. Baby, don't stop." My hands guided her hips just the right way so I could unload inside her. Preoccupied with my powerful orgasm, I didn't notice hers. Satisfied, she collapsed on top of me, so I assumed she did.

We stayed fused by our sweat. My arms held her tight against me. I was never letting this woman go. "Princess, that was the best sex of my life. Fuck woman you are...."

"I know." She smiled and kissed me again. I rolled her to my side, so I could continue to kiss her properly. We were amorous the rest of the night.

CHAPTER EIGHT

Jeppson Malört

My heart was happy and content. Ben was the light I was missing from my life. He naturally kept away the darkness by his mere existence. Sex was spectacular with him because of our profound connection. I could feel him inside me beyond a physical release. Brief naps dotted my night, only to be woken with Ben between my legs, eating me like a starved man. We were mad for each other and utterly greedy in our desire. Whenever I tried to sneak back to my room, he would pull me back to bed and pounce on me frantically. My white knight had a passionate, dirty side too.

Even though we had spent the night together, I almost skipped down to breakfast, elated to see him again. My heart was full, and I felt whole. The feeling was so foreign it was unsettling. Ben was magnificent. I wanted him more than any other man I have ever known. He had snuck in and settled in my soul in a matter of days—a feat no mortal man had accomplished.

Securing a small table on the patio, I searched for two expressos and a large plate of fruit and pastries to share. Sunday was the last day of the retreat, and the guests would leave shortly after breakfast. Ben and I had plans to have lunch in Newport before he left. Dating him felt right.

The ladies and Tanner were gossiping as usual in the dining room. My name was always a prime topic.

"Zelda's an idiot. An affair with Ben isn't possible. His father-in-law won't allow it. That man is a tyrant and abhors his good name tarnished. Ben is too good for her anyway."

"Did you go to the wedding?"

"Who didn't? The event was the wedding to aspire to five years ago...."

My hiding place behind the expresso machine was disturbed by Marilyn. "Zelda, how are you doing this morning? Land's End agrees with you. Did you sleep well, darling?" I passed my brewed coffee to her as my brain processed the ladies' conversation. "Theo, doesn't Zelda look rested?"

I turned to my uncle, needing his help. "Zelda, what is it?" His perceptiveness gives him credit. I pressed him into the sunroom.

"Is Ben married?" I whispered as his arms drew me into a hug. He kissed the top of my head affectionately. I stiffened at what was coming.

"Please, honey, don't judge him too harshly. I haven't seen you this happy in years. He's good for you. But yes. Technically, he is married…"

"Excuse me, please." I pushed myself away from him and sprinted to my room. I was an idiot. He didn't lie. I just never asked. I thought my adversity to lying, cheating partners was clear from our first conversation. All men are narcissistic. Where was his fucking wedding ring? How did I not read his marriage on him this whole weekend? I was blinded, fucking feelings.

Back in my room, I packed as quickly as I could, throwing random outfits and toiletries into my suitcase until it was full. My leather bag filled with cash was back in my room. Tucking my poker bracelet into the side pocket, I flew down the back staircase with my stuff.

Just inside the garage door, everyone's keys dangled from hooks in the order they were parked. The Aston Martin Vanquish Zagato Speedster was parked perfectly for my escape.

Theo and Ben came bolting down the driveway as I opened the trunk. "Zelda, please wait. I can explain."

"Explain what? That you deceived me? You're married, Ben. I feel betrayed. I …"

"I love you."

"Sorry, Ben. It doesn't work that way. You made a promise to someone else. I thought you were honorable, different. You knew how I felt about infidelity."

"Please, princess, tell me you don't feel the same. We have…"

"We have nothing, Ben. Nothing."

"Zelda, honey, no. I can't let you go yet. You have…" Theo pleaded.

"Watch me." I spat and climbed into the Aston Martin Vanquish Zagato Speedster, roaring it to life. I put it in gear and sped out of the driveway. With a fun car, I took the scenic route along the coast back to the city. Stealing a car just made the whole escape more satisfying. Stealing it from Lincoln was the icing I needed.

* * *

"Fuck Theo. What do I do now?" My hand rubbed my face as we watched Zelda take off down the road.

"You love her?"

"We belong together. She has my heart and soul. I love everything about her."

"The darkness?"

"There is no darkness when she's with me."

"I know." Theo placed his hand on my shoulder. "She's worth it, my friend."

"I have no doubt."

"Who the fuck took my car." Lincoln flew outside in a rage. Again. His nose was egregiously swollen, and he failed to look in my direction.

"Zelda. You disrespected the wrong woman. Revenge will be long and limitless. Never underestimate her abilities." Theo stated as he rubbed his jaw.

"She stole my fucking car!" Lincoln belted out. Theo was unmoved by his temper.

"Your dick and balls are intact. You should feel grateful right now." I couldn't help chuckling at Lincoln's expense.

Theo led me back into the house. As soon as everyone left, we had matters to discuss.

* * *

"How was the Gentleman's Retreat?" James was in my office chair first thing Monday morning, playing finger drums on his foot. "Who was there?"

James was like a brother to me. We grew up together on the same street. My mother left when I was five. He never knew his father. Neither of us had siblings, and we were both latchkey kids rotating between houses, holed up playing video games most days after school.

"Hughes, Kelly, Harris, Abbott, Fisher, and Theo Alexander, of course." I paused to store my bag. "Wives and a couple of kids."

"Fantastic and ….wait. Hold on. You had sex." James read me like a book.

"I met Zelda."

"Zelda Alexander? You know her father, Grayson Alexander, was the first investor in my company. Let me see her picture." I pulled out my phone and showed him photos I had taken when she wasn't looking.

"See those black diamond earrings..." Zelda always wore a beautiful pair of black diamond earrings her father gave her.

"You created the tracking device and this App?"

"The code name for the device is called the *magic compass.*"

"What the fuck, James. From *Legend of Zelda*? This all seems like an unbelievable coincidence."

"How do you have the App? It is specific to the device."

"Theo gave me the code."

"I don't understand."

"I love her."

"I don't understand. Ben, what is going on?"

"Theo visited here just before the retreat. The App went off, and he bolted to Vegas. Zelda had overdosed. He brought her back to Land's End."

"Still not sure what this has to do with you?"

"I researched her. She is amazing. A picture of her was posted just after she completed her first job and before her parents died. A voice inside my head told me to save her. To save Zelda. Rescue her. She was meant for me."

"A voice?"

"A woman's voice."

"You know how odd this is. Being in a sexless marriage is causing you stress and trauma, manifesting fantasy. No man should go that long without sex."

"This isn't about sex. Well, I did have the best sex of my life with Zelda. Meeting her was life-changing. She called me out on my life, deeming myself unworthy of her."

"A drug-addicted orphan thought you unworthy? You?" James' disgust was heartwarming. "She rejected a brilliant, rich, handsome, well-connected, and fit, thanks to me, man. She sounds defective."

"She isn't. She's magnificent and doesn't value those characteristics. Well, she did appreciate my fitness, so thank you."

"Then how did you get her to sleep with you?"

"I beat her in Poker. Then we were partners in a pitch tournament." An odd thought suddenly occurred to me. "Theo and Marilyn seem awfully supportive of our time together. They know my marital position."

"And Theo gave you the tracking App. Ben are you sure you know what you are doing?"

"I've never been more sure in my entire life. James…" I looked at James. Our brotherly connection spoke without words.

"Oh no. I see your plan in motion. I'm not going up against Daddy Roberts. Your father-in-law is a ruthless son-of-a-bitch." James' shoulders slumped with my easy defeat. "I would like to see you extradited from his clutches." Our eyes connected again while we reviewed the plan. "Is she worth it?"

"Yes."

* * *

Lincoln Fisher was a coward. Most bullies are. He stole back his car weeks later in the middle of the night. I took pleasure in imagining the ride back to the city with his wife and her lover, the chauffeur. I had fun with my stolen property while the car was mine.

The shock never left me the whole ride home from Land's end. The condemnation and censure I was perseverating on were making me ill. Failure was an infrequent emotion. I kept replaying our interactions, evaluating what I had missed.

My current residence is at a Library Condo at Riverton in the lower east side. The historical 1905 public library building had been restored and converted into eleven condominiums. The building façade consists of square Corinthian columns linked together by an elegant entablature. The brick walls and repurposed wood beams were accented by high ceilings and long windows designed to maximize natural light. Natural stone kitchen and bathroom accents gave the space a rustic contemporary feel. The top-of-the-line appliances were for decoration more than use. I never cooked.

My home was minimally filled with furniture and decorative items. I preferred clean, uncluttered spaces where my brain could relax with less stimulation. Comfortable brown leather couches and chairs dominated my open living room. The dining table had been commandeered as an office. Guests were infrequent to my home, and I never entertained. This space was my refuge.

My immediate community was full of restaurants, bars, and local shopping areas. My favorite bar, the Chemist, was tucked unassumingly down a side alleyway a few blocks away. Long lab-style benches were arranged like a classroom, with the main bar mimicking a mad scientist's laboratory. I appreciated the genius of the owner Jeb's creativity, whimsy, and wit when creating his menu of drinks. Odd and unique flavors were mixed with unusual spirits and served decoratively. A new menu was created every couple of weeks. Jeb's mood was always transparent.

Sitting with my thoughts grew exhausting. By the end of the week, I parked myself at The Chemist for a distraction. This week Jeb seemed to be processing love lost. His menu consisted of Lilith's Revenge, Elixer of Evil, Sweet Poison, Homicide Hangover, and Mengele, to name a few. I ordered Mengele, the angle of death, which also seemed fitting for my current state. Juniper berries dominated the vodka infusion of orange, lemon, and ginger. The cocktail was nearly translucent but packed with flavor. A spicy jalapeno afterburn lingered threateningly on your tongue.

"You're surprised?" Jeb came back to me for my evaluation.

"Always." I took another sip to confirm the experience. "One is lured into a false sense of security by the citrus and berries. The Angle of Death seems appropriate as the torment of the finish is harsh but addictive. A proper tribute to a serial killer's nature. Well, the ones who hunt anyway."

"So few get me, Zelda." He tapped the bar and continued filling orders.

I liked the diversity of the clientele of The Chemist. No one was here by accident. As a hidden gem, Jeb didn't need to advertise. His loyal patrons kept him busy enough. People came here to reflect rather than party. Groups were rare, and no one usually bothered a person sitting alone. My nirvana.

"You okay?" Jeb kept an eye on me. He seemed to sense when I would dip too far into my own chasm.

"We are suffering from the same affliction." He nodded in understanding. Nothing more needed to be said.

My third Mengele went down too fast. I was chasing the numbing effect of a good cocktail. "Zelda?" *Fuck.*

The man in my thoughts appeared. "What do you want, Ben?" Disdain flowed so easily from my lips.

"I need to talk to you."

"Well, I need you to pretend I don't exist. How did you find me?" My downfall was looking into Ben's face. God, he was handsome. My body betrayed me instantly. My eyes locked on his full lips. My heart rate became erratic as I recognized his scent. Ben saw.

"Zelda, everything alright?"

"Yes, Jeb. Thank you. This is Ben. He was just leaving." I couldn't tear my gaze from Ben.

"I'll have a Sweet Poison, please," Ben ordered, but Jeb waited for my nod freeing me.

Jeb brought me another drink and a glass of water with Ben's drink. He nodded at me again with a twinkle in his eye. The drink should be called Jeb's Revenge. Ben took a sip and almost spat it on me.

"Holy fuck, what is in this? The description said whiskey-based."

Jeb chuckled, "For you, I used Jeppson Malört. Seemed fitting."

"How so?" Ben was more intrigued than angry.

"Brutal to the palate and bitter," Jeb smirked at me and walked away.

"Wow, your fan club is vindictive. I expect nothing less." Ben took another sip to confirm. His face scrunched in pain. "Zelda, I meant everything I said at Land's End…"

"It's what you didn't say that vexes me." I took a sip of my delicious drink.

"The whole time at Land's End, I did not once think of my wife."

"How magnanimous of you."

"That's not what I meant. Please, Zelda, let me explain." I gave a subtle nod. I was curious. "I'm technically married, yes, but I have not seen my wife in two years…"

"Ben, you still have a wife. The explanation ends. Your feelings for me are inconsequential as long as you made a vow to another woman. I don't tolerate infidelity." I downed my drink and got up to leave. I would settle my bill at a later time.

Ben beat me to the door, blocking it. "Zelda, I love you. I need …"

"Step away from her. She has nothing to give you. The only thing you need is to leave her alone." Jeb was my champion. He gestured for me to move to the back room behind the bar. Without glancing back, I complied.

Several minutes later, Jeb came in and sat down. "Who was that joker?"

"He's married, so not for me." I couldn't keep the sadness out of my tone.

"You love him."

"He is not mine to love."

"Have you had dinner?" Jeb became a friend in my world devoid of friendships. We ate heartily and talked about theories of love lost in the back of the bar. He gallantly walked me home in the early morning light since his apartment was above the bar.

My heart could still feel Ben's presence. A shadow of amity was lurking, making sure I got home safe. Even though I dismissed him again, my soul still siphoned off the light Ben had brought with him. My demons settled back into the depths of my mind. I felt peace knowing Ben was in the world.

CHAPTER NINE

Voltaire Aerospace Design

Working a job consumed me. Right now, I needed to be consumed by something. I was berating myself for not seeing Ben more clearly. Of course, he was married. Self-loathing crept in, admonishing myself for thinking a white knight would want to date someone like me.

I loved going to work. My brain would figuratively link with the systems within a company. Once I had assimilated, a pragmatic audit could be completed. Patterns were easily seen. Weak spots were detected. Depravity was rooted out. The best strategy I used to figure out a company's intricate workings was infiltrating as an entry-level secretary. Only the person who hired me would know my real identity. Secretaries knew all the gossip and were too low on the totem pole to be a threat.

Voltaire Aerospace Corporation was my next assignment. Even though Stamford, CT was just over 30 miles outside NYC, the commute would have taken up to two hours from my apartment. The company had corporate housing near the main campus. Hal Williams, the board chairman who hired me secretly, had enough influence to secure a studio apartment.

My position was to assist Mr. Barnes, a senior vice president of Corporate Operations on the 9th floor of the main building on campus. A PA position gave me access to everything. Mr. Barnes was intelligent and no-nonsense. He asked. I delivered. We had a great relationship that involved minimal talking. The job was easy, giving me lots of time to make friends and gather data. The major players made themselves known quickly.

Gloria, the general receptionist for the whole floor, was my first friend. Her desk was near the elevators, adjacent to a waiting room where she fielded most incoming calls and greeted visitors. She was lovely. As wide as she was tall, her small stature didn't mimic her large personality. Gloria latched on to me immediately, declaring we were long-lost sisters, even though she was Cuban and I was Caucasian. We had lunch together daily and the occasional dinner out.

Brennan was the PA for another vice president, Mr. Lyman. Like Mr. Barnes, Mr. Lyman was rarely seen. He was either hiding in his office or off campus. Brennan was tasked with more than the usual PA work. He took it upon himself to make sure I was doing my job. His self-importance repelled most of his colleagues.

Our interactions were strained but typical. I had a hard time acting as his subordinate. Constantly swallowing my rebuttal to Brennan's commands made me look compliant. Next came the sexual advances. His behavior was textbook. The tension he brought to every situation made my nerves on edge. Not all human behavior patterns were eloquent.

After hours was when I did most of my sleuthing, and Brennan was the first conundrum I wanted to crack. I snuck into his office after stealing the master key from the janitorial staff. His desk was immaculate, profiling him into a slew of categories. Files were color-coded and meticulously labeled. One drawer on the left side of the desk was locked. The lock was a new addition and not part of the original desk hardware. Without hesitation, I knew the key would be buried in the fake flower pot on his desk. A trace amount of dirt remained in the lock.

A drawer full of defense contracts lined the files. *Odd*. Since Mr. Lyman oversaw research and development. I took a couple of pictures of the files before I was interrupted.

"What are you doing in here, Zelda?" Shit. Brennan had never left for the day.

"The light was on, and the door open. I came looking for you?" I back up against the wall, literally. "I was hoping you were still here."

"Why?" He took the bait and leaned his hands on either side of my head.

"Research." A finger grazed against the bulge in his pants. His eyes closed as I undid his zipper and reached in, wrapping my fingers around his unremarkable cock. "You walk around here with such importance and confidence. My theory is that you have a giant cock to match." I stroked his not-so-giant cock to maximum hardness.

"Only a matter of time before we fucked, Zelda." He moaned as I jacked him off. His hands stayed on the wall as I played with him. Too soon, his head jerked back as he released into my hand unimpressively.

Taking a tissue from the box on his desk, I wiped him off my hand, leaving him to secure himself on his own. "Let's go to my place." He was so unaware of his deficits. My ruse made me sick.

"No, thanks. My research is done for tonight." I scurried out of his office, grabbed my things, and was on the elevator before his pants were zipped. *What an ass.*

* * *

My friend group grew considerably over the next month. Gloria's acceptance of me made other friendships easier. Jen was a contract editor on the same floor, and Sam was her assistant. Sam had a partner, Brian, who worked in research and development. He was only available for our lunchtime antics occasionally.

On Mondays, our group ate in the break room to debrief about the weekend. Tuesdays, we ordered takeout. We took a long lunch on Wednesdays since all the VPs had afternoon meetings on the top floor. Thursdays, we spent the lunch hour arguing about where to go for happy hour, and Fridays, we ate pizza and salad, preparing for the weekend activities. Lots of gossiping took place at our lunches. Gloria and Jen were always game to seek out single men in the different areas on the campus. The guise gave me the pretense to observe how the company was set up.

"Research and development is prime real estate." Jen was excited about the day's mission. "Nerds with potential. I call them."

"I don't mind a little redecoration, but if their vocabulary is too unfamiliar, I lose interest instantly." Even though Gloria recently celebrated her twentieth wedding anniversary. She liked to play along. My friends were fun. At times, I almost believed that this life was real.

"What are you three doing here? This is out of your pay grade, ladies." Brennan was always where you didn't want him to be.

"You're here and have the same pay grade as us, big man." Gloria loved fighting with Brennan. "My girls need real men to look at during their day."

He growled, especially at me. His retaliation later would be unbearable. He stalked off in the same way he came from. *Interesting.*

Back at the office, Brennan backed me into the supply closet as soon as the opportunity arose. "Zelda, did you see any real men today? He was angry and aroused."

"Step away from me, Brennan. I've told you repeatedly I'm not interested." Brennan came closer instead of backing off. "If you touch me, I'll knee you in the place you hold so dear."

"You know you like my attention. My little touches to your ass. My little brushes against your tits. You want to be fucked so bad you are teasing me with other men."

"The only reason you're not constantly on the floor in pain is that I like my job. Your narcissistic egomaniac ways would blame me for your advances."

"So you see your position then."

"Sexual gaslighting is for cowards. Blackmailing for sex means you can't get any on your own."

"You loved having your hand on my dick, Zelda. Don't forget that."

Like a knight in shining armor, Sam opened the supply room door. "Zelda, Gloria said you have a meeting." He looked at Brennan and frowned. "Now."

I extracted myself away from Brennan again while Sam ensured he stayed put. God, working in corporate sucked. The game was less about contributing to business and more about threats and favors. My time was coming to an end. In the last month, I gathered intel that I could never have collected off a report or graph.

My life in Stamford was a perfect distraction. Girl talk was invaluable. My new friends commiserated with me about dating a guy and then finding out he was married. They all had similar experiences. I failed to mention this man was like no other. With our connection, I couldn't imagine Ben having a life with another woman. There had to be details I was missing. Theo and Marilyn were so eager to put us together. No one could be that cruel, even to me.

The next few weeks, I followed the same routine, gaining opportunities to observe most parts of the campus. I pretended to take a class at a community college to cover for my probing questions. People were more helpful in assisting a damsel wanting to better herself. Brennan stayed annoyingly close, monitoring my every move, making him my number-one suspect for defrauding the company.

CHAPTER TEN

Mill River Park

Mill River Park was a short walk from the Voltaire campus. On the other side of the park, Columbia Street was packed with nightlife opportunities. A tradition at Voltaire was that once a month, a department was tasked with creating a 'golf course' on Columbia Avenue. The event was modeled after the Oxford and Cambridge legendary college pub crawls. The nine-hole course mapped out specific places to drink and the scoring conditions for that hole. For example, in hole 1, drink your beer in three sips to par. Hole 2, drink one shot of your partner's choice, etc. Bars and eateries lined both sides of the street, creating a perfect pub crawl atmosphere. The Marketing Department was responsible for the 'golf course' this month.

Each department was allowed to begin at a different hole since over a hundred people participated. We also had slightly staggard start times to not overwhelm each establishment. Corporate Operations was to start at hole 1, at 5 o'clock. Mr. Barnes graciously let our group leave early. Ten people from our floor had signed up for the event. We all had to keep score for a partner. Gloria insisted we sign up together.

"Come on, Z. Girl power. Brennan can find someone else. You need a break from him always riding your ass anyway." I choked on my coffee as Gloria unknowingly called him out. "He's in the same position as you, just longer. He acts like he's your boss, and it pisses me off." I loved Girl Power.

Our group walked to Columbia Street together. In a couple of hours, we stumbled more than halfway down the list.

Hole 1: Drink a pint in five sips at The Stagg

Hole 2: Drink a pint with a stranger at The Bulldog

Hole 3: Drink a pint without using pronouns at
The Wheelhouse
Hole 4: Drink a pint in three sips at Mcleod's
Hole 5: No bathroom usage at George's Tavern
Hole 6: Drink a pint, then use the bathroom at The
Blue Door

Hole 7 was to be completed at the Federal. The swanky bar was in a brick mission-style building that had several floors. We were all pretty drunk with six drinks down.

"What's the par for hole 7?" Gloria yanked on my jacket so hard she ripped a seam. "Oh shit. Sorry Z." She could barely differentiate words at this point. The only people left in our group were Gloria, Brennan, Jen, Sam, and me. The bathroom omission at hole five did the rest of our group in.

"And then there were five," Brennan whispered in my ear, giving my earlobe a little nibble. He had a great seduction all mapped out for himself. "Three more holes and your holes are mine." His crude lines were wearing down my patience as the course continued.

"We have to drink a beer and do a shot you've never done before." I tried to ignore Brennan by studying the map.

"I can't drink any more beer. I'm too full. Can I do two shots instead?" Gloria complained.

"Of course," I said.

"Of course not," Brennan barked at the same time.

"Stop being you." Gloria bit back at him.

"Fine, it's my turn to get the drinks anyway." Brennan sped off to the bar as the rest of us found a table. The bar was hopping. Lots of twenty and thirty-something professionals were letting loose after the work week. The music was a mix of techno and pop, making everyone's body move. Brennan came back with ten shots. "Each of you has to do a blow job and a screaming orgasm. I took a chance you all were virgins."

"Well, I am." I took one of the shots and tossed it down my throat.

"Good to know you swallow, sweetheart." Brendan leered. The others followed suit.

"Hey, Z. The sexiest man I've ever seen is staring at you. Fuck he's hot." Gloria nudged me, but everyone looked. "Right there at the end of the bar."

Fuck. I looked away before our eyes connected and tossed down my other shot. Brennan turned to me, "You know that guy?"

"Yes." Luca met my eyes, curled his index finger toward himself, and summoned me. There was no use ignoring him, but I tried.

"I think I just came watching him walk towards us," Gloria said too loudly.

"So that guy has an expensive suit. Women are so materialistic." Brennan snapped.

"We are fantasizing what is underneath, ass wipe." Proper Jen surprised us with her quip.

Luca approached the table, and all the ladies and Sam began mewling. Brennan was vibrating with anger. "Zelda, I need to speak with you. Privately." Luca was politeness masking rage.

"No, Thank you. Everyone, this is Luca. He lives in Vegas." My flippant behavior rattled him for a moment.

He pulled a chair from another table and sat down next to me. "Can I get everyone another round?" Everyone said yes, but Brennan. The cock fighting was about to begin. The bartender appeared with two more shots for everyone and a tumbler of whiskey for Luca.

"So how do you know our girl Z?" Gloria dove right in as she moved closer to him, wiping the drool from the corner of her mouth.

"Intimately." He stared, looking at Brennan. We all did another shot to avoid the obvious tension. Luca leaned back in this chair and gripped the back of my neck. He was angry and barely keeping it together. "So, how do you all know each other?"

"We work on the same floor at Voltaire. We are on hole seven of a golf course?" Jen piped in to get his attention. As she continued explaining the course details, Luca began possessively stroking my neck. His fingers pressed into the scars he made previously with his pronged ring.

Other than blowing my cover, I wasn't afraid of Luca. I was afraid of what Luca could do to others. "Zelda, I didn't know you worked?" He was being an ass.

"Of course, I work. Everyone works, Luca." I snapped but then decided none of this would end well unless I took control of the situation. "Fine, Luca. Let's go talk." I nodded to the group and pulled him toward the back of the bar. We slipped into a small storage room. "What the fuck do you want...." Before I could finish, Luca's lips were devouring mine. His anger was transferring to lust. My body betrayed me instantly, opening up for him to ravage me.

We didn't talk. He pummeled me against the wall, shaking all the contents of an adjacent rack to the floor. His harsh, brutal rhythm had us both climaxing quickly. We half kissed, half panted into each other's mouths as we caught our breath. "You have to come with me. Now."

"Where?"

"Hotel. Not far." I nodded. Luca always won. Not that I wanted to lose. I excused myself to the bathroom.

I peeked out the door, hearing Luca's menacing voice. He had Brennen by the throat outside the men's room. "You will not touch her, talk to her, or even look in her direction. Understand. Or I'll be back, cut off your dick, shove it down your throat, and then put a bullet in your head. Zelda is mine." Brennan had been served. Luca did have his uses. I went back to the table to finish my last shot.

The golf course was abandoned. After we all said our goodbyes, Luca and I walked to his hotel at the end of Columbia Avenue. We still didn't talk. He gripped my hand possessively, making me feel desired.

In his hotel room, he unzipped my dress and peeled off all my clothes. Moving me to the bed, he positioned me on all fours. His hand came down and smacked my ass harder than I have ever been hit. The momentum thrust me forward, and I screamed. Pain radiated from the point of impact over my cheek. Another equal assault was executed on the other cheek. My dark knight was still angry. Very angry. The only reprieve given was when Luca removed an article of his clothing between hits. When he was naked, he was done, and my ass was on fire.

"You're a bad girl, Zelda. I expect you to obey me."

"No." He growled and impaled me. He was so hard he could have torn me open. His pace was as brutal as it was in the bar. His fingers flexed into my burning flesh, holding me still as his punishment continued. My moaning only increased his thrusts until our orgasms took hold. Our waves were crashing violently. Instead of withdrawing, he pressed his body on top of mine. He held my hands in his, parallel to either side of my head, and began thrusting again. Each thrust pushed me further into the mattress, causing friction on my clit. The weight of his body on my back and his power and control over me sent me into oblivion again.

After his release, he flipped me onto my back and dragged me to the edge of the bed. Opening me wide, his face settled between my legs. Another punishing pace ensued. He licked me to another climax with only my nub. Then he added fingers. Then his palm rubbed me. After each release, he would immediately begin again. I was captured in torture masked in pleasure. Tears streamed down my face as Luca continued relentlessly.

"Luca, please." He ignored me, eager to continue until he was hard again. He dragged me back up the bed and laid his body on me. Dominance and submission were the game. He was too strong, and my body was still betraying my continence.

Grinning like a madman, he played his game through the night and into the morning. My body was so depleted I could barely move to use the bathroom. With the conditions of my punishment met Luca was a different lover. He curled me into his body, and we slept until late in the afternoon.

"Let's go to dinner. I can't talk to you when you are naked." *Yeah. That was it.* By the time we had showered, a package had been delivered containing a complete change of clothes, a selection of toiletries, and new make-up. Luca could be a beast, but he also liked to take care of me in his way. I was sure about two things at this point. One, the dress in the box would be stunning and fit me perfectly, and two, Brennan would never bother me again.

* * *

Luca secured a booth in the back of a five-star steak house. We ordered several appetizers, salads, and dinners. Being out with Luca made a woman feel cherished and secure. In public, he was a gentleman who exuded sex appeal and subtle manners that made everyone jealous of me.

"Rowan has a job for you?" Luca began.

"You could have called?"

"I prefer having this conversation with you in person."

"You prefer having access to my body." A ghost of a smile was his only response.

"Rowan needs you to play in a poker game and determine the validity of the game."

"Deception?"

"Maybe. The game is set for the third weekend in October in NYC."

"Who's playing?" Luca ignored my question and dragged his fingers over my thigh underneath the table. "What if I say no?"

"We have your blood." His fingers inched their way between my legs. "I won't insult your intelligence by explaining our hold on you."

Rowan had a vial of my blood. He could run me through CODIS, plant evidence, submit false evidence, or frame me for several jail-worthy crimes. DNA was the evolved way to blackmail or keep a person under your control. *Clever*. Depravity is as sophisticated as the education of the holder.

"How did you find me?" Luca continued to play with me as if it soothed him.

"Fingerprint. Your employer put you through AFIS a few days ago." *Fuck*. Someone was investigating me.

"You have access to AFIS? That's a federal database." Luca ignored my question again.

"What do I get out of this favor?" His knuckle was circling my clit. I knew the answer but still wanted him to say it out loud.

"Me." His cocky smile knew that would be enough. I didn't care about money.

Seated on the couch back at the hotel, Luca tested his Pavlovian training on me. "Zelda, come here." My brain fought, but my body didn't want to endure another night of punishment. The plethora of orgasms did not outweigh the mental angst. I obeyed. "Zelda, take off your clothes." Again, almost in a trance, my brain turned off, and my body submitted. Luca unbuttoned his shirt and put a line of coke on his chest. "Blow me, Zelda."

Traditionally, my body craves the effect of drugs when I'm at an emotional low point. Luca had fed my ego, satisfied me sexually, and given me the intimacy I'm rarely bestowed. My hunger for escape was absent. "Now, Zelda." My hesitation was noted.

Justification is a great tool of the human brain. My brain instantly conjured images of Ben: his betrayal and my undeserving of such a man edited away any good feeling Luca had planted. My destiny was to live in darkness, unworthy of love from others. I knelt between Luca's legs and followed his commands for the rest of the night.

The consequence of submission, when defiance is more natural, is regret. The false euphoria streaming around my brain wasn't enough to shield me from the condemnation I felt. As soon as Luca passed out, I fled. I escaped down Columbia Street into Mill River Park. The adrenaline seeped out of my body, and my steps slowed. Emotions flooded my system as I tried to find my way back to myself. A dip in the grass caused me to crash to the ground, where I just folded into myself, sobbing.

Life was getting too difficult again. Ruled by expectations and reminders of sorrow, I prayed for this life to conclude. I settled into the grass, wallowing in my grief.

Strong arms cradled me to his chest. The gentle momentum of his rocking gait and the scent of bergamot, sandalwood, and jasmine lulled me back to sleep. I woke late in the afternoon back in my studio apartment. Bottles of water, Gatorade, and aspirin littered my bedside table. My dress was hanging in my closet. I could still smell Ben's cologne on my skin. Dreams did not leave evidence.

* *. *

Upon my arrival at work on Monday, I could sense everything had changed. Brennan changed direction when I approached. The 9th floor avoided me not because of Luca but because someone leaked my true identity, and my cover was blown. Mr. Barnes called me directly into his office.

"I'm disappointed, Zelda. I thought I had found a sharp PA I liked. Hal would like to see you at the top floor conference room. My guess is you'll be working up there from now on. I hesitate to say it was a pleasure to know you. Don't want it affecting my evaluation." Mr. Barnes winked at me. This was as good as it was going to get.

"Thank you, sir." I shook his hand and left. The friendships I had developed evaporated as I walked to the elevators. Even Gloria ignored me. I was a spy, and their jobs were dependent on my report.

The fifteenth floor housed the CEO, CFO, and the board of trustees. Hal was waiting for me as the elevator opened. "Sorry, luv, I hope a month was enough time to collect your anecdotal data. We can go through SOPs and reports from my office."

"I'm not sure how I was compromised?"

"You had an admirer. Your skills and intelligence threatened him."

"Brennan?"

"And Brennan's boss. Mr. Lyman was feeling exposed when your inquiries hit a nerve."

My rejection of Brennan caused me to be a suspect. Infiltrating Mr. Lyman's computer was never detected, a lucky guess on Brennan's part. Lyman was selling pre-patent product ideas to the Department of Defense and other companies. The loss of revenue from the patents caused Research and Development's balance sheet to be disproportionate to what was happening in the department.

After my report to the board, I handed over all the evidence to have Mr. Lyman and Brennan arrested for trade secret theft. Their contacts were also arrested in the scandal. My other minor recommendations would only add to the company's readjusted profitability.

A month and a half at Voltaire Corporation was a welcome distraction from my life. The consulting jobs were so consuming I almost forgot I had another life. Rowan sequestered my next job. As I packed up my studio apartment, the unsettled feeling of injury made me self-conscious. My former friends thought so little of me now. I added this to the road I was paving to perdition.

The casualty of my strategy was the loss of friends. My intolerance of others made friendships difficult to foster in my daily life. The work environment made it more manageable since you were forced to interact with other people. The aliases gave me permission to step out of character and embrace the normality of life. My effect on others began to become a sin.

CHAPTER ELEVEN

New York Mafia

When I arrived home, a large box with a satin red bow sat outside my door. Inside was a beautiful deep blue dress with a black lace overlay, a black lace bra and panty set, and black Louboutins. A card was attached. *I'm picking you up at eight, as agreed. Luca.*

Outrage and defiance should have filled my emotional palate, but the present represented value and respect for my services. My body wanted to see Luca again, especially in this sexy ensemble.

I stepped out of the apartment building at exactly eight. A black limo was parked outside my door, and a tall, dark, and handsome man was patiently waiting with an open door for me. The driver came to the stairs and helped me to the car as I balanced on my four-inch heels. I could smell Luca before I could touch him. My eyes dilated instantly.

"Zelda, you look beautiful." Luca bent his body to kiss my cheek as I passed. His arm flew out, preventing my entrance to the car, while his nose traveled slowly from behind my ear down my neck. "You smell delicious." He licked at the space between my neck and my shoulder. My body shivered, and he bit.

"Fuck, Luca!" Wildfire spread between us. He pulled my lips to his while pushing me into the car. We groped each other shamelessly. Decorum and civility were absent. The spark was lit, and we were consumed with primal need.

Luca's hand dove between my legs and found I was drenched. He ripped off the lace obstruction and moved my hips, so I straddled him. With our lips locked, I stroked him until he was in the position I wanted. "Fuck, Zelda!" I lowered myself slowly on his pulsating maleness until I was seated as low as I could go.

His eyes were black as he panted with need. Luca made me feel powerful and sexy. He looked at me like I was a goddess, and he was humbled to be in my presence. He knew my body better than anyone and fed the depravity it craved. My dark knight allowed me to dwell in my darkness, unconditionally accepting this part of me. We were kindred spirits.

Our routine increased until we were yelling each others' names. We barely slowed, coaxing another orgasm out between us. One was never enough for us. With our foreheads connected, we waited until our heart rates slowed. As if the intimate moment was offensive, Luca lifted me off of him and set me down as far away from him as he could. My dark knight had to swallow feelings. I understood, having my own shields always intact.

The limo was now parked in front of a large brick townhome. I hadn't realized or paid attention to what part of the city we were in.

"Luca, where are we, and what are we doing here?"

"Uncle wants you to play with one of his associates. We think he cheats, but we don't know how."

Luca handed an invitation to a man at the door. We were allowed through, only to be stopped by Rowan. He embraced his nephew but only nodded to me. They took off connecting with friends and acquaintances.

Luca left me to wander the room alone. I looked through the family's bookshelf and the art on the wall. As I made my way to the mantle, the owner, Bruno, joined me. "You have a handsome family. You must be very proud."

"That's my son Matteo. He works with the Navy Seals, outfitting them with devices of his design. He's a genius. You know his tech helped remove the rest of Bin Ladden's regime."

"That's amazing. How long has he been in the service?"

"His four years turned into eight. We miss him, but he visits when he can." Bruno looked me over. "You are here with Luca?" I nodded. "His heart is stone, that one."

"He only shows a heart of stone. There is a difference."

"A good woman can root out all the secrets of men."

"True. Luckily for Luca, I'm not a good woman." Bruno continued to look at me, unsure of what he was missing.

Bruno excused himself as Luca approached with a drink for me. "You look beautiful, Zelda." His hand stroked my neck possessively. His eyes darkened as they met mine. Luca was intense. He could commandeer my life force for his desire. Everyone feared him so. I cherished him—my dark knight.

* *.*

Eight of us were seated around a table set to play. Rowan and Luca watched with about twenty other spectators. The buy-in was $50,000 each for the seven mob bosses and me. I didn't like playing with other people's money. Expectations became a variable I didn't want to influence my skills. No one questioned my participation in the game, especially Bruno. His overconfidence in his scheme would be his downfall. A brazen ego led to careless mistakes. Mistakes led to detection. Whether you were a serial killer, bank robber, or scammer, once you were comfortable with your success, pride would open an opportunity for capture.

Within a few rounds, the plays weren't making sense. Six of the players were easily profiled. Most of the other bosses tried to mask a tell with an intentional movement. Their actual signatures were always buried subtly underneath. Bruno was winning or folding on wims. The data didn't fit with how he should be playing. His tells were obvious, but his strategy wasn't until I looked beyond the table.

Clever man. Or should I say, clever son? I put my theory to the test holding my cards tight to my chest. Bruno's eyes would concentrate intently on his cards without moving his head. The unnatural way he would process his hand was definitely interesting. As the hands progressed, I began to win again. Bruno was becoming more irritated with my new method of play.

"Cards on the table beautiful. One might think you were cheating, coveting them like you are."

"Sorry, I do that when I get nervous." I put the cards back more naturally in front of me, and Bruno relaxed considerably. I need to check to make sure my data wasn't circumstantial. I needed to be sure. Soon, my chip pile decreased again. Interesting.

"Are we going to take a break soon? I have needs." I looked at Luca mischievously. His eyes darkened. Rowan got pissed.

"Sure, beautiful. Let's take a half-hour intermission. Back at the table at midnight, everyone." I leaped from my seat, dragging Luca in search of a bathroom, preferably on another floor. Rowan called my name as we climbed the stairs. We ignored the most powerful man in the room.

Luca already had my dress pooled at my feet on the floor. His hands massaged my breasts from behind me, pinching my nipples as he kissed my neck. "Rowan will be furious if you can not…"

"The mission is solved. I need my reward." Lucas's hand dipped between my legs, playing with my already swollen nub.

"Baby, you are always so needy. You need a marathon fucking."

"Yes, please. That's what I want for payment." Luca laughed as he continued to work my body.

"If I am payment, what does that make me?"

"A rare commodity." Luca made me come three times before we rejoined the group. My relaxed state made me arrogant about the situation.

"Zelda!" Rowan was beet red mad as he watched Luca and I approach. I leaned in and kissed his cheek, then uncharacteristically hugged him. "You know?" He whispered in my ear as he hugged me back.

"Of course. Childs-play." My after-sex glow put a dumb smile on my face.

"Well, my dear, do you want to enlighten us?" Rowan was now more accepting of my current state.

Luca, Rowan, and I were alone in the corner of the room. "Matteo, Bruno's son, is in tech support that outfits the Navy Seals. Bruno is using one of his prototypes to cheat. High-resolution surveillance cameras are set up around the room and detailed enough to see our cards clearly. The data is being sent back to the microprocessor on Bruno's contacts. We can never bluff, and he knows if his cards are …"

"Ingenious." Rowan spat.

"He must always have card games here. The system is elaborate." Luca added.

Rowan kissed my cheek before leaving to talk to the other bosses. "I guess his cheating days are done."

"So is his life," Luca said darkly.

"Luca!" My mind went into a panic. "I can't be responsible for this." I looked to Rowan, speaking with the other bosses. "Luca, please. I didn't know." Luca looked at me like I was insane.

"What did you think would happen?" His tone was curt and unkind. I race to Rowan in horror.

"Rowan, please. Please." Rowan ignored me as the bosses began to tear Bruno's home apart, looking for the cameras. "Rowan, please, he has a son that he loves. You can not take him away from Matteo." Rowan softened at my hysteria. "Please, Rowan."

"Bruno knows the penalty for defrauding the families. He made the choice, not you. Not us. This is our way, little one." My knees buckled as two enforcers secured Bruno. Luca was there to catch me.

"Time to go." Luca carried me out as I sobbed into his chest. The limo whisked us away from the premeditated murder that was about to happen.

We arrived at the Plaza Hotel late in the night. Luca carried me through the lobby and right to his room. He gingerly removed my dress, leading me to the couch in the room's sitting area. After taking off his jacket, tie, shirt, and belt, he poured me a glass of whiskey and threw a bag of coke on the table.

Time to forget the consequences of my actions yet again. He made a line on the top of each of my breasts, kissing me before he snorted them. After licking the remnants of the white power, he popped a nipple in his mouth and sucked hard. His teeth bit as two fingers pumped into my channel. He gave equal attention to the other breast. As he bit again, I came. Pain was my gateway to pleasure tonight.

We reversed places, and I mirrored the same sexual tactic. Always greedy, I did an extra line on his pulsating dick. Tears streamed down Luca's face as I played with his sensitive erection. We fucked several times before I was completely numb. Luca had passed out as I stayed up to finish the bag.

I woke the following morning in my own bed. My hair was tied on top of my head, and a nightgown covered my body. My face felt clean of makeup, and a couple of Gatorade bottles were on the nightstand, with a few aspirins on a napkin. *What the fuck.*

Attentive blackouts were not a thing. I do remember wanting to go home. Maybe even walking the streets at some point. The rest was blank. I tried to capture the scent of Ben's cologne, but nothing was detected.

CHAPTER TWELVE

A Moment of Peace

Theo's office was in the Financial District on the southern tip of Manhattan. Most of the larger finance companies were in proximity to Wall Street. My apartment in Rivington was about a half-hour walk to Uncle Theo's office. In between jobs, I would often meet him for lunch. Gladly sitting through an interrogation for a chance to walk down Bowling Green.

The area's architecture was rooted in the Guided Age. My favorite building was The United States Customs House. The building displayed French neoclassic designs with sculptures from twelve different artists. This was a great example of how art and architecture were once united to create unique structures.

We would always eat at Delmonico's. The steakhouse has been in business since 1837. Beyond the Wall Street titans, celebrities, athletes, and entertainers frequented the famous restaurant. The busy establishment entertained Theo enough to keep his prying questions at a minimum. Today was an exception.

"Zelda, darling, how was your last assignment?" The interrogation was to begin as soon as we ordered.

"You read the papers, Uncle. You know how it went." I never liked talking about events in the past.

"Did you have any complications or interesting twists in your detective work?"

"Not really. The patterns were simple. Too simple. I was a little bored, but…"

"Zelda?"

"I made friends. Friends I liked."

"Well, that's good?"

"Good until they found out I was a spy. Then the friendships ceased, and they looked at me like I was a traitor." Unwelcome tears pooled in my eyes.

"Darling, you can make friends when you're not a spy."

"I can't, really." My self-awareness shut down the conversation. Diving into my psychosis was not an option. Theo knew me well.

"Would you like to come to Land's End for Thanksgiving?"

"No, thank you."

"Marilyn loves you. Please at least try to …"

"No, thank you." Thankfully, our meals arrived. Theo's shoulders shrugged in defeat. I was feeling more of a burden than an appreciative niece.

"So Ben…"

"I don't want to talk about Ben. You and Marilyn deceived me as well." My patience expired. "Thank you for lunch, Uncle." My mood went from contentment from my walk to angst about my life. I left Theo at the table with my untouched meal. Neither I had ever abandoned before.

My walk home led me directly to The Chemist to see what mood Jeb was in. He seemed to be as dramatically mercurial as I was. I appreciated the way he was able to process his emotional palate therapeutically and creatively. My visits began to routinely end with a midnight dinner where I did not mind stating my thoughts. We became allies in an intolerant, mundane world.

CHAPTER THIRTEEN

The Black Knight

Iddless fed the darkness. I arrived back at the Horseshoe the Tuesday night before Thanksgiving. My darkness was consuming me. I knew I would be dancing with death. My actions and my brain were not usually as aligned as they were presently. The hopelessness I felt needed to be replaced by drugs, depravity, or death. I always started with drugs first.

My methodology wasn't completely lawless. I never used my own money for my vices. If I was successful at the tables, my reward was drugs. Drugs usually led to risky behaviors that fueled my desire for sex. The Horseshoe Casino provided me with a comfortable, nostalgic way to make money. I knew how to get the good drugs here, and deep down, I knew I could get Luca to do anything I wanted.

Thanksgiving weekend at the casino would be a popular destination for people who wanted to either avoid their families or take a vacation with them. The casino would have lots of opportunities to entertain the masses. "Do you have a list of the organized gameplay for the weekend?" I asked the woman at reception as she checked me in.

"Yes, Ms. Alexander." She hesitated, and I smiled. "Umm."

"You can let Rowan know I'm here." I took my key and let her finish checking me in. Her calls to me fell on deaf ears.

I was settled into a high-stakes game with five yahoos from Texas by nine pm. In several hours, I was up 100,000 dollars. My comrades were sweating from the exertion of opening their wallets so often. No man ever wanted to admit defeat to a woman.

"Zelda, are you playing nice with the oil barrens from the great state of Texas." My black knight had sought me out.

"Nice? When have I ever been nice? Nice is not in my wheelhouse.

Right, fellas." They all grumbled, refusing to make eye contact.

Luca bent down and whispered, "I think you're nice when you let me slide my cock inside you anytime I want." The man sent shivers through my whole body, pumping blood to my core in response.

"Go away, Luca. I'm busy." I tried to bat him away, but he took my hand and seductively kissed the back, garnering everyone at the table's attention.

"Boss wants to see us."

"You mean me."

"Nope, us."

"Sorry, gents. I have to cash out. Bigger fish to play with." Most of the men sighed in relief.

"You're calling Rowan a fish?" Luca chuckled.

Luca waited patiently as the dealer transferred my winnings to a slip of paper and entered the amount into his computer. I could cash out later. As soon as I put the slip into my clutch, Luca grabbed my hand and pulled me away. Being part owner of the club, he knew all the secret doors and passages. He had me through one, pressing me up against the wall in moments.

My arms were held high above my head as his lips assaulted mine. My dark knight, I craved him. I rubbed my body up and down his. A growl escaped his throat. Luca's hands let go of mine, which went right into his hair. I pulled it as if it steered his desire. His member was freed, and my lacy thong ribbed off me. "Fuck me, Luca."

Luca was my servant, complying with every request. He did his work magnificently. "Harder. Faster." He served me well. "Fuck, Luca. I'm coming." He gallantly waited for my waves to cease before releasing his own.

Our foreheads pressed against each other as we caught our breath. "Zelda, you are mine." *Whatever.* We both knew the truth. All men were narcissists with big egos. Claim as you will, my knight.

Luca brought me to an employee bathroom to clean up. My face looked brighter and more alive as I looked in the mirror. He entered the ladies' room as his patience expired. I gripped the edge of the sink, knowing he wasn't done with me. He lifted my dress and rubbed between my legs, still without underwear. His fingers dug into my thighs as he spread me to accept him. I looked into the mirror, watching as desire commandeered his features. Black eyes dominated his taunt face as he thrust into me possessed.

Luca took what he wanted when he wanted it. He found equanimity in me as a partner. We fueled each other to the extreme. This time, his orgasm was unleashed first. Thrusting through mine seemed painful to him, not that I would allow him to relent. Pain was our thing.

Rowan had summoned us to his office. I was here the first time I got in trouble for winning too much at one of his poker tables. He seemed to remember the same thing as we walked in.

"Three years, Zelda, and not much has changed. You're still in trouble cleaning out my tables." Rowan looked at us closely. "Luca, I told you to bring her to me. Not fuck her on the way…twice."

I smiled at Rowan. I was proud his profiling skills were increasing. "It's Zelda's fault." Rowan rolled his eyes at Luca.

"I need you two for a mission this weekend." Rowan also wore a different hat as the chairman of the Nevada Gaming Commission. He was tasked with investigating fraud or illegal gaming within the casinos—a thief in charge of a bank vault.

"What do you mean a mission? I'm still upset about the last one." I pouted.

"You're here to at least Sunday. I want you and Luca to go undercover for me at the Bellagio. There's a tournament this weekend. I want you two in it. Tournaments can't be rigged, or no one will come and play in them. Bad for business."

"Husband and wife first anniversary. Prefer to be away from families. Etcetera. I'm sure you two can play the part. Here are your aliases. Your rooms are booked starting tomorrow night. Luca, take Zelda shopping. This is an upscale high-roller event. I'll front you the amount you need. Zelda already has some play money you can start with. Zelda, I ordered some new luggage for you. It was already sent to your room."

"Come on, *il mio gattina*. I can't wait to buy you some sexy dresses." Luca purred into my neck.

"And shoes. I want the good stuff. And underwear. I'm sick of replacing the ones you destroy."

"Yes, dear." Luca smiled, and Rowan laughed.

"I think I like my kitten better." This was going to be a better weekend than I could have imagined.

* * *

The Horseshoe had a boutique in the shopping area, but the next morning Luca took me to a couture house he preferred. I was excited to be spoiled. The last time I went shopping was with my mother.

"Jasmine Harrod has the best dresses on the strip. She's a friend.

We'll get a good deal." Rowan gave us a porche to drive around in.

"What kind of friend?" My jealousy was transparent.

"I send a lot of business her way. Don't worry, *il mio gattina*. I only have eyes for you."

"I think I'm going to like to be married to you." The thought warmed my heart. Even if it was roleplay, we were both into it.

"Baby, I'll treat you right. You'll never want to let me go."

"I like kitten. I'm glad our aliases are not too different. Luke and Ella Mancini seem too real."

"Mancini was my mother's name."

"Where do your parents live now?"

"They died when I was a teenager. Rowan took me in when everyone else failed."

"I'm sorry. I didn't know that. We are kindred spirits." Luca gave me a loving smile. We never talked about my parents, but he seemed to know already.

"Come on, *il mio gattina*. Jasmine is waiting." It seemed I had nothing to worry about. Jasmine was a beautiful woman in her seventies whose adoring husband Melo shuffled around the store as her servant. I liked her immensely.

Luca talked to Melo as Jasmine showed me around. "You are playing poker. You must sparkle and distract your competitors with your beauty and body." Her accent added credibility to her words. I was in. She brought me to a dressing room, where she rotated in and out until I had ten dresses to try on. They all fit beautifully. Couture was a different level of clothing.

"*Gattina*, can I come in." Not that Luca waited for an answer, but the intention was thoughtful. "What are you deciding between?"

"Well, this one." The one I had on was a black sequined disco dress. The large sequins flashed when the light hit, giving off a silvery flashing effect.

"I like the deep neckline." Luca snaked his hand into the front of the dress and began playing with my nipple. "I like the thigh length just under your ass." His other hand lifted the back of the dress so he could slide his fingers between my legs. His lips sucked the mark on my neck he had made prior. Luca worked my body until I was coming so hard he had to cover my screams with his hand.

"Let's try another dress on." He was an enthusiastic shopper in the dressing room. We spent the rest of the afternoon in a similar fashion. I left with five dresses, two pairs of Jimmy Choo heels, and a bag full of new lingerie that Jasmine and Luca picked out. Rowan was mad we were getting to the hotel so late.

We checked in under our aliases. I let Luca lead. As long as he called me kitten, I wasn't as worried I would forget my fake name. "My wife would like to see the event list for the poker tables this weekend."

"Have you played here before?" The clerk asked us. Luca answered all her questions while I stared at his transformation. His stern, brooding, dark countenance was replaced with a friendly, outgoing, fun man. He was wearing a baseball hat backward and wore a sexy but casual cashmere sweater with jeans.

"I have several years ago. My wife has never been here. Right *il mio gattina*." I smiled and nodded in agreement. Luca was so cute. I hugged his waist, loving being married to this man. "We told our respective families we were spending Thanksgiving with the other side. We escaped to Vegas to avoid the 'grandchildren talk.' We've only been married for a year."

"We are happy to have you both. Enjoy your escape. Here is the list. If you need assistance, this is Derek Bucannan's number. He can organize a game for you."

"Thank you so much." Luca picked up my hand, kissing it before guiding me to the elevators. The bellboy followed behind us with our luggage. Rowan was right. Having luxury items instantly gave you a different hotel experience.

We showered and changed for dinner and a night of gaming. I wore my black sequin dress with Jimmy Choo sparkly shoes. My goal was to get noticed and from more than just my husband. We ate a delicious dinner at a Japanese sushi restaurant. Luca's protests were ignored. *Happy wife, happy life*. I kept reminding him.

We were having fun. My black knight was on vacation and was enjoying being married. Luca had called Derek Bucannan's number and got us into a high-stakes game that night. We did what we had to do. Show them the money, win enough but not too much, and have a great time. As soon as we got our invite to the tournament, we snuck back to the room and rewarded ourselves. Partying hard through the night, where we slept all Thanksgiving day.

* * *

We emerged from our room just in time for a late dinner and to find some fun in the casino. I still had all my play money and some from last night's winnings. Luca didn't fare as well, which was his motive to play again tonight.

We wandered around looking for something unscripted, but nothing caught our interest. The lounge was empty, so we took a seat at the bar. Luca excused himself after ordering a drink while I sat and chatted with the bartender. Bartenders knew everyone worth knowing. He asked a lot of questions about us.

Luca came back, practically growling at the attention I was getting. I laughed and gave him the affection he needed. Men were such babies. A couple of kisses and possessive caresses, and they settled right down.

"There is a game tonight that needs a couple more players. The GM can't seem to find the right fit being a holiday. Do you two want in?"

"What is the buy-in?"

"20,000 a seat."

"Come on, baby, let's play. My mad money can cover it tonight."

"Okay, *il mio gattina*." He kissed my forehead and mouthed *Happy wife, happy life* to the bartender. Who was this man?

The bartender oddly showed us upstairs to a private room with several tables, a bar, and trays of appetizers laid out. He made the introductions and organized us into groups. Luca paid the buy-in for us and got our chips.

"Skirts don't usually play here." A man complained to the bartender.

"They are a couple." He pointed to Luca, who bowed.

"Can you keep her in line?" An audible gasp left my mouth at his comment. Luca's grin kept me from retaliating.

"With pleasure." My husband spoke so mischievously that I was getting wet.

"Well, separate the happy couple. Put her at my table. I'll keep an eye on her. We're playing no limit." The man smiled and winked at me more in a grandfatherly way. "It separates the men from the boys, missy."

"You okay *il mio gattina*?" Luca kissed me as I nodded. "Okay, have fun and play nice with the other players."

The old man harrumphed and gestured for me to sit beside him. Let the games begin.

With the no-limit betting, I cleaned out my table within the hour. Just the old man and I were left standing. We got ourselves a drink and waited for the others to finish. "You count cards, missy?"

"Not really. I pay attention. I look at how my opponents are playing. Most of it is intuition. You know woman's intuition." He laughed but was still not thrilled about having me as a competitor.

Luca made it to the final round with two others from the other table. The room was reset. "Are you having fun, *il mio gattina*?"

"Ugh. You two are married what a year?"

"Yes, just. Why do you ask?"

"Honeymoon phase. He still cares about your well-being. Soon, you'll be driving him crazy enough that having fun will be taking separate vacations."

"Oh, *il mio gattina*. I'll never want separate vacations. We won't be able to fuck."

"Skirts are everywhere to fuck. Boy."

"My gattina is special. I can't imagine wanting to be with anyone else."

"Yep. Honeymoon phase." The old man chuckled.

The bartender was back playing host and setting us up at the finals table. Luca was having fun talking with the other men. He checked in with me continuously with a wink, nod, and smile. I had never had so much romantic attention before in my life. He made me feel safe and adored, a feeling that I perseverated on instead of getting my head in the game.

The finals round went a little slower. All the participants were good players who were focused on winning. "Kitten, are you looking at me or your cards?"

"You. You're so handsome and sexy."

"Are you drunk?"

"No, darling."

"Are you two going to flirt or play?"

"Are we due for a break? We have been playing for several hours." Everyone agreed to a 15-minute break.

"Come on, *il mio gattina*. Let's get some air." Luca gallantly took my hand in his, pulled me down the hall to the ladies bathroom, and locked the door.

"You make me so hard when you look at me like that." Luca's eyes darkened. "I need to spank you and fuck you. Hard kitten." I purred at his request. He leaned me over the arm of a small couch and lifted my dress over my hips. His long fingers wound around my thong and tugged it, rubbing me with the pressure. I began panting with need.

His other hand kneaded my cheeks to get the blood flowing. "*Gattina*, you're so wet already. I have been neglecting my wife." A hard smack landed on my ass. Luca pulled my thong as he hit me, so it rubbed directly against my throbbing nub. God, that felt good. He continued until my ass was burning red hot to the touch. The thong evaporated as he spread me apart. "My wife needs a good fucking. Huh, kitten?"

"Baby, please. I need you." Luca impaled me. His cock was like hot steel driving into me. Punishment felt so good I couldn't wait to misbehave again. His hands pressed on my lower back, forcing me to submit. Luca was a sex demon designed just for me. He rubbed between my legs just before he came, propelling me into my own screaming orgasm.

He stilled debating another round. "Baby, let's go finish this so we can fuck like this the rest of the night." I moaned my approval.

"God, I love my wife. Come on *il mio gattina*." He kissed me and then bent to pick up the shreds of my underwear. "We need to buy these in bulk."

The men were all waiting when we returned. "You got her in line, boy?" The old man tried to be funny, but it came out snarky.

"Yes, sir. All women just need a good spanking and a hard fuck when they misbehave. Don't you agree?" Shock quieted all the men.

"I'm not so sure about that, darling. I was thinking what more I could do to deserve such an erotic punishment." I licked Luca's lips before gingerly taking my seat. "Well, maybe not right away. Are we going to play gentlemen, or are you going to stand there with your mouths hanging open?"

Luca and I threw the group off their game enough that he won easily. I knew how to keep my man happy.

CHAPTER FOURTEEN

Dancing with Death

The tournament was to take place Friday night. Luca and I were both entered. We were having a hard time figuring out who was running the show. Someone had inside knowledge about the players and enough balls to manipulate the result.

"Hey, our favorite honeymooners. What else have you been doing this week?" A man looked up from the reception table at the entryway to the gaming room.

"Practicing making babies," Luca answered while I looked stunned.

"That is a great excuse if your inlaws catch your deception." The bartender from the other night winked at us. *Fuck!* He gave us our assigned first-round tables and wished us well.

"Luca?"

"I know. Keep watching. Stay alert. Find the pattern, Zelda." Luca kissed the top of my head as if he was scouting for danger. His arms went around my body, and he hugged me tight. "Be careful, *il mio gattina.*"

"You too." Luca tentatively let me go.

Our goal was not to win the tournament, but we had to make it to the last round. My opponents were sinfully easy to beat. Almost too easy. Luca was having a more challenging time. He barely made it to the second round. There was an hour break between rounds in the schedule in case a game went over. My next round ran the same as the first, so I was able to watch Luca's match. Again he had very experienced competitors who seemed to be communicating with one another, but I couldn't quantify their signs. Luca was defeated in round two. We had a few minutes to ourselves before the next game. We compared our observations.

In the third round, I finally had competition. Not enough to be challenging, but at least I wasn't bored. In my peripheral view, I could see Luca changing vantage points using his magnificent powers of observation. He was focused and intent on finding deception.

My intuition was focused on the bartender. He has a more significant role in this event than his position would naturally lend itself to. The third round ended while Luca was nowhere in sight.

"I think your husband is upset he lost so early." The bartender was looming near my seat.

"Probably. My Luke tries to be gracious, but don't all men hate when women beat them? Even indirectly."

The bartender frowned. "Maybe you're just lucky."

"Lucky? That is what a man would say if a woman just beat him." I laughed as my inquisitor got mad.

"Well, good luck in the final round. You're going to need it." Although my evidence was only anecdotal, I knew my theory was correct. Especially when he began talking with the clerk who checked us in. A man's ego is often his demise.

Luca found me just before I sat down for the final round. As he kissed me good luck, I whispered my theory to him. "Leave it to me, *il mio gattina*. Maybe you should win this event. I saw a Harry Winston black diamond necklace displayed in the jewelry store downstairs. I think it will look beautiful on this sexy neck of yours." Luca stroked my neck possessively, sending shivers down my body and causing an ache between my legs. "Win the tournament, and I will fuck you the rest of the night with nothing on but the necklace." He kissed me again, releasing me only as the Gaming Manager called for us to take our seats.

Luca was off again as I focused on the Harry Winston black diamond necklace. Want, desire, and need were all great motivators. I settled in and observed my opponents. After a few hands, their pattern became clear. Tics and tells were my specialty. Memorizing the cards and weighing probability wasn't as crucial in this game as learning the other players' language. Four of them were communicating their hands to each other. The other three were keeping to themselves.

Once I broke their elementary code, the game was mine. Their strategy was cooperative play. Illegal in a strictly non-cooperative game. I used their own signals against them. My victory was that much sweeter when I was declared the tournament winner. No one wanted to shake my hand, especially the group from which I took the million-dollar prize. The Gaming Manager and the bartender were the only ones present for the ceremony. The Gaming Manager graciously handed over the check asking me what I was going to do with the money.

"A Harry Winston is calling my name." The GM laughed.

'Too bad for you, the price just went up to a million dollars on that piece." The bartender spat at me as he texted someone on his phone.

On cue, Luca draped the necklace over me, fastening it possessively. "Here you go, kitten. Congratulations. You did remarkably. Do you like your prize?"

"I love it. Thank you, baby." Luca kissed me, stroking my neck and claiming me as his. We needed to wrap up the loose ends so we could celebrate.

The bartender was beet red in having been thwarted again. "Oh, and thank you for the help. Not that I needed it, but I didn't have to work as hard in these games." He continued to stare in shock at my thanks. "Your friends' signs were easily deciphered. Again thanks. I love my necklace."

Luca moved in front of me as a team of police arrested the bartender, the four players, and quite a few other employees. The scheme was devised unusually by low-level employees running a racket. It was clever in essence but transparent in the end.

The gaming representative was on site and shook Luca's hand. Their conversation was taking too long, and I was getting impatient. "My kitten is restless. She needs her prize." Luca said goodbye to Rowan's colleague and guided me through the hall to our room. "We have plans, huh *il mio gattina*."

* * *

As promised, my Harry Winston necklace was the only thing I wore for the next two days. The police briefed Rowan and Luca and I were left alone. The high from the tournament win and the mission solved was continued by ingesting large amounts of drugs.

Luca and I ate little, fucked constantly, and drank too much. He pushed my sexual boundaries with new toys and positions that drove me wild. Luca, the sex demon, turned into a sex devil.

"God, I love my husband. I never want to be parted from your magnificence." My finger drew on the sharp planes of his face. Luca was uncommonly handsome.

"Oh, kitten, you know we are getting a divorce tomorrow night." He tried to say the truth playfully, but reality pierced my heart.

"I don't want a divorce." I couldn't mask my feelings. Luca looked at me with a tinge of pity that destroyed my soul. "I'm not good enough for you, am I?"

"That's not true. I... The family...." He looked scared to explain the rest. "Kitten, we did great this weekend. You..."

I didn't need accolades. I wanted to know his true feelings. "A divorce is pragmatic. I have other lovers to get back to." Luca's face dropped into pain and then anger. That's what I thought.

Luca rolled on top of me and growled, "I'll kill you before I let another man have you." There's my dark knight. My servant. My protector. *Prove it.*

He pulled a new bag of coke out from his suitcase. "I had this specially made for this weekend." He put two lines on his chest for me and one on his cock. This was our new norm. I sucked and licked him until he was primed. I wasn't as addicted to Coke as I was to Luca. Cocaine was more of an avenue to the intensity we had for one another.

"Arms up, kitten. He secured my wrists to the bedpost and placed his lines on my chest." Luca played with my breasts as I arched, offering myself to him. He ingested his lines off of me, licking me everywhere. Feeling higher than usual, I began to make demands.

"Bite me, Luca." He slowly sank his teeth into my flesh, imprinting me. "Again." The pain was good, but I wanted more. "Bite me harder, baby. Claim me." My dark knight obeyed. He ravished my body, doing everything I asked him to do. "Cut me, Luca. I need to bleed." Sharp razor cuts were placed artistically over my body. The pain drove out every good feeling I had and replaced them with despair, inadequacy, and sorrow.

Luca made me climax, but I didn't get euphoria. I experience loss. I couldn't keep my dark knight. Self-loathing predominated my thoughts. He didn't want me, nor did his family. I began to perseverate on loss. "Luca, I need more." Still tied to the bed, he let me snort more of the good stuff up my nose. I needed to banish loss before it overwhelmed me. I wanted more, but he gave me sips of whiskey instead.

Luca put the bag on the bedside table and mounted me. He kissed my lips and jaw before settling on my neck. He sucked on the holes he made last year. My body ached for him to do it again.

"Suck me again, baby." He hesitated, but I pushed him. "Take me. Drain me. I need to be inside you." Luca took out his ring, and one prong pierced my neck. Blood streamed out the hole and down my body. The relief was immediate. Luca licked the blood off my neck and kissed me with wet lips.

"Again, Luca. Fuck me to peace." Luca, the obedient servant, thrust inside me until I came gloriously. He did it. He broke through the wall of darkness into another place. A place I had never been. I was set adrift.

My mind calmed, my body relaxed, and I felt the peace I desired. Luca was absent from this place. Everyone was absent from this place. I tried to conjure images of my parents, but I could not. Before I panicked, I felt the trickle of my blood over the planes of my body and focused on that. Sleep was close.

Ben was here.

CHAPTER FIFTEEN

The White Knight

Housekeeping couldn't open the door fast enough. Fuck knocking. Zelda had never stayed at this hotel. Too many patterns were being broken. My stomach was so tight with anxiety I could barely breathe.

"Sir, my card isn't working." The maid I grabbed on the way up here was too nervous.

"Use your override key." I knew she had one. They all do in case of an emergency. Like this. "Give it to me."

"But, Sir." I took the key from her hand and pushed the door open so forcefully that it banged against the wall. The room smelled like death. I spotted two figures passed out on the bed.

"No, no, no, no." My greatest fear, the one I had suppressed all these months, was unfolding before me. "No, no, no. Call an ambulance!"

Sprinting to Zelda's side, she looked dead. Her face was pale and withdrawn. A thin layer of blood was smeared over her mouth and jaw. Dark purple skin circled her eyes. Cuts and bite marks covered her naked body. Blood was streaming from her neck, soaking the bed underneath. She looked drenched in blood-soaked sheets—my Zelda.

Lifting her eyelid, an immobile, tiny, dark pupil stared at nothing. I cradled her head as my tears dripped on her lifeless face. My hand wrapped around her wrist in hopes of finding a pulse. I couldn't detect anything. My Zelda. I failed her.

The man lying naked next to her was of no concern to me. He looked to be in a similar shape. He killed my Zelda. He should die as well. Fucker. Absently, I put the almost empty bag of drugs into my pocket as if taking it away now would help my girl.

The blood from her neck began to trickle instead of stream. *Fuck.* Dead bodies don't bleed. I ran to the hallway and grabbed a clean sheet from the housekeeping cart. Wrapping her up, I sprinted to the elevator and pressed the button to the lobby.

"Come on, baby. Hang in there. It's Ben. For me. Please, baby, don't leave me." I placed soft kisses on her temple, willing her to live. "Please, Zelda." The elevator opened to the lobby, and I ran out haphazardly, knocking people out of the way.

An ambulance pulled up at the entrance, and I commandeered it. "This is the girl from the call. Possible OD and severe loss of blood."

"We heard there were two?" I growled loud enough with a crazed look in my eyes that set them in motion. The back of the ambulance was opened, and I set her on the gurney. The EMTs put a line into her arm and began fluids.

"What type of drugs?"

"She usually does cocaine. Here." I pulled the bag from my pocket. "This was left in the room."

"The EMT tested it."

"Yup. Coke. The good stuff but…" They gave Zelda a shot of Narcan and worked on her until we arrived at the hospital. The driver must have called ahead. A team of doctors and nurses was ready as we parked. They whisked her away through a multitude of doors while I was stopped by an administrator.

"Who are you to that young woman." His tone was condemning.

"I'm her guardian." He looked skeptical. "I have the paperwork."

"Follow me, please." The man went through a different door. I looked to the opposite hallway where they took Zelda down. My heart was catching up to my brain that I might never see her again. All I could do was fall to the floor and sob.

* * *

My body felt heavy. Too heavy, like the air was holding me down. Voluntary movement was not attainable. I was stone. My brain was active but slow to make sense of my situation. The elements of death began to give me anxiety. Reconciling, I had to be dead. My body vessel expired, so was this my spirit that was still conscious? I couldn't reason through my current state.

"Zelda?" Ben? Was I in heaven or hell? Maybe purgatory was a torturous place where you faced your sins. "Zelda, baby. Come back to me." Ben? The scent of bergamot, sandalwood, and jasmine made me commit.

My eyes fluttered open, excited to see Ben, only to be thwarted by bright overhead lights. I tried again, and the room was dark. Ben sat beside me, looking like shit. He was disheveled and unkempt and not in a good way. Purple bags laden his eyes, and his skin looked discolored and taunt.

"Ben?" My voice did not sound like my own. I stared into his hurt eyes. Anything I said would bring forth the onslaught of disappointment and condemnation waiting on Ben's tongue. I wasn't feeling brave at the moment and closed my eyes again. *Fuck. Not dead.*

Ben placed his hand in mine, and we stayed in silence. He began to rub tiny circles with his thumb over my writ. His touch was soothing. My thoughts betrayed me that I was happy to be alive and to feel Ben's touch again. *What the fuck happened?*

The need for sleep pulled me back under. Periodic fits woke me as I thrashed in the bed. Ben was always there to soothe the journey. I had never felt so removed from my own body. My mind couldn't complete a thought, and my body fought itself. Only Ben's words guided me like a beacon in a storm. I began to believe I was in hell.

"Princess, are you in pain?"

Of course, I'm in pain, you jackass. My darkness was resurfacing and needed a punching bag. I just nodded and tried to stay mute.

"The doctors have been giving you a sedative intravenously. They're beginning to wean you off. Your body has to purge all the toxins on its own."   Well, that sounds fucking fantastic. Yup, still mute. Ben translated my care and needs to the doctor as I watched from a surreal position.

The third day was the worst. I can't imagine if I felt the withdrawals in full force. My chest was tight, I was nauseous, and my muscles cramped while sadness and panic set in. I couldn't reason through my symptoms. I never had this type of withdrawal before.

The doctor was back answering my unsaid concerns. "The drugs you took were cut with fentanyl. Your body craves the drug more intensely now that the medication has stopped." Ben looked at the doctor as he spoke. Thankfully, they were not passing judgment on me. "Zelda, today is going to be a tough day. We usually bind a patient, so self-harm isn't an option. Your nervous system will realign if it is denied drugs. There are too many variables to predict how long this will take, but I'm hopeful you'll feel better by tomorrow." Ben was forcing me to live. I was too tired to be defiant. My body was not my own.

Ben was my champion through the long night. Whatever fentanyl was, I never wanted to put it into my body again. This was an overdose legends were made from. I had never felt worse in my entire life. My body shook, and I cried. Ben held me curled up on my tiny hospital bed. I wanted to hate him. Blame him for taking me away from the place of peace—the place where selfish murderers went to die alone. Hell was not a place you went to. It was here on Earth.

* * *

The fourth day was tolerable. Jello was edible, and I could sip on rehydration packets and ice water. Ben looked even more like shit, despite changing and showering. His lecture never came. I expected a full disclosure of how I had fucked up. He looked defeated. I had that effect on my guardians.

We sat in silence. The light I usually felt in Ben's presence was absent. Maybe I sucked it all out. He looked at me, ready to give me bad news. Luckily, I was already building my shields of disdain. "Zelda, you're going into the next phase of your treatment. For the next five days, you'll be in the psyche ward completing therapy while your body continues to heel."

His delivery was full of deception. There was so much more he wasn't telling me. "Where will you be?"

I hated to admit that I needed him. Ben made me live, and now he was abandoning me. I forgot. I wasn't good enough for Ben. Hell on Earth was no longer a theory. I was living it.

He still failed to meet my eyes, and his shoulders were hunched in defeat. "I have to get back to work." He bent down and kissed my forehead. "Take care, Zelda."

Abandonment. Despair. Inadequacy. Sorrow. Loss. My new team was assembled and ready to take on hell. Or at least the baffoons running this place.

The days were long and the nights longer. I lived inside my head, trying to recall better times. Reliving the joyful memories from my childhood through college gave me moments of reprieve followed by a flood of regret. My own punishment was designed for my ruin.

The 9th floor of the hospital was just like jail. We were marched to breakfast and then corralled into therapy circles. We were marched to lunch and then given indoor recess. Afternoon sessions were one-on-one with a doctor, and then we were marched to dinner. Nighttime activities were therapy masked in games. Jail was better. In jail, there were fewer questions hurled at you.

Security was similar. Metal bars were replaced with locking white doors that only biometric keys could open. I began to entertain my escape once my body was stronger. All I needed was the index finger from one of the doctors, and I would be free in minutes. My intolerance for stupidity rose to new levels as I watched the professionals incorrectly diagnose almost everyone and engage in counterproductive therapy. Profiling wasn't the only discipline I studied at Quantico.

With my mask in place, I was a good patient and marched in line. I was undisruptive, compliant, and kept my comments to myself. That was the best I could do. Their questions remained unanswered, and I refused to play their games. The enemy in white was easily defeated.

* * *

"She's not responding to any form of treatment. She barely eats or sleeps and refuses to talk to any of us or the other patients." *Fuck Zelda.* "If she doesn't complete our recovery program, with her record, we have to put her in a long-term inpatient facility. We have no indication she won't self-harm as soon as she's released." The team of doctors gave me their report. Zelda was being obstinate.

Leaving her was a mistake, but I was depleted. The trauma of finding her lifeless body was too much for me to process. I understood Theo's reaction to the alarm from the Magic Compass app. Nightmares plagued my sleep. Visions of a world without Zelda scared me to my core. I was right there with her as she endured her withdrawals. The reprieve was necessary.

"As her guardian, can she be released to me?"

"We need evidence."

"What kind of evidence?"

"Progress."

"If I can get you the progress you need, will you release her to me?" The doctors were dubious. "Put us in an observation room where you can watch the whole session. I'll wear an earpiece so you can ask your questions. The only difference is the delivery. She has trust issues. A barrier that has yet to be alleviated."

The doctors were easily convinced. Zelda exasperated everyone quickly. Except me. I have never been more patient or committed to more than anything in my life. James thought this was too much for me and begged me to stop. He and his wife had to breathe life back into me. I was so emotionally drained when I returned home. I was still dedicated to Zelda.

My love for her bloomed stronger than ever. She was broken but illogically so. Princess Zelda needed me, and I knew I could save her.

The orderly brought her into the observation room. She looked bored but eyed the room, ready to make a move if there was an opportunity. I smiled at her opportunistic tenacity until he unceremoniously sat her in a chair.

Fire danced just behind her eyes as she assessed her prey. Intolerance and irritation masked her face, but I could see her raw beauty underneath. *My Zelda.*

"Why is she cuffed?" I was already irritated with these doctors.

"Mr. Walker, we can not assess her, so we assume she is a threat." The two doctors looked at each other.

"You're scared of her? Jesus Christ." I never asked about her training at Quantico. She completed an internship at the BSU before going into the academy. I assumed she completed the FBI training curriculum. Maybe not. A third doctor entered the observation room as we watched. Zelda stayed stoic, pretending not to hear his questions. After a time, she gave him her full gaze. Unnerving him with her intensive study.

"Ms. Alexander, your current diagnosis is substance abuse disorder…" She looked into the one-way window as if she could see us. A sardonic grin played on her face at us before her monologue began.

"Really, doctor? What scripted online certificate program did you pay money to for a subpar degree? My increased intolerance is due to your self-importance and incompetence. I'm not dependent on drugs. I use them as a means of avoidance of behaviors and memories I want to forget."

The doctor fidgeted. Zelda's disdain and impatience could be felt through the one-way mirror. "Just because I use my gray matter more efficiently does not mean I have a narcissistic personality disorder. I can adhere to social norms. I just chose to challenge them. So cross that one off, too." She peaked again at his clipboard, "You omitted the pronoun 'I' from my diagnosis statement. Clearly, you lack conviction. Are you just showing off for your colleagues or the pretty nurse you eye fuck every day?"

She looked him up and down, stared into his eyes, and chuckled. "Shall I continue? You're the one who wanted to talk." He was rattled and left abruptly.

"She is hostile and completely deranged." The attending doctor flew into the observation room.

"You mean she made you feel uncomfortable unveiling your

secrets." I had to chuckle to myself. I was getting the picture quicker now why Zelda was uncooperative. "I'm going in."

For a moment, my beautiful girl lit up when I entered. My heart soared at her response. A frown appeared as she locked herself down again. I unlocked her handcuffs and rubbed her wrists for a moment. She tried not to respond, but I affected her. *Good.*

"So they're bringing in the big guns." She looked me up and down. I let her process me willingly. "Give it your best shot, hot stuff. Then you can leave the hotel room with the uncomfortable bed. Were your neighbors partying all night or just during your rem cycle?" She tapped her fingernails on the table. "And take that earpiece out. I'm not talking to strangers." She sat smugly back in her chair.

"Zelda, why are you here?" The lightness in the room turned dark. Her teasing tone turned to rage instantly. She leaned towards me and locked eyes, boring into mine.

"Because you could not let me go." She made no movement beyond her lips. The clever girl went right for the knife into my heart. She immediately made me relive the worst memory of my life. The PTSD knocked me off my game already. I held her gaze until the pain was too much.

"Ben, you are such a fucking white knight. Did it even occur to you that I did not want to be rescued? My death was exactly how I wanted it. Sexy, deprave, and peaceful."

"Suicide gives you an eternity as a servant in hell." I had my own words ready for the battle.

"Fuck off, Ben." She lost eye contact as I began to make her uncomfortable.

"Your parents are in heaven. Your desire for suicide is counterproductive." I had a kill shot of my own. My girl crumpled instantly, but her rage came back in full force.

"You fucking left me, Ben. You rode in on your white horse and left me an empty shell again. Stop doing that. Just let me go. I can't tolerate …" Agitation was letting her mask slip.

"You can't tolerate what, Zelda?"

"No one loves me. I can not tolerate when they pretend they do."

"Zelda, that is not true."

"Name one person."

"Theo."

"Theo feels guilt, not love. He never showed interest in me growing up. Now, with dead parents, he becomes the doting uncle. I don't think so."

"Marilyn." Zelda did not dignify that with a reaction. "You have other family?"

"Oh, you mean the family that hired lawyers before the funeral was even over to stake a claim on my parent's wealth. They even took most of my stuff. Theo got their books and me. At least he got a good book collection for Land's End."

"Friends?" Again, Zelda did not qualify my questions with an answer. I knew it would be just as cruel.

"I love you, Zelda."

"Fuck off, Ben." A sadistic grin erupted on her face. She had another kill shot. "I'll concede my dark knight loves me."

"Luca Moretti? Codependency isn't love, Zelda. As Edith Warton said, true love brings out the best in each other. Seems you two are nothing but toxic." Zelda was cracking. I could see the fire burn out in her eyes. Unfortunately, sadness replaced her rage. She screamed in frustration and pain, but I was not relenting.

"Why are you here, Ben? I release you and Theo of your guilt. He can go fuck Marilyn, and you can fuck your wife without regret or responsibility to me. I'm no one."

That was it. My girl didn't feel she mattered to anyone or was cared about. She didn't give value to love. Love died and left you alone in her mind like her parents did.

I moved toward her, but she shut me down. "No. Don't touch me." Tears welled in her eyes. I almost had her. "In fact, leave. Now." She could sense her fractures. "Leave Ben. Stop following me. Stop having me followed. Stop rescuing me. Stop putting Gatorade and aspirin by my bedside table. Stop interrupting my death. Just leave me alone." Her voice ratcheted up with every declaration.

"No." It was my turn to bore into her eyes.

One word unleashed the dam, unlocking Zelda's shields. A cry quickly turned into a wail. She screamed as if she was being repeatedly stabbed. Years of pent-up emotions erupted from her body. Her body shook and vibrated with pain. The pain of loss, the pain of love, and the pain of reproach. The insurmountable energy she had needed to keep her shields up for so long flooded out of her. She writhed and doubled over as defenses released. The spectacle was clinically beautiful and heart-wrenching.

As her body deflated, I scooped her up and set her on my lap on the couch. Her head rested on my chest as she continued to sob. I became her shield, encasing her against my body.

"Tell me, princess." I kissed her forehead and petted her hair, trying to soothe her.

"They're dead because of me. My parents are dead because I charted their flight. I surprised everyone with a vacation to Saint Martin with my first big paycheck. Theo and I ended up not making the flight. They died, Ben. They died, and I didn't. It was all my fault."

Zelda sobbed harder while she relived the event. As she got to the funeral in her memories, she whispered, "No one touched me—the whole time. No one hugged me or held my hand. My value ceased without them. I was set adrift without help. Theo had Marilyn. Where the fuck did she come from? I had no one. Vultures. Everyone was a vulture. No one cared about me. Everyone knew it was my fault they were gone. Ben, please." Her cries shredded my insides.

"I know, baby girl, this hurts. Keep going." I hugged and kissed her head, urging her to continue.

"I have nothing left of them. The vultures took everything. I need to feel them, and I can't anymore. They would be alive if not for me. My torment needs to end. I'm not strong enough." Heaving sobs began to slow. "Ben, just let me go."

"No." My resolve was firm.

CHAPTER SIXTEEN

The Guardian

Ben stayed with me that night. I trusted him to keep me safe. My shields had been decimated, and I had no energy to build them again. Periodically throughout the night, I woke in a panic waiting for the devil to drag me to hell. Now everyone knew I deserved to be there.

Ben organized my discharge the following day with a list of conditions from the doctors. I agreed to them all without properly listening. My escape from rehab was imminent.

"Ben, why are you listed as my guardian?"

"I've been promoted."

"You mean demoted. Theo? Why are we flying into Providence?"

"Your uncle had surgery. He is recuperating at Land's End."

"Ben. Look at me. What happened?"

"He had a heart attack. He'll be fine with some rest and ..." Ben paused, pretending he did not say 'and.'

"And what?" I shrieked. "Reduced stress. You mean get rid of me."

"He had a blockage. They put a stint in. He and Marilyn are expecting us."

I stood my ground, folding my arms in front of my chest. I wanted to cry but displaced tears with anger. "What's in it for you? Don't you have a job? A wife? A life? I'm sure the position doesn't pay well."

"I love you."

"You are a ridiculous man Ben Walker."

Ben booked us on a direct flight later that day. He had already secured my luggage from the room at the horseshoe and the room at the Bellagio. I wasn't brave enough to ask about details. He knew all my secrets. Except...

"Ben, do you have my Harry Winston necklace?"

"What does it look like?"

"48 carats of black diamonds in a pear-shaped and round cluster choker set in platinum." Ben just raised an eyebrow at my details. "I won it. It's worth $180,000." He choked on nothing in particular.

"I should have had it on when you found me at the Bellagio."

"You didn't have a necklace on. Trust me. I would have noticed moving it aside to stop the blood streaming from a hole in your neck." Ben uncharacteristically spat at me. I stayed quiet until we boarded.

Before taking off, Ben took my hand in his. He closed his eyes and fell asleep, never releasing the tight grip throughout the flight. I stayed awake watching over my white knight, having a lot to process.

* * *

Ben's car was already in the airport lot when we arrived late Friday night. Even though he slept the whole plane ride, he still looked exhausted. I had that effect on my guardians.

"You'll sleep well at Land's End." I cupped his face before he opened the car door for me.

"I can stay until Sunday. Then, I'm expected back at work." I knew I needed to thank Ben but was not ready to. The only thing I could give him at this time was an absence of disdain.

As we approached the 10-mile drive, I began to get nervous. "Ben, what am I to expect at Land's End?"

"Theo and Marilyn are already in bed. I have a key. We'll see them in the morning." The closeness we had on the plane had dissolved. The rest of the trip was dutiful.

Ben unloaded our luggage before parking the car in the garage. He opened the front door allowing me through, then secured the deadbolt. "Do you need anything?" He motioned to the kitchen, but I shook my head no. I trailed after him as he deposited my bags in my room.

"Good night, princess." He kissed my forehead, careful not to touch any other part of my body, and left for his room. He knew many protocols at Land's End and even had a preferred room.

After a long hot shower, I was still restless. The truth was, after all, I had shared with Ben, I was uncomfortable not being in his presence. My feet took me to his room before my brain caught on. The door opened before I knocked. Ben was as restless as I was, except his excitement was showing through his tight briefs. I forgot how magnificent he was. Licking my lips, I pushed him back into his room. The security and aura of Land's End allowed us to be together. Edith protected soul mates from condemnation, at least in my mind.

"My Zelda." Ben breathed my name as his lips touched mine. We were lost to one another for the rest of the night. Desire fueled need. Need complimented passion. And the bed knocked against the wall all night long. We stayed entwined, dosing through the early morning hours.

"We should go have breakfast with Theo and Marilyn." Ben tried to rouse me.

"No," I stated my resolve. Ben chuckled, rolling me under him.

"We'll need a nap later. You know to catch up on our sleep." He kissed my neck as I drew him closer to me.

"One more round and I'll concede." Ben obliged instantly. We didn't rise until lunch.

* * *

Ben insisted we shower together, making sure I was nice and clean for lunch. He claimed it was his role as guardian. Who was I to correct him? My anxiety about seeing Theo increased the closer we got to the great room.

A fire in the large fireplace gave the room a warm glow. Theo and Marilyn were in large wingback matching chairs like a king and queen holding court. I was grieved at the sorrow I had caused them. Penitence was not usually an emotion I coveted. Standing in the doorway, I felt Ben behind me. I could do anything with his support.

Theo stood with a long tube secured under his nose attached to an oxygen tank beside his chair. I rushed into his awaiting arms. The tighter he hugged me, the more I cried. We embraced for a long time as a litany of I am sorries was said into his chest. Marilyn had moved to Ben, where he wrapped his arm around her shoulder. Rage wanted to slash at her, but I swallowed the words down. I didn't like her touching Ben. *Fuck.*

"My beautiful girl. I would be lost without you. Please do not leave us." Tears were streaming down Theo's cheeks. "I love you, Zelda. I'm sorry I haven't been what you needed."

"Uncle, I didn't even know what I needed." As our tears began to slow, I felt the contrition he deserved. "I love you too, Uncle Theo. I'm sorry I have been such a brat. I just miss them so much."

"I know, baby girl. Me too." I was reduced to feeling like the juvenile I was, so I had no problem climbing onto my uncle's lap and continuing our embrace—time to take what I needed. Marilyn began sobbing into Ben's chest. A growl escaped from my throat before I could stop it. My uncle chuckled.

"Ben Walker is devoted to you, my darling. Marliyn will not take him away from you."

"She took you from me." He pet my head much like Ben had done to comfort me.

"You and I are more alike than you think. Losing my brother and my beloved wife was too much for me. Marilyn was a friend of your mother's. She stepped in, making me live for you. She saved my life, and I fell in love with her. If it weren't for Marilyn, you wouldn't have me. Not that I'm without faults, but I did my best."

"Why did you allow all the vultures to take Mom and Dad's estate?"

"I got you. The rest was just money and property. Marilyn secured the books, photographs, and any sentimental item she could. I was in no state to help."

"I didn't know that."

"She's not as evil as you believe." I stayed curled up on my uncle's lap until Marilyn and Ben called us for lunch. Thoughts in my head were trying to find the evidence behind Theo's claims. After lunch, my preoccupation worried Ben.

"I think Zelda is still recuperating. Come, Zelda. You need rest." Ben stood and offered his hand gallantly.

"I'm not a child, Ben. A guardian of an adult does not mean you have to treat me as a toddler."

"Do you not want a nap?" His gleam was mischievous.

"No, I do," I said too quickly.

"Then your defiance is obsolete. Choose your battles wisely, princess." Ben leaned in and kissed me in front of Marilyn and Theo. He snickered at my hesitation. "They know I love you, Zelda."

I chose to stay quiet and allowed Ben to tow me back to his room. We didn't emerge until dinner.

* * *

My heart opened to Ben again. I knew the repercussions would be grave, but my body didn't care. I needed and loved him, not that I was ready to admit it. Ben and I were constant bed partners. Our bodies were connected in some way every moment of the weekend. We said little, probably in fear of saying the wrong thing to ruin our blissful existence, knowing it was coming to an end.

"Princess, how do you feel about staying here through the holidays?" I was hoping he would say next that he would be back. "Theo asked me to invite you. I won't be able to see you for a while."

"How come?"

"I can't keep you safe if we are seen together. Land's End is safe. But if I frequent it too much, it will draw attention."

"How is it you are here now?"

"I told my boss I was using vacation time and the holiday to help Theo as a friend. Everyone knows he had a heart attack but not everyone thinks helping a friend is an appropriate holiday." Ben looked sad in contemplating his acquaintances. He held me tight as we swayed together, almost dancing. "Princess, I'm so proud of you for how far you have come. You're so brave and wonderful. Theo would love to spend more time with you. I would be happy to know you are here and safe."

My juvenile side hadn't been totally exorcised away. I wanted to throw a tantrum because I wasn't able to see Ben again. "Please, Zelda. I need this from you."

I could not commit with words but squeezed my answer. Ben was not mine. There were risks in us seeing each other that I didn't understand. I wanted to stay with Theo, but I wanted Ben more. A tantrum was inevitable at some point.

CHAPTER SEVENTEEN

Loss in Las Vegas

Leaving Land's End was hard for me this time. I stayed a month. Theo and I were in a new place in our relationship. Misinformation had been detrimental to the processing of my parent's death. Marilyn accepted my apology with the understanding my natural inclination to hate her would still be present. I was friendliest towards her when no one was around. My juvenile tendencies were ever-present.

My apartment held little interest to me, even being in the city. A suicide attempt was leaked to the newspapers, tainting my consulting business. My next job wasn't until the following month for a company that one of my father's friends owned in Jackson Hole. Drugs were off the table as a distraction. Since alcohol led to drugs, my vices were limited. Although, sex was still an option.

Ben made it clear he could not see me for a while. Understandable. He was married. My condemnation never came from having sex with him at Land's End again. I believed in the ghost of Edith Wharton. The hospital and rehab event was so intimately shared between us that the physical nature of sex was second. I excused the infidelity.

My black knight was unavailable to me as well. Luca survived our last night together, but we were ordered to stay away from one another. Rowan and Ben had met in the hospital that week and agreed that we were too toxic for each other. They were not wrong.

My thoughts went next to Mason, the hulk of a delicious man. He would serve my needs perfectly. I texted him to inquire if he was available.

> Me: Steak. Godiva needs a steak. Bad. Are you available this weekend?

> Mason: Godiva. I am available for you anytime.

Me: Catching a flight tomorrow. See you at your place around 8.

Mason: I will kick everyone out by then.

Me: Excellent. I hate muffling my screams of ecstasy.

Mason: Fuck. You have me already painfully hard. You will be punished.

Me: Lovely, a little pepper on my steak.

Shamelessly, I took a four-hour plane flight for great sex. I checked into my room at the Horseshoe under an alias. I didn't need to draw attention to my presence. In hindsight, I should have stayed at a hotel further down the strip. Old habits rarely die.

I had time to take a long shower, wax all parts south, and give my muscles enough time to relax after the trip. New lingerie always made me feel sexy and ready for a night of passion. Mason would appreciate my efforts.

Deciding to hop a bus down the strip seemed efficient and untrackable. Mason's house was only a block from the stop, but the humid, dusty ride ruined my clean, fresh, just-showered feeling. I walked up the stone pathway through the back yard getting the feeling in my stomach that all was not well.

As promised, there wasn't a typical party going on, and most of the lights were off. I knocked on the back screen door twice before pushing myself through. "Mason?" I walked through the kitchen, hoping he was already waiting for me in his room. As I appeared in the living room, a solemn but beautiful man sat on his usual throne.

"Mason?" I expected a better greeting as I moved towards him.

"Zelda?" A familiar voice barked from the other side of the room, stopping me in my tracks.

"Luca," I whispered, trying to understand the situation.

"Zelda, why are you here?" Luca was angry, but I couldn't figure out why. Then I saw the gun in his hand. My head turned back and forth between Mason and Luca. Self-preservation kicked in, and I tried to take a couple of steps back. "Oh no, you don't. Zelda, tell me why you are here. How do you know Mason?"

Mason and I stared at each other. I was trying to read from him what the correct answer should be. "Zelda. Are you here for drugs?" I shook my head in defiance. "It's my understanding that if you are caught doing drugs, you will be locked away for a long while." I agreed to his admonishment, not knowing what Ben and Rowan had told him.

"So if you are not here for drugs, then you are here for...." Rage replaced Luca's curiosity as the evidence clicked into place. "You are mine, Zelda. Marked by me for the Moretti family. You belong to us."

"That is the most ridiculous thing you have ever said, Luca. We aren't even allowed to see each other." My hackles were evoked at his declaration. "I've done some jobs for Rowan. You and I like to fuck. That's the only association I have with your family." The memory of his rejection was still raw. "Go away, Luca. I came to see Mason." Luca pointed the gun at me for my insolence.

Quicker than I could track, Luca pulled the trigger and put a bullet through Mason's forehead. "You're not fucking him tonight." Shock paralyzed my screams.

Luca pocketed the gun and dragged me through the house, out the back yard to a parallel street where his car was parked. He opened the passenger side like a gentleman and tucked me in. I was still frozen inside and, at times, forgetting to breathe. We sped through the back streets until we came to a local house party. Luca parked in an open spot near the entrance and escorted me in. This was an alibi for tonight.

The large house was full of people having a grand time. The music was thumping, and drinks were flowing. Luca nodded to a few people while towing me toward the back of the house. His hand gripped me tighter as his body began vibrating. Abandoning his destination, he had me pressed against a wall in a hallway. My hands were held by his high above my head as his body leaned into mine. He rubbed his erection into my crotch while bending his head so his lips could meet mine.

Luca was not usually loving. He took. No kind words. No gentle caresses. Raw sex to satisfy his desire. His desire was always me. Kissing became more urgent and fevered as his desire grew. He pressed his lips harder into mine, trying to light the spark in me. I was never far from being ignited around Luca. The shock in my system slowed the progress.

Luca's assault left my lips and continued on my neck. He sucked on the marks he had left on my neck, driving me wild. "Luca, please." My needs soon matched his.

Without hesitation or propriety, Luca entered me in the hallway. He held me against the wall, thrusting into me like a man possessed. My dark knight was a sociopath. Societal norms did not apply to him. He took, and it felt so good.

"Luca. I'm coming, Luca." He pressed into me harder and faster, intensifying my climax and letting loose his.

His lips were back on mine as I slid down the wall. Still, no words were said. Without fully reassembling himself, he brought me into a room, barely closing the door before stripping me of my dress.

Luca tossed me on the bed and ripped my thong off, promptly tying my hands behind my back. My ass was in the air, and my chest was firmly on the bed. He held my tied hands as a hard slap hit the right cheek. Fuck that felt good. He did it again, and I could feel my juices leaking down my thighs. Luca spanked my ass until it burned. My demons danced excitedly, waiting for the punishment to continue as he fucked me hard.

Luca did not disappoint. Menacing. Punishing. He was relentless in giving me what my body needed. Being lured back into the darkness, I was disappointing my white knight. The bad girl was coming back. Luca and I fucked all night in a place I didn't know. Usually, I was high as my excuse for making bad choices. Now, I was sober, making bad choices. Reprocussion be dammed. Luca felt too good.

Morning came, and he still had not spoken a word. After our morning urges were satisfied, we dressed, and he towed me out of the house. "Luca, I'm hungry." He nodded and settled me into his car.

"Baby, what do you remember from last night?" His knuckles pet my jaw as he spoke.

"Lots of fantastic sex. You're a sex demon, Luca." He smiled and kissed me.

"And you are my goddess."

After breakfast, Luca took me back to my room. We showered and climbed into bed. I lay in the crook of his arm with my head on his chest. Uncharacteristically, he delivered light kisses to my forehead, holding me tight.

"Baby, I'm sorry I gave you drugs laced with fentanyl. I know you had a hard time afterward. You almost died."

"Luca, I wanted to die." He stilled. "My black knight admirably consented."

"The fentanyl made me crazy. I would have never knowingly killed you." He stilled again. "Zelda, why do you crave death?"

"Not so much anymore. But they have taken all my vices away but one." I turned and began licking Luca's neck.

"Mason made the lethal dose of product. I asked him for something special for our party that weekend."

"He did it on purpose?"

"Yes."

"Why?"

"I may have learned a few things from Chase and paid him a visit."

"Luca, I don't like causing so much trouble. Now Mason is dead…"

"Mason is not dead because of you, strictly speaking. He tried to kill me. Indirectly you. You have been trouble for me since I first saw you sitting at a high-stakes poker table. I have craved you constantly since." Luca flipped me over and maneuvered on top. I opened for him automatically.

"You know we are not allowed to see each other."

His lips kissed my ear and whispered, "Then close your eyes." Slowly, he entered me to the hilt.

"Luca, you feel so good." His progress was slow and steady, kneading my core. He planked above me, driving into me expertly. Luca was strong and intense in all things he did.

"I know, baby. I love to make you feel good." Lowering his hips enough that the pubic bone rubbed the right spot and sent my orgasm into high gear. I ground up into him, extending the pulses. He continued with his rhythm until I was ready again. We released together. Sometimes Luca didn't always take.

* * *

"I'm hungry again." Luca and I had taken a long nap. Usually, he is on the move and leaves me after sex, or I'm running away from him. Since our husband and wife stint, we lingered.

"Get ready. We can eat in the lounge. I have to check in with Rowan."

"Rowan won't be happy to see me."

"Rowan won't be happy to see us."

We dressed quickly and made our way down to the lounge. As expected, Rowan was holding court at a table in the back. "Is he waiting for us?"

Luca laughed, "Probably."

We approached the table, and Rowan gestured for us to sit. "We have things to discuss." He was not happy.

"I'll talk about anything you want as long as there is food." As I said the word food, an assortment of dishes was placed in front of us. The server took our drink order, giving Luca an extra long look.

"Luca, you are a rumpled mess. This is not the way we present ourselves." Rowan barked at him.

"It's Zelda's fault. I'll change after I eat." He mumbled as he shoved food in his mouth.

"That's not how I'm remembering last night." I protested.

"I'm sticking to it. He likes you better, anyway."

"That's not true. You're his nephew." Luca rolled his eyes while continuing to eat. I looked at Rowan.

"Yes. I do. I have no children and three nephews. If I had a daughter, I imagine her to be like you." Tears welled up as I processed his statement.

"Luca, you need to go change. I need to talk to Zelda." Luca looked to me oddly for permission. I nodded. He stood and gave me a lingering kiss on my cheek before he walked away.

"Ben called. A lot." Rowan began. I choked on the lemon chicken currently in my mouth.

"I didn't know you two exchanged numbers." Rowan's phone rang. He looked down at the caller ID and smiled.

"Rowan. Yes. Yes. Yes. She is right here." He passed the phone to me.

"Zelda." Ben was pissed.

"Ben." I was unamused.

"Why are you in Vegas?"

"Truth."

"Please."

"I came here to have sex. Sex is my only vice left." I know I was being mean and insensitive. Too bad Ben was married.

"Why aren't you answering your fucking phone?" Ben was barely holding it together.

"Same answer. I guess. Lots of sex."

"Give me back to Rowan." I handed Rowan back his phone without saying another word.

"Ben. Yes. No. No. No. Yes. I will. We can do that too." The line disconnected, and I readied for my lecture. "Ben loves you. You're behaving like an adolescent."

"True. Too bad he's married."

"Zelda. Ben loves you. Luca loves you. I love you. Theo loves you."

"What's your point?"

"You know my point. You think you are going through this life without love. Even though you are a pain in the ass and sometimes treat people poorly, we still love you. We love you when you make mistakes. We love you when you shine. We love your spirit. We love you on your darkest days." He placed his hand over mine. "You'll not be better off with your parents. You're meant to be here with us. Living."

"You were there?" I didn't consider Luca to be in the same shape I was, probably in the room next door. Rowan must have heard my breakdown with Ben.

"Yes."

Tears were steadily streaming down my face. I had nothing to say. Rowan continued. "You know you and Luca aren't good together. Oil and vinegar. Delicious but incompatible. You two court each other's demons. Ben and I can't survive another time when we almost lose you both. Luca is set to marry the daughter of another boss. The union will unite our families, and she is very docile. A good match for Luca."

"No!" My heart constricted instantly.

"You'll not be allowed to see each other anymore." Luca emerged at Rowan's proclamation.

"I haven't agreed to this, Uncle."

"No need. I agreed." Rowan stared Luca down. Family was business. Luca looked at me with my tears still active and pitched a fit.

"I'll marry Zelda. She can be the daughter you desire. Her skills will become the family's."

Rowan looked to me for support. Luca sat down next to me at my request. I took his face in my hands. He was so handsome and sexy. I finally felt his love when he looked at me. Now, I had to let him go.

"My handsome dark knight. I love you. Our time together is never healthy. We feed off of depravity and each other's demons. Our passion is epic, and sex is extraordinary, but you know we can not commit to one another. You'll marry a beautiful girl, have many babies, and be the protector and provider you yearn to be." I kissed him, but he didn't kiss me back. I could feel his pain.

I loved Luca enough to set him free. He almost lost his life because of me. I was toxic to him, and he had a chance at a better life.

"Take tonight. Say your farewells. Make sure Zelda is on the 1 p.m. flight back to New York tomorrow." We nodded and abruptly left for my room.

Giving up Luca would be denying a part of myself. My dark knight woke the passion lurking beneath my decimated light. The darkness we shared as kindred souls made life worth living. My brain understood the necessity of letting him go, but my heart never would.

CHAPTER EIGHTEEN

Birthday Gift

Theo and Marilyn had been calling me all week, wanting me to visit Land's End for my birthday. I was still mourning the loss of Luca, my dark knight, and didn't particularly like celebrating anything without my parents. Without light, the darkness crept in easily. I felt like I was floating on a sea of loss again. My Vegas playground was off-limits, and I needed a distraction. My distractions weren't usually mentally or physically healthy.

Pounding on my door pulled me from my reverie. I wasn't expecting anyone. "Who is it?"

"James."

"Is that supposed to mean something to me?"

He laughed. "I guess not. Your guardian has sent me. Fuck, it's cold out here. Can I come in? I come bearing gifts."

I opened the door to a tall, extraordinarily handsome man ladened with wrapped boxes. He tried to smile but was arrested as our eyes met. "Fuck. I'm married."

"Come in, James, married friend of the guardian." He clumsily came through the door and deposited the stack of wrapped boxes on my table.

"So what got you to let me in? My voice? The fact it was cold or the gifts?"

"You smell good. Serial killers don't smell good. They are too preoccupied with their fantasies and preparations. They forget hygiene."

"You're fascinating. Did I mention I was married?"

"And a friend of my guardian." I laughed.

"I didn't mention Ben and I were friends."

"Ben would never send anyone he could not completely trust to my apartment. He also sent you to spy on me when he could not."

"Spy is such a loaded word. How about enamored interest." James took off his coat and continued to rearrange the pile of presents. "My wife was pissed at first, but you know Ben. He can charm the fleas off a dog."

"So he made her spy on me, too?"

"Yeah, we had shifts for a while. He's obsessed but endearingly so. I see the lure."

"Too bad you are married."

"Married. Right." James's smile left abruptly. "I love Ben like a brother. I held him as he cried after returning from finding you half-dead in Vegas. Then again, after he left you at Land's End before Christmas."

"I know. You don't have to say it." Tears began to pool in my eyes at my effect on Ben.

"I think I do."

As I prepared for his heartfelt speech, James's phone went off. He answered, and I could hear Ben yelling at him. "What do you mean by what is taking so long? I just got here. She wouldn't let me in. She thought I was a serial killer. You could have mentioned your BFF once in the last six months." He looked at me as he was listening to Ben. "She said I smelled good. Serial killers smell bad, apparently. Only your girl would know something like that." His girl? "Okay, I'm hanging up." James put the phone back into his pocket. "God, what a grouch. He needs to have sex." His hand flew to cover his mouth. "Oh, sorry."

"No, I get it. So what's the program?"

"Well, happy birthday, princess." James leaned in and kissed me on my cheek.

"Not you, too. I have been called Princess Zelda since I was in elementary school."

"I was called mustard face. Consider yourself lucky. One time. One. I ate a bologna sandwich at lunch, and boom, forever labeled." James smiled again. His mischievousness returned. "Anyhow, Princess Zelda is the theme of your present. I think you'll come to appreciate her."

James was tall and lean with masked tone muscles beneath his long coat and sweater. His carefree smile engulfed his whole face. He had piercing blue eyes and blonde hair that was gelled back. His dark-rimmed eyeglass frames only made him more handsome. Nerds with potential. Yum. He continued as I studied him.

"You understand Ben can't be seen with you or even have a digital trail connected to you. I thought of this solution myself." He handed me a heavy box. "Open."

The first present was a large 16-inch laptop. The next present was a headset and a Nintendo Switch. James wouldn't let me open the third box until he left: "This computer can only be used for one purpose. Do not use it on any other network except the one installed. Understand?"

"I'm not sure I understand. I have a computer."

"Come." James sat me on the couch while he set up the computer. He installed the headset and handed it to me. "The Legend of Zelda is already loaded."

"Ben got me a computer game?"

"This is a well-equipped gaming console. Here is the remote. Ben and I played this game endlessly growing up." James laughed at my confusion. "Oh, did I mention you would be playing Ben?"

As the program launched, Ben streamed in from his computer. "Hey, baby. Nice to finally see you. Happy Birthday."

"I was just getting to know your girl…"

"Get out!" Ben and I said in unison. We were already devouring each other through the screen.

"Zelda, I've missed you. This method allows us to see each other all the time."

"Thanks to me."

"Why the fuck are you still there, James."

"See Zelda. Grouchy."

"Not for long."

"Now, that is my cue to leave. Unless…"

"I'm calling your wife," Ben yelled, and James flew out the door.

"Open your other gift, princess." Ben purred. I opened the last box while Ben watched. His eyes darkened as I pulled out nipple clamps, simulators, lube, and a vibrator that matched his cock perfectly.

"So we aren't playing Legend of Zelda?"

"Virtual sex first. Computer gaming second."

"This is a great birthday present."

"I know."

* * *

Ben and I were connected virtually most nights and weekends. My white knight was sinfully erotic, entertaining me. For the next few months, my mood was exceptional. Being able to see and talk with Ben daily kept my darkness away. Virtual sex was surprisingly satisfying, especially with Ben's sultry voice loud and clear in the headphones. Physical touch was replaced with words and ministrations empowering self-orgasms.

Plus, it was Ben. Our connection only got stronger the more we talked and shared our lives. I never asked where his wife was. My selfishness sidestepped the emotional infidelity. I edited out that virtual sex was immoral. Ben was mine.

"Time to play, Zelda." He chuckled through the mic. "Pun intended. You need to learn what all the fuss is about when people have called you Princess Zelda."

"I've never played video games."

"That's okay. We'll be playing together. I have completed most of the series except *Breath of the Wild* and the latest ones."

"You say that like that is impressive? I lack reference, remember?"

"There are 30 games available in the franchise. Some are rereleases. James and I have conquered many of them."

"I feel there is more to this game than nostalgia."

"You're correct. You only have three of them loaded onto your computer. James should have shown you how to hook up your Nintendo Switch. The Switch is the controller, and the screen on your laptop will allow us to play together or at least side by side. We'll start where it all began. 1986 *The Legend of Zelda. Ocarina of Time* was released in 1998. The *Breath of the Wind* is one of the more recent ones. At least to start." Ben winked his inner nerd surfacing. It was weirdly hot.

Ben and James had configured the computers, so we had shared screens. Half the screen was Ben's gameplay, while the other half was mine. A live camera feed placed a video of each of us in the corners of our corresponding games as we talked into our headsets.

"This seems elementary. Like a kid's game."

"These are kids' games. Remember, this was 1986. This was revolutionary for 1986."

"If you say so." We played the first game for the rest of the weekend. I mirrored his moves. We got to the end pretty fast with Ben's experience."

"So Zelda is a weak heroine that always needs saving from the male character. Are all the games a similar trope?"

"Remember, this is the cultural view of women in the eighties. I always felt like there was more potential for her. Male Nintendo creators oppress her."

"She's a former goddess. Doesn't she have some powers tucked away?"

"Zelda, all little boys want to be the hero. To save the beautiful princess from evil villains. Most of the games had a similar trope." Sensing my vexation, Ben continued. "She guides Link and keeps him on the right path. In the end, Link and Zelda defeated Ganon together as a team."

"The team is severely unbalanced. Would Link rescue her if she was ugly and had green skin with warts all over?"

"What did you like about the game?" Ben did not dignify my comment with an answer.

"The music. Navigating the dungeon layouts was cool. So were the fight sequences. I guess the storyline and mix of puzzles added to the gameplay. I liked that side quests were available and gave you rewards."

"So not that terrible."

"The three parts of the Triforce, power, wisdom, and courage, mirror Zelda, Link, and bad guy Ganon. Link is in service of Zelda and collects the shards of the Triforce to save her. Still elementary and chauvinistic."

Next week we started *Ocarina of Time*. In this version, Link has to use a magical flute to access the Door of Time to save the kingdom and Zelda from an evil king.

"Wow, what a difference a decade makes. The graphics improved considerably. So with each game, the main characters' souls are the same, just reincarnated in different bodies?"

"Basically. mystic sages help them defeat the evil king and save the kingdom of eternal darkness and monsters."

"Link is the hero of time, but Zelda is more participatory in this game." We played for hours, actually forgetting about virtual sex.

"She has to become a male in order to become a warrior and battle side by side with Link? You know how deranged and oppressive that is."

"As Sheik, she shows depth as a character."

"She can only kick some ass when she is in a male form. She had to disguise her authentic self. You realize when Zelda is back as a woman, she gets captured. Sheik would never need saving in this game." My arguments continued without validation.

"Yes, the troupe of the story. All men want to save the princess and be the hero. It's in our DNA. On the Y chromosome. There have been studies."

"Yes, as a man. Even though she is the leader of the Sages, she is still dependent on Link."

"Sometimes in life, people need another person to become complete."

"Weak people." My insensitive comment flew out of my mouth before I realized we weren't talking about the game anymore. The hurt in Ben's eyes made me regret my words.

He shook off my crassness and continued, "But neither Zelda nor Link can defeat Ganon alone. That is the troupe that everyone fails to see. This game is really about teamwork."

"Zelda is useless with her ceiling-protecting powers. The elements of teamwork are still unbalanced."

"You are putting too much value on Link and not seeing what Zelda is contributing. I think you are disvaluing Zelda because she is a woman. Her role is no less heroic." Ben was clever.

"I think if Zelda and Link traveled together in her true form, they would fuck. A lot. No saving the kingdom. No saving the Triforce. Just pleasuring each other for the rest of time."

* * *

Next, Ben and I played *Breath of the Wild*. The first game in the series Ben hadn't previously played. Our main characters were back after a century of limbo. Zelda had been using her powers to keep Ganon caged. The arc is the same, but the story has evolved to nonlinear open-world gameplay. Ultimately, Link and Zelda must collect artifacts and beat quests to gain enough stamina and power to defeat a giant dark beast before he destroys the world.

While Ben was at work, I watched countless YouTube walkthroughs, tips & secrets, and online conversations between gamers. I didn't want to follow anymore. I wanted to lead. The map was huge and hard to navigate because it was so vast.

"You forget Zelda is fierce and powerful, wise beyond her years. She has psychic abilities and magic powers. Does this remind you of anyone?" Ben liked to tease me by wildly pointing out the parallel consistencies between me and Princess Zelda. I was always annoyed.

"My profiling ability is neither psychic nor magic. It's based on scientific evidence and personality patterns."

"Psychic and magic to us commoners. Zelda has keen insight and judgment beyond mortals. "

"Link is still the playable character. I thought with the progress feminism has made over the last few decades. There could be a choice at this point. You realize Zelda is still the prize. Saving the kingdom from evil for her. At some point, the game needs to progress where she and Link have equal footing.

"She is evolving. She rejects the restrictions placed on her by her father and develops scholarly interests."

"That's still medieval thinking. I guess the healthy depiction of women is too subtle for me. The responsibilities of the stature of a princess are too linear. I like the chaos she brings and how it's up to her to save the kingdom."

"Remember, we have been playing the Legend of Zelda. Not the Legend of Link." Ben thought he was so clever.

* * *

In the final battle, courage, dedication, and destiny helped defeat the evil villain and save the kingdom. Ben was right. They had to work as a team more in this game than any other, but Link was still the player. The world was trying to evolve. I was not.

In The Legend of Zelda, I saw a female ruler repeatedly having to be rescued. She was a weak heroine, and the plot focused on her incompetence. The damsel in distress trope began to grind my nerves. She was always in peril from the evil Ganon, a force of darkness. Zelda was stuck in her character role, and so were Link and Ganon, for that matter. For each game, my assessment was on repeat.

The inherent plot resonated with me. The storyline ran parallel to my life's themes, although I would never admit this out loud. The woman always has to be rescued by the male character. The incentive in the story was to save the beautiful princess and save the world. My male characters were only saving me from myself. The repetitive plot I called episodes.

Link as the light was not lost on me. Calling Ben my white night perpetuated what Ben already saw in himself. He had to prove himself worthy. The little boy inside Ben wanted to be the hero and save Princess Zelda. I was not Princess Zelda. Except for a handful of people, I wouldn't be missed.

Luca, I called my dark knight. I succumbed to death in his presence. Living in the darkness was easier than living in the light. Presently, I was only avoiding the darkness. I was still on the road to perdition. True to my word, I abstained from drug use. In the recesses of my mind, I was conjuring other ways to punish myself for my continued existence.

Ben gave me a great birthday gift. A fine distraction. Time with him. A skeleton to analyze my life. Having been called Princess Zelda most of my life pissed me off even more. Weak. Powerless. Dependent. This is what the world thought of me—even Ben.

Powering off the computer, I needed distance from Princess Zelda and Ben. The reality of our playtime made me consider Ben in a different manner. I would be on a flight to Luca if I weren't meeting a potential client in Chicago this weekend. In the absence of love, depravity sneaks back in.

CHAPTER NINETEEN

A Step to Redemption

A client requested an in-person meeting prior to the assignment. A necessity at times, especially if the client feels compromised digitally. I offered to meet him in Chicago on the way to Jackson Hole. A friend of my father's had been anxious to engage my services for his mining company. I was highly suspect he had ulterior motives.

Ben had me so wrapped up in conquering the Legend of Zelda I devoted little time to my business. Money was never a pressing issue for me. I lived simply and didn't spend much. Food was probably my biggest expense since I hated cooking and was always hungry. My clients paid me well, and I also had my poker winnings in a separate account if needed. Outside of tournaments, I won enough to always have large amounts of cash on hand. I was very fortunate not to have money as a stressor.

The Chicago company was a large motorcycle shop that assembled, fixed, and sold several major brands. The campus had a well-known retail store for biker merchandise and memorabilia, as well as a bar, restaurant, and tattoo parlor. The destination concept was brilliant and, from my research, profitable.

I sent a large suitcase ahead to Jackson Hole. Joel, my father's best friend, was insistent I was prepared for the winter climate even though spring was approaching. This way, I could pack a carry-on for my detour to Chicago. The client bought my plane ticket and booked a reservation in the historic Drake Hotel. I loved staying in places that linked to the past. The Drake has been a haven for celebrities and significant figures through the decades. Even renovated, the structure still held the old-world charm. That alone brought value to the trip.

Drake had sent a car to pick me up at O'Hare airport. The company attended to details to ensure my services. Their respect was better than that of the Fortune 500 companies I had worked for. Still shaken from the flight, my mind was elsewhere instead of noticing unusual patterns.

Check-in was effortless. An itinerary was handed to me at reception from the client. I was escorted to my room even though I only had a small bag and a carry-on. A car would be waiting for me in an hour to take me to the meeting off sight.

After a quick shower to erase the travel grim, I put on a deep purple silk dress keeping my hair down. The thick waves would act as a blanket in the frigid Chicago air. I assumed the meeting would continue to a dinner engagement and maybe even into the Chicago nightlife. Securing a long black cashmere wrapped around me, I headed to a bar called Mercy. Odd name, but I enjoyed the owner's wit.

The night air was brisk, and it felt cleansing being out in the world. The past month I had isolated myself in my apartment, playing with Ben. A fine distraction, but I couldn't hide from my life forever. The car left me right in front of the old bar, miles from the city center. A motorcycle enthusiast would fit right in with the rough interior and shady customers that lined the dark wooden bar. Still, no alarms were going off as I looked for my contact. I figured this was a test of my ability to assimilate into any environment. Until I saw Mateo sitting at the bar.

* * *

Self-preservation never came naturally to me. One of the reasons my father was so overprotective. Even in elementary school, I would confront a bully to understand the true motive behind their acts. In college, I continued to add to the carousel of behavior patterns by watching people's reactions to stress. The environment was usually on the verge of being illegal.

My opportunity to retreat vanished when his eyes met mine. The pictures from Bruno's mantle didn't do him justice. Mateo's eyes lit up at my recognition of him. Bruno's son, the Navy Seal tech, was not easily forgotten. I was in front of him before my thoughts concluded. "You're much larger in person than in your picture."

"Yes."

By the look on his face, I had already thwarted the well-rehearsed plan in his head. I sat down next to him and ordered a tumbler of Macallan whiskey, always preferring my death to be sexy and classy.

Mateo watched me consume my drink without saying a word. His scrutiny was profiler-worthy. I ordered another drink, letting him settle the conflicts swirling around his head.

"I'm sorry for your loss. Bruno was so proud of you, talking about your accomplishments. He missed you but understood your absence was for the greater good." Pain flitted over his face. He was feeling guilty about his father's death.

"My parents died three years ago. I miss them every day. Some days are crippling, knowing they're not in the world anymore." The burn of the whiskey felt good.

"Tell me what happened to your parents." Mateo's voice was commanding but kind. I expected him to drag me to the back of the bar and put a bullet in my head. Talking seemed surreal.

"After my first client, I surprised my family with an island trip to thank them for their support. The chartered flight crashed, and everyone died. I missed the flight that day. Most days, I wish I hadn't."

After another period of silence, Mateo spoke again. "Tell me what happened the day my father died." My hesitation didn't go unnoticed for long. "Please, I need to know."

"I was asked to play poker with your father and the other bosses one night. They knew Bruno's winning streak was from foul play. Rowan asked me to investigate." My account was vague. I didn't want to point out his father was using his tech equipment.

"Is that it?"

"I was removed before he died. I don't know what happened after the game."

"I know what happened. You would rather assume responsibility than state my dad was using equipment I had set up?" His hand wrapped around my neck. His anger was displaced until he found the scar from Luca's pronged ring. "Fuck." He released his grip as his thumb pet the closed holes. "You were blackmailed."

He continued stroking my neck. "I know you tried to stop the bosses. I still want to blame you."

Mateo sat and stewed as he sipped his drink. My empathy for him had stalled the analysis that was waiting for attention. Mateo was solid without an ounce of body fat. He was powerful but not overly bulky. His beard had grown to the length of his military haircut, creating a sexy dark shadow around his face and head. He smelled of fresh soap, moss, and a hint of patchouli.

"Closure and acceptance are an important stage of grief." He looked at me like I was a nut. Do as I say, not what I fail to do.

"You would give your life to resolve mine?" He thought for a moment, "Or are you trying to get me to do what you have failed at?" If he could not beat me up literally, he would do it figuratively. "I've assembled quite a large file on you, Zelda Alexander." I prepared for the beating.

"Odd that you missed the society pages. You only scanned the first page of Google." The death of my parents seemed a strange detail to miss.

"Let's start with your file at Quantico. You were expected to enter the FBI after your BSU internship and academy training. It's interesting how they let you go. A genius in mathematics and personality mapping. They listed you as a high-functioning savant. Your inability to process grief is understandable. Isolation, intolerance, and ignoring social norms are personality traits of your kind. The suicide attempts illude me. Most savants can reason beyond what stresses them, but you get stuck." Mateo continued to inspect my reaction to his claims.

"The attention to detail you possess is from hyperawareness and acute sensory sensitivity. You were a child prodigy, but your parents forced you to have a normal life while they encouraged your skills at home. Poker is not an honorable way to use your powers."

Mateo was just getting started. "Have you ever thought about the consequences of your career choice? You shake up multi-million and billion-dollar corporations. Your discoveries put people in jail, lose their jobs, or at the very least, end up in divorce court. Your mask of disdain, arrogance, and disregard can only protect you from emotion, not a bullet. I'm surprised you have stayed alive this long. Is this the life your parents hoped and dreamed about for you?"

Mateo's analysis continued, "Sex and drugs are your coping mechanisms to suppress feelings. I bet there is less than a handful of people that would mourn the death you seek."

"Then you should feel little guilt about killing me." I was firm behind my shields, but his opinions hurt. "All your research and planning shouldn't go to waste."

Mateo looked at me for a long time. We sipped our drinks, waiting for his resolution. "Misinformation and context. I needed to see you and talk to you myself. All the bosses made you the executioner."

"Even Rowan and Luca?"

"I was on my way to Vegas tomorrow. Unless?"

"Unless what?"

"Have dinner with me. Tomorrow night." Mateo couldn't have said anything more random if he tried.

"We can have dinner tonight."

"Not possible. But I will feed you. You already look hungry. I expect you were ready for a night out in the city. Change your flight to Sunday, and we will go out tomorrow." Mateo didn't wait for an answer as he called for the bill and paid.

His hand took mine, pulling me outside. The night air felt refreshing as the turmoil continued in my head. Mateo led me to a motorcycle and handed me a helmet. Nothing was said as I blindly followed his orders. Part of me was waiting for the bullet.

The back of a motorcycle was exhilarating. Few road norms were followed as we sped through the city. My fingers were laced around Mateo's torso, allowing me to feel the planes of his abdomen and chest. My cheek rested against his firm back. I closed my eyes, letting the sensations wash over me.

In no time, we were parking in a garage under the hotel. Sensory overload continued to make me compliant with what was happening. He picked up my hand again, moving us quickly up a flight of stairs, through the lobby, and to the elevators. Still, without a word, he pressed the button to my floor, avoiding making eye contact. The bell rang as the doors opened.

"How do you know my room number?" We stalled outside my room.

"I'm right next door." He finally looked at me. His eyes were almost black. "I plan for every contingency. The rooms are adjoining." His mercurial threat was so sexy. He even had a key.

My body was immediately pushed up against the door. Mateo pulled my hair, forcing my chin up and neck open, where he dove into inhaling my scent. His lips dragged around my jawline, ending up hovering over mine. My tongue reached out to coax his in. With permission granted, he devoured me. His lips assaulted mine. Hands stroked my body. His body pressed into mine. We were both vibrating with desire.

I tugged his shirt off, revealing a masterpiece of muscle definition and ink. He was covered in intricate tattoos. His movements could only be categorized as suppressed stealth. His eyes never left my face as my clothes were methodically removed. Patience was not one of my virtues. Pants or no pants, I made my needs known. Mateo growled as

I rubbed up against him. In moments, his thick shaft was sheathed with a condom teasing my entrance. He took me against the door. His thrusts echoed in the room. We continued to vibrate until I was screaming through my climax. Round one quickly rolled into round two.

By round four, I was starving. Without a word, Mateo ordered room service. Several dinners and a box of condoms appeared as round five concluded.

* * *

Mateo and I had missed the morning, ordering breakfast in the afternoon. We had yet to speak a sentence to each other. Our post-coital embrace sent us spiraling into our own thoughts. We seemed to be only waiting for our desire to return. Our day continued to be out of physical need.

"Can you be ready at seven?" I nodded, feeling weird to break the silence. Mateo kissed my forehead before vacating the bed. He used a key to open the door between our two rooms and disappeared.

By seven, I was ready, wearing a flowy dark green dress that would allow my legs to spread on the motorcycle. My cashmere wrap was still the warmest coat I brought. Mateo knocked before he entered. His appearance took my breath away. Dark dress slacks hung low on his hips. A steel-colored dress shirt made me drool as I scanned his chest. He had a leather jacket draped over his arm.

"Zelda, you are so beautiful." He was appreciating me as I was him.

"That was a lot of emotion flitting over your face to settle on beautiful." I laughed at his expense.

"The other adjectives were too rude to say to a woman. I was taught to be a gentleman." We both recessed into silence again after his comment. Bruno had taught him to be a gentleman.

After an exhausting dinner, we gave up all pretenses of wanting to stay in public. We were back in the room by ten. Sex was now less fevered and more composed. Our bodies knew each other now. Climaxes came quicker with more intensity. By midnight I was exhausted.

Mateo gripped my hands above my head, nuzzling his nose into my neck and inhaling my scent. His mouth settled by my ear while his other hand roamed methodically over my body. As we relaxed, he began to whisper.

"Zelda, who does your body think you are betraying?" My silence didn't deter him. "You hesitate before each time we have sex. My research never found a partner or lover. Well, except Luca Morelli. He just had his bachelor party in Vegas." Mateo planted kisses on my neck and behind my ear as he spoke. "My guess is you both were ordered to stay away from one another after your failed suicide attempt. Do you miss him, Zelda? The cold-calculating mafia underboss who used you for immorality." His knuckles began tracing circles around my breasts. Signals between loss and arousal were getting crossed. My brain and body were acting independently.

"A grown woman who has her uncle as a guardian. Do you feel he won't love you without a court order?" Mateo continued, "The marks on your neck where others claim you could have been easily removed. Yet you wear it like a badge of depravity. Depravity is for the weak mined, Zelda."

He kissed me in between each declaration. His observations were tortuous. "Your mask slips, and I see you. You are living an incomplete life." His knuckles moved down my stomach and over my mound. Rubbing between my legs, his seduction was making me moan while tears formed in my eyes.

"You have to forgive yourself if you want to be whole. No one can do that for you. Sex and drugs only give you a temporary feeling of well-being. It will not fill your soul. Death isn't the answer." His whispers became demands, and my body obeyed. "Zelda, come for me." I came hard and long as he rubbed me through my release. As promised, emotional well-being disappeared quickly, allowing the waiting sadness to filter in. Tears were ejected from my eyes.

Weeping turned into howling. Loss and abandonment consumed me. Shrieking horror escaped my mouth while I was shaking in despair. Mateo's words were reviewed again and again in my head. His calls to me were unrecognizable. My mind was in turmoil. I was free-falling.

Ben had cracked through my mask once. I felt more anguish exposing my pain than suppressing my demons behind shields. Ben pushed me to acknowledge my remorse. Mateo stated it to me. I'm not sure which was worse. My body was not my own as I sunk owning my life. I thrashed and vomited as if possessed.

Mateo tried to wrap his arms around me, but I couldn't be contained. The devil was knocking on my door, and I wanted to go with him. Breathing became a chore. My mask was breaking again. Torment and recrimination flooded out, leadening my body. I looked around for something to take it all away.

Mateo's eyes met mine in alarm. He threw himself on me, knocking me back to the bed. His body planked over mine incrementally lowering, keeping me weighted down. My body eventually tired and stilled as I wept. He tried to get me to mirror his breathing while forming a connection through my eyes. Once calm, I set my mind adrift.

The sun began to rise, flooding the room with light. Mateo had moved us to his room during the night since my room was trashed. His body was wrapped around me so tight that he would wake if I moved. Soft kisses were placed in my hair, lulling me back to sleep.

The next time I woke, Mateo sat in a chair beside the bed, staring at me. His elbows were on his knees, and his fingers were steepled into a triangle. "Zelda, I have to get back to my base. My leave has ended." His demeanor was solemn and pained.

"I had no business interrogating you about your life. I'm sorry." He sat back in the chair before he continued. "You became a challenge, and I consumed you like a drug. I've never been so physically and emotionally drawn to someone." His eyes roamed my face. "My only regret is leaving you." Mateo stood and bent down to kiss my forehead. "Stay safe and well, Zelda. You're an extraordinary woman."

Mateo left. Part of me was unsure if I had experienced penance for causing his father's death. I stayed in a hot shower, slowly building my shields and fitting my mask. After breakfast, I lay in his bed, processing the weekend. Being profiled was raw and unbalancing. It sucked. I never had empathy for my subjects. They were the means to attain a goal or practice my skills. Clever but unkind.

Mateo was a kindred spirit. He used me to process his own grief, allowing the information he gathered to come to terms with his father's choices. I envied his skill. How could I have missed that Mateo was trained at Quantico?

CHAPTER TWENTY

Jackson Hole

My next job was for a coal mining corporation in Jackson Hole, Wyoming. The Rocky Mountain Mining Corporation was one of the largest coal mining companies in the United States, employing over a thousand people across several states. The company had hundreds of working mines whose production covered over 60% of the United States coal supply.

Joel Nelson, the CEO, was a college friend of my father's. The fact almost made me decline his contract. Work was for me to escape haunting memories, not face them with strangers. Joel was persuasive in his pitch that I was the only woman for the job and promised a side vacation to the Grand Tetons. Interestingly, after news of my suicide attempt hit the society pages, Joel was persistent in my extended stay and moved my temporary residence from a hotel to his house near the Teton Village. Reasons extremely transparent.

Jackson Hole Airport was small and catered to private, charter, and small commercial planes. Unwilling to navigate the emotional trauma alone, I flew on a jumbo jet into Salt Lake City International and took a five-hour train to Jackson Hole. My brain emptied from my time with Mateo. As the train rolled over majestic mountains and through the plains of the valleys, I compartmentalized and stored all that was said.

Nature's beauty was a therapy I had never previously considered. My concerns were inconsequential to the history displayed before me. The eons of time it took for glaciers and volcanos to sculpt the land was amazing to see. The pine forests edging around the alpine meadows created a beautiful habitat for the creatures of the temperate ecosystem. Large mountain peaks stood tall in the background as if guarding the sanctuary. I imagined Native American tribes hunting buffalo. Cowboy mining towns with saloons and ladies dancing the can-can. The Rough Riders galloping over the plans and Teddy Roosevelt's tour of the West, which understandably led to the preservation of sights I was seeing. Maybe I was narcissistic.

Joel was waiting in the terminal upon my arrival. "Zelda!" I recognized Joel from previous events with my parents. He was tall, fit, and graying at the temples. Before I could stop him, he engulfed me in a tight hug. "Zelda, I would know you anywhere. How's my girl?" His hug failed to release as he spoke. I uncharacteristically embraced him back. Thanks, Teddy.

His refined good looks didn't diminish with age. He made me instantly think of my father. "Joel." We stayed entwined entirely too long as we silently processed his connection to my parents.

"Come, you must be starved. I remembered how you were always hungry."

"That has not changed." I tried to laugh but was still choked up, remembering the last time we were all together. Joel took my bags, and I followed him out of the terminal.

"I'm glad you are staying with me. I'm sorry I wasn't able to go to the funeral." He stopped in front of his Range Rover, "The truth is I couldn't face the event. I'm sorry, Zelda."

"I understand. I wish I didn't have to face the event." He opened my door but failed to meet my eyes. He was uncomfortable and knew he should have been there. I placed my hand on his, making him look at me. "Dwelling in the past is destructive. I can attest to that daily. Forgive yourself, and we can be friends." Do as I say, not as I do.

Joel searched my face and finally settled on my eyes. "You are even more beautiful than your mother. I see a lot of your father in you as well. The piercing eyes and firm jawline. I have followed your impressive career. They would be proud."

"Of my career, perhaps." The suicidal and destructive elephant was standing between us. Bravery wasn't one of Joel's strengths.

Joel lived in an enormous, beautiful stone and log cabin in the North West Bank outside of Jackson Hole. Having never been to the area, Joel broke into a monologue about the geography and economy of Jackson Hole. The ride to his house was breathtakingly beautiful, with the Grand Tetons always in the backdrop. A long stone driveway snaked towards the house hidden among the pine trees. In the higher elevation, snow was still part of the landscape.

"Since Marla left me, I hired a housekeeper and cook. Dinner should be waiting." He took my bags, and I followed him inside.

"I don't remember ever meeting Marla. She never accompanied you to New York?"

"She never accompanied me anywhere. She gave me Gavin. For that, I'm indebted and will gladly pay a huge amount of alimony."

"I don't think I have ever met Gavin either?"

"No. You haven't. He was either away at school or vacationing with his mother. Marla lives in Palm Beach now.   Gavin is with me. He earned a degree in business and geology and is training to take over the company. You'll meet him tomorrow." I didn't like the gleam in Joel's eyes. Transparency abounds.

After we ate the prepared dinner, Joel showed me to my ensuite. The large room had a four-poster bed and a desk that looked out to the mountain range. A gas fireplace dominated the room, accented with two cozy oversized armchairs that begged to be curled up in. The bathroom was predominately grey stone. A large clawfoot tub was set by bay windows that looked out to the mountain range.

"I may never leave." I stood in awe at the beautiful room.

"Good. I would be honored to have you." Joel kissed my head and said good night. My heart felt lighter than it had in a long time.

By mid-morning, we were en route to his office. The half-hour drive took us through Jackson Hole and out to Miller's Bute. The corporate office complex was more sprawling than tall. They had a modern design with clay-looking metal rooves and black windows. Only about one hundred people worked at this campus. The lab was a separate building, and so was the processing plant. The remaining employees were spread across Wyoming and bordering states near the mines.

"We'll meet with Gavin in the conference room at eleven. Let me introduce you to my main staff." Joel made introductions, and I observed. The first meeting always gave you the most information and a baseline for a person's mannerisms and micro-expressions.

Belinda, Joel's PA, met us as we entered the building. She spoke rapidly, giving Joel an update on pressing information. She averted her eyes in my direction, but curiosity eventually won. "Belinda, this is Zelda Alexander. We've hired her as a consultant. She is staying with me for a month or so." I nodded to Belinda, steeling my eyes. Establishing my dominance early made the rest of the job easier.

"Ms. Alexander." Her voice quivered and slowed. Mission accomplished.

"Zelda, please." I shook her hand too firmly, never relenting my gaze. Joel chuckled behind me.

"You are your father's daughter."

"Next." My intolerance was surfacing. Joel led me down a hallway to grander offices.

Joel rapped on an open door. "George, meet Zelda." He turned to me as George stood. "Zelda, this is George Hewitt, our CFO." I nodded again and met his eyes.

"Ahhh, the infamous Black Diamond. You grace us with your presence. I hope you find us a well-oiled machine." His eye contact never faltered, and he began to mirror my actions. He was trying to assert dominance over me while simultaneously trying to build trust. I smiled at the move. *Commoner.*

The only other introductions of the morning were the three vice presidents. Sam Turlott was the VP of the environmental engineering group. Gloria Henrich headed the supply and demand division, and Nolan Brown oversaw all the mine production. Each introduction gave me an interesting baseline to process. Joel led me to the board room for our meeting.

"Gavin's not here yet. I'm getting myself a coffee. Can I get you something, Zelda?"

"I need to make some notes. Take your time. I'll have hot tea. Thank you, Joel." Joel tapped the door frame, leaving me to type on my laptop. I wanted to ensure my first impressions of the leading players were well documented.

Distracted by my thoughts, I didn't hear Gavin come in. I felt his presence but chose to ignore him, letting him observe me.

Joel came in several minutes later, "Gavin. This is Zelda Alexander. You met her father, Grayson, a few times." As Joel spoke, I stopped typing and stood, moving to Gavin for the introduction. He stood oddly mute, watching me approach.

"Gavin, great to meet you." I held out my hand, but he stayed frozen in place.

"Gavin?" Joel admonished him for his poor manners.

"You're Zelda Alexander." A whisper came out of his mouth.

"I'm aware." Scanning his face, I couldn't understand his duress right away. "Ahhh. We've met before. How many Zelda Alexanders do you think there were when your father told you my name?"

"I didn't realize until this moment. You won Event #2: $25,000 High Roller Six-Handed No-limit Hold'em at last year's Word Series. You were the last woman standing."

"Yes." Joel was watching us with a shitty grin on his face. "Nothing personal, but I play to win."

"Why didn't you play in the championship round? There were rumors..."

"The rumors were true. Now, let's get this meeting on track. I'm very expensive, and time is money." Joel chuckled and directed us to our seats.

Gavin was just my type. Tall, intelligent, and handsome. His scent was fresh linen and ambrox. The woodsy musk was mixing with his perspiration, making me ache. Although this company was a major corporation, the dress code was mid-western casual. Fine sweaters and dress pants to flannels and jeans seemed the norm. Gavin wore a light blue cashmere sweater that pulled under protest as he moved his muscular upper body. Black dress pants hung loosely on his narrow hips. Bright blue eyes were still watching my every move. He was enamored. I was already annoyed.

* * *

"Typically, when I investigate a company, I begin as a secretary or PA to get perspective. The lower-level positions give me insight into the problems quickly. Since my presence and role are known, I'll have to observe the company's workings less covertly."

"Zelda, what do you need?" Joel was letting me lead.

"First, I need to know why you called me. My guess is that you initially employed my services to check up on me to honor the memory of my father. Theo could have a hand in this, as well, as a way to try to keep me too occupied to have an episode. I'll not pretend you are ignorant of my issues. But now I believe you have stumbled on some business issues that don't make sense, and a systems audit is warranted."

Father and son looked at one another, confirming my guess. "I'll need a long desk with a few chairs to be placed in a central location. Rather than an office, I want access to as many people as possible. I have a cursory understanding of how the company works and would like to visit a mine, especially one on your radar. And I'm always hungry."

Lunch was brought in as we continued our closed-door meeting. Gavin continued to stare uncharacteristically, according to Joel's discomfort. "Gavin, you have questions?"

If his pupils were dilating solely on lust, I was going to be disappointed. "You never lost." I continued to eat my sandwich as I listened. "You defeated me so easily. Then I watched you. Your playing was like you had magic powers reading everyone's hand."

"I don't read cards. I read people."

"Zelda was trained at Quantico." Joel looked sheepishly, knowing that information.

"I balance game theory, probability, and profiling. Deception and affirmation are as easily read as a smile or a frown. My secret weapon is being a woman. Men hate to lose to a woman."

Their attention never waivered, so I continued. "There are 44 facial muscles that give nonverbal cues to about twenty universal emotions. When I challenge a person, they involuntarily leak or reveal true feelings. Most poker players think they are good at suppressing their tics and tells. They are not. I find it quite amusing, really."

"What is my tell?" Gavin was engrossed.

"One of them is that you compress your lips when uncomfortable. Not a true form of deception, but your body is trying to suppress an emotion."

"Which emotion?" Gavin was brazen. I raised my eyebrow in condemnation.

"Gavin. Please, your father is present." I winked at him as his father chuckled.

"You date Luca Moretti." Gavin was punching back. "I saw you and him at the bracelet ceremony."

"No, we do not date." I sent Gavin a warning glare.

"Looked like you were dating." He deadpanned, knowing he had found a weakness.

"So Zelda, are you dating anyone presently?" Joel tried to smooth over our tryst.

"No." No, I wasn't. Saying Ben was not mine out loud pained me. Pain turned to rage. "Are we done with my nonexistent love life interrogation? We have embezzlement and shady deals to uncover, and I would like to be in a hot bath watching the sunset over the mountains by six o'clock tonight."

"You think someone is embezzling?" Joel gasped at my statement.

"Yes. Now, let's start with what I know about your coal operation." I walked around the room as if lecturing to students. I needed to find the holes in my understanding.

"The mid-west has huge reserves of coal that formed around fifty million years ago. This area consisted of vast freshwater swamps that nurtured the formation of peat. The woody plant accumulates and decomposes into a carbon-rich gel layer. The geothermal heat from the volcanic activity heats the layer and forms coal." Both men nodded. I continued.

"Wyoming coal, your coal, is sub-bituminous. A category given to coal that contains less sulfur and can burn more cleanly and up to 8,800 BTUs per pound. Your mines are reliable, and the coal is of such prime quality that other countries desire it since the specs meet their environmental objectives. The freshwater swamps known in this area make the best low-sulfur coal. Your coal beds are seemingly endless, being 250 feet thick and thousands of square miles wide. Fantastic job security."

"Now, explain the general process of mining to me." I peered at the wall maps as I made my request.

Gavin sat back in his chair and began. "The top layers and the overburden are removed by scrapers. Large machines remove the dirt and topsoil to be reclaimed or backfilled once the mine is exhausted. The overburden rests on top of the coal layer. The coal is removed and brought to a plant, similar to the one behind this building, that extracts contaminants like rock, ash, and other substances. The coal is screened for quality and size. Clean coal is then transported by trucks and trains in containers."

"What happens to an exhausted mine?"

"The reclamation of an empty mine begins right away. We work with environmental engineers and the EPA to return the landscape to its original state. The reclaiming process begins with redistributing the overburden, backfill, and topsoil. Replanting and monitoring flora and fauna can take years as the stages of succession reclaim the land. We pledge to monitor the mines until they are fully restored."

"That seems noble but expensive." Maps of Wyoming and boarding states covered the walls. Different colored labels not only identified the mine's geographic position but also what stage the mine was in. There were more active mines than ones under reclamation. "Who has voiced concern about the amount of money and resources dedicated to your philanthropy?" Father and son chose to stay silent. "Listen, we can work together on this, or you can make me the bad guy. You two talk it over while I have a look around."

"Zelda, we haven't even told you about our concerns yet." Joel and Gavin were not keeping up.

Candy. Baby. I loved this moment. "This is a twist on the great

Diamond Hoax of 1872. I'm sure you are familiar. I just need details and players." A satisfied smile sat on my face as I watched their mouths hang open.

"How do you know that?" Gavin whispered through his mouth again.

"Your company is always in the black. You offer good wages and benefits. Not being publicly traded means you don't answer to a board and can gain as much wealth as you want. Look at all the wall maps in this room. Nine of the ten largest coal mines in the US are here in Wyoming. You also have several mines in neighboring states and smaller producing mines scattered about. With over fifty active sites, it's unlikely you can intimately track activity." The theme was so common. How could they not see? "Power and money are the roots of all evil. Someone within your company is exploiting the fact you trust your process."

"I don't quite understand how the Diamond Hoax has anything to do with this?" Gavin was trying to follow.

"I have a completely plausible and brilliant theory, but I need more data. You two talk. I'll be back in an hour." I scooped up my computer and left the room undeterred by their parting comments.

"Dad, I love her."

"I know, son, me too."

* * *

An hour later, father and son hadn't moved. "After meeting five people and spending an hour in the board room, you're confident in your theory?" Gavin was dubious.

"Yes. I gave you all the variables. If you calculate the probability, only a few scenarios fit. I always defer to money and power as a motive."

The following week, I lingered at my desk in the great room, gathering data to support my theory. Interviewing the staff was not necessary, but I wanted to appear thorough. I loved Joel's house and riding to and from work with him. He wasn't as intrusive as Theo into my life but seemed genuinely interested. Of course, I edited.

Gloria was the least deceptive when interviewed. The deception was not in her job performance. She was in love with the VP of mining operations, Nolan. They worked closely together. She tried to hide her feelings. In my opinion, Nolan talked a big game but was lazy. His charm and electric smile fooled most. He hired competent people to run the individual mines to keep his workload minimal. The mines weren't monitored enough.

Sam was a bright environmental engineer who gave me additional insight into the depth of the reclamation process. His wife ran the lab in the building to the left of the main offices. She was also impressive with her chemical and geological knowledge.

The CFO, George Hewitt, had the most obvious deception. His huge ego was easily stroked, and he saw no value in having me audit his finances. An obvious red flag. He was quick to anger when I demanded his time and access to his computer. I didn't need his permission. I wanted to see his reaction and what he would subsequently try to hide.

Joel invited Gavin to stay at the house, giving me opportunities to come and go at different times. At least, that was the excuse. Gavin was looking for ways to interact more with me. His rugged good looks and Midwest charm quickly stirred my libido to dangerous levels. The bottom floor of Joel's house had a suite where Gavin typically stayed when he visited his dad. The drawers and closets were full of his clothes and personal items. Outside the suite was an entertainment area encased by oversized couches and chairs.

Joel held off playing matchmaker until the third week. "Gavin, why don't you take Zelda to dinner? I have the town council meeting tonight. I'll be late." Gavin and I both nodded. My reserve expired. A woman can not exist on brain work alone.

"Let's go now and grab some takeout."

"You don't want to go out to dinner?" Gavin looked surprised.

"No. Voyarism is not my thing." Quick to understand, Gavin towed me out the door and to his car, leaving all of our belongings behind. We never stopped for takeout, making it home in half the time. As we parked, I could tell Gavin was nervous.

Unbuckling, I climbed over the seat and straddled him. He relaxed a little as I traced his mouth and jaw with my fingers. Hovering over his mouth, my tongue licked his lips as he hardened underneath me. My lips pressed into his, and we ignited, ripping the clothes off each other's bodies in a fever. Suppression had fueled our fire.

I released his erection, and it stood magnificently at the ready. Slowly, I impaled him while we locked into each other's gaze. He was panting with need as I clenched around him. His hands wrapped around my ass, helping me up and down his shaft. God, I loved sex with handsome, rugged men.

"Fuck, Gavin. I'm going to come." His hips thrust himself deeper.

"Go, Zelda, I'm holding back for you." My climax immediately pulled him into his. "God, Zelda. You feel so good." We stayed connected as we began to make out.

"Let's go to your lair. I've been known to be insatiable." I laughed. Gavin opened the door so I could unfold myself from him. The clothes were ruined. There was no sense putting them on again. We walked practically naked through the house, scaring the housekeeper Maria.

In Gavin's room, he pulled me toward the bed, maneuvering himself on top of me. "I'm clean. I haven't been with anyone since Christmas."

"I take shots for birth control. I usually tell lovers I have syphilis so they use a condom. Two of them saw through my rouse." I smiled, bringing Gavin's lips to mine.

"Do you have many lovers, Zelda?" His lips began sucking on my neck.

"Define many?" My hands were back rubbing his erection, making him mute. We didn't talk for the rest of the night.

Joel called down to us in the morning. Gavin yelled he would bring me in later. We didn't make it to work. Finally, around dinner time, I threw on one of Gavin's flannels and tried to sneak to my room. Joel caught me. I could sense his smile even though I didn't make eye contact.

"Dinner is in a half-hour." He called out to me as I disappeared down the hallway. Gavin and I were sneaking into each other's bedrooms for the rest of the week.

* *.*

Towards the end of the month, my presence began to unravel the guilty. "You wanted to see me?" George motioned me in and to close the door. I failed to sit upon request. Malintent was easily read on his face. I had been name-dropping exhausted mines for the last week to see if any produced a reaction from him.

"I just wanted to check in on how you are fairing?"

"The job is interesting."

"Not the job. Luca Moretti was married this past weekend. I understand you two were close."

"I don't understand your concern?" *Interesting*.

"Before you came, I did a little research. You're an interesting woman, Ms. Alexander. Very Jekyl and Hyde. There are videos of you and Luca, shall we say, embracing. The passion you two had was intense." George looked genuinely thoughtful for a moment. "I had a love like that once. She got married to someone else. I was never the same." Unexpectedly, he opened his briefcase and tossed a bag of white powder across the desk.

"My condolences. A gift from a fellow jilted soul."

"You know I'm an addict, and Luca getting married would be a trigger. One would think this gesture to be more self-serving than commissary. How do I know it's not tainted?" Without pause, George opened the bag and made himself two lines on his table. He snorted one up each side of his nose.

"That is the good stuff never cut." His motive was transparent, but I played his game. Wrapping the bag in my scarf, I nodded my thanks. *Ass.*

I met Gavin in the hallway, "Ready to go?" He had my bag and coat in hand.

"Yes, I'm starving." Gavin chuckled. "Which one is George's car?"

"Over there. The red Cadaliac SUV."

"I'll meet you in your car. I want to leave him a note." Gavin looked perplexed but didn't challenge me.

Predictably, on our way to dinner, we were pulled over by several police cruisers. We were handcuffed, and the car was searched. Gavin was pissed, more at me than the cops.

"The car is clean." Disappointment plagued the officers' faces.

"You wouldn't happen to be looking for a 10g bag of cocaine?" Four officers snapped their necks in my direction. "The call you received was staged as an attempt to direct your attention away from the real suspect." As they unlocked our cuffs, I continued. "Red Cadaliac SUV. George Hewitt. I saw the bag in his briefcase at the office. We work at Rocky Mountain Mining."

"What's going on, Zelda?" Gavin was still pissed at me, not understanding the sting I thwarted.

"Call your dad. Have him meet us for dinner. We have to get to the Streeter Mine ASAP."

An hour later, we were seated at a table at the Jackson Brewery. "Zelda, my CFO, has been arrested on cocaine charges. He said you planted it." Joel tried to look amused but was clearly shaken.

"Interesting how only his fingerprints were lifted from the bag."

"Interesting how you know that." Joel missed nothing.

"I hit a nerve. He was trying to get me out of the way. Gavin and I need to get to the Streeter Mine and check out what is happening there.

Investigate any unusual correspondence from George's computer. I suspect Sam is an accomplice."

"An accomplice to what?"

"I believe George is selling off barren coal mines as potential gem mines. He and Sam are pocketing the cost of reclamation earmarked for the land. Look up the activity of Rocky Mountains Mining Corporation. They thought no one would notice the added 's' to Mountain." Joel and Gavin were shocked. I ordered for all three of us.

"The mine is over an hour away by helicopter. I can have it here first thing in the morning."

"No. No helicopters. Gavin and I will drive. We can spend a night or two." Gavin smirked at my offer. He was game as long as there was one hotel room.

CHAPTER TWENTY-ONE

The Great Diamond Hoax

The promise of wealth from the West began with the California gold rush and evolved into a diamond hunt. News of a Diamond Rush in South Africa prompted the Great Diamond Hoax of 1872. Tales of diamonds, rubies, and other gems being plucked right out of the ground caused wealthy businessmen to take a chance on speculation. A couple of grifters sold land salted with planted gems to prominent men in San Francisco and New York, even getting the owner of Tiffany's to authenticate the find. The mines were empty of gems.

Diamonds are made from pure carbon. Coal is too impure to make a diamond, although a common misconception. Diamonds require high pressure and high temperature to form. The only place within the earth's layer where these gems can form is in the uppermost mantle, almost 200 km beneath the surface. The age of most diamonds is about 3 billion years old. They are transported closer to the surface in molten rock from volcanic activity. Northwestern Wyoming sits on top of an active supervolcano that constantly moves and erodes geological layers over time.

The salting scheme was apparent as we approached the east end of the Streeter Mine opening. Gems were scattered so investors would find them. Diamonds in this area should be found in bedrock, not on disturbed topsoil. Some of the stones showed signs of cutting, which never occurs naturally. The most important observation is that the diamonds were found with rubies, emeralds, and sapphires. These stones never coexist in nature. This was Geology 101.

Reality met lore as we walked around the exposed crater. Gavin's geology degree came in handy as he pointed out the different geological layers exposed by volcanic movement around the depressed crater.

"See there. There are several fractures radiating out from this point. This is all volcanic rock from the mantle." The mineral analyzer was placed on an igneous rock, instantly emitting a loud noise. "Zelda?"

"That was my guess based on the way these kimberlites are shaped. They are a perfect host matrix for diamonds."

"This area is littered with them. If we could find these so easily, why didn't Sam?"

"He wasn't looking for them. He was blinded by the hoax and focused on the easy payoff."

We took samples and pictures of the salted and misplaced gems along with our discovery. We went out for a celebratory dinner near our motel.

"Dad put a lien on all properties until the lawyers can sort out how long this has been going on and what mines were affected. The Attorney General's office has flagged the Rocky Mountains Mining Company pending the investigation."

"Glad to hear it." We saluted ourselves with a tumbler of fine whiskey.

"Zelda, you saved the company millions and found a new resource to earn us millions more."

"Indeed. Remember that before you complain about my fee."

"You understood the dynamics of this the first day you were here."

"Yes." We ordered another round with our dinners. "Patterns. Once you understand the pattern and calculate the probability of that pattern being true, conclusions are easy. The evidence will surface. It just takes time."

I continued after our drinks were delivered. "We still have to link George and Sam with enough evidence that their conviction will hold up in court."

"Dad will be crushed. He feels like his company is family."

"Family members can be full of greed as much as anyone."

"Zelda?" A second door opened to my road to perdition. The pain of Luca's marriage was still pressing on me to be explored. My demons were awakening as my brain powered down. Gavin's sexual boundaries were going to be tested tonight.

The motel was the best in the area but still only a two-star. *Perfect.* Immorality didn't deserve luxury. Gavin's inexperience made the evening less elegant. "Zelda, what's changed?"

"I have needs. I'll walk you through it." Gavin was submissive and easily trained. He was smart but didn't possess the superior intelligence I needed. He was neither light nor dark. Our tryst would not last much longer.

Gavin was not Luca or Ben. Although he tried, he was not willing to commit to what I needed. The depravity was too tender, and my demons were not satisfied. Gavin was used to nice girls who just laid under him, where I continually shocked him.

The battle between fucking and making love was constant in our short relationship. Tonight, I wanted raw aminal sex that rode the pain pleasure line. Being dominant, I won at Gavin's expense. He didn't understand.

"Are these marks on your neck from other men hurting you?" I consented to cuddling after our last round. "Your body has several small scars. Their placement dosen't look accidental?"

"The events were consensual."

"Tonight at dinner, it was like a switch was flipped, and you went into the darkness?"

"I have triggers." Gavin sweetly tried to kiss my mental anguish away. I would always love him for that.

We were on the road by mid-morning. Gavin was deep in thought for most of the ride home. I had pushed my mountain man too hard. Just beyond the Teton's Pass on Route 22, we had cell service again. Both our phones were loaded with calls from Joel.

George was out on bail from the drug charge. Even though they found more contraband at his house, it was still his first arrest for drugs. Joel told his team we were checking out an active coal mine in Casper. Sam wasn't completely clueless. Large amounts of data were being extracted from the company's main frame. Trusting no one, Joel covertly hired an IT consultant to track their digital trail and security in case of trouble when all this came to a head.

We were instructed to go directly to campus. Joel had everyone assembled in the largest board room. Gavin and I were the last to arrive.

George growled as I walked in. I winked at him in return, needing him nice and agitated. Joel nodded to us. We all had our ducks in order. "Our meeting today is not a joyous one. One of you created a clever scheme to milk millions from this company to line your own pockets. I'm grieved and disappointed. Zelda."

"An employee with a high-security clearance has been moving large amounts of data off our server this past week. We are looking for an external hard drive or a laptop that potentially houses this data."

"Check out the new IT guy. The timing of his hire can't be coincidental." George barked.

"You're right, George." Gavin gasped, but Joel quickly understood this was a technique. "Jail gave you a great alibi."

"I would like to say that whoever stole the database, they should bring it back." George's deception was unmasked in his words. Why use *whoever* when we just established that it was the new IT guy? Why use *they* when we were referring to one person? There is no mystery, according to George's subconscious. He failed to think through his concerns. The spontaneity betrayed the lie.

A brief look at Sam caught him focused down and off to the right. A running internal conflict dialogue was speeding through his thoughts. He was trying to create new information and prepare a response if questioned. He was under stress. No one else had apparent signs of discomfort beyond their normal baseline. Anxiety and curiosity were not deceptions.

"The genius of the Great Diamond Hoax of 1872 was that many influential players were on board. The ignorance of the buyers' knowledge of geology and mineralogy allowed the grifters to prove the validity of the mines' prosperity. Nolan. Would diamonds and rubies ever be present in the same geological layer?"

"No. Of course not."

"Sam. How much money is budgeted for a complete reclamation of a small mine?"

"Up to half a million dollars."

"Nolan. If a mine was sold before reclamation has begun, would it be the new owner's responsibility to complete the process?"

"The only condition that would fiscally apply would be if the mine was still active."

"Agreed. Let's say, for example, the Streeter Mine. According to the company's records, the mine was exhausted and ready to begin reclamation. Then, a handsome geologist finds numerous kimberlites in a Devonian layer. He shows his lovely assistant they are full of grade diamonds worth hundreds of millions."

Sam and George both gasped audibly. "We would be grieved to have sold the property, especially as a hoax." Nolan offered.

"George, as CFO, can you calculate for me the cost of the reclamation of the Streeter Mine, the mine's property value, and the worth of several uncut diamonds and gems, as compared to hundreds of millions of dollars?" George was beet red and taking fast, short breaths. He wanted to pummel Sam for not discovering this on his own.

"What the fuck, Sam?" George blew. Sam tried to take himself out of the equation.

"Rocky Mountains Mining Company doesn't mimic the quality and integrity of the company it's stealing from. Don't you agree, Joel?" I played with my prey long enough.

"George and Sam, we have enough links to prove you own Rocky Mountains Mining. All of the company's activities have involved stealing property and money from us. Your positions are terminated, and the state attorney's office has collected all the evidence. Sam, your wife will be removed as well."

Security was available, but the police were already here to make the arrest. "My wife has nothing to do with this," Sam begged.

"Sam and George created a shadow company to embezzle?" Gloria was dumbfounded.

"Yes, item one of my audit. Anyone else want to come clean before I continue my investigation?" The room became eerily silent. No one met my glare. Joel's chuckle broke the silence.

"You're definitely your father's daughter."

* * *

With the job done, my brain was allowed to process Luca's recent marriage. I had suppressed the event when George threw it in my face. Curled up by the fire in my room, I had the Grand Tetons to lean on for support.

A mafia prince and princess wedding was a big deal. Hundreds of video clips were posted from different parts of the day. The first sight of my handsome dark knight in his tux tore my heart open. His stern, disapproving mask slipped to show joy and contentment. I continued to torment myself, watching video after video. Despair. Sorrow. And love lost. I sunk into the abyss of the final proof that I was not good enough for Luca or Ben.

My body craved serotonin. The pain of rejection and despondency created a chemical imbalance. Grief was going to tow me under. Hating my promise of abstinence from drugs, I grabbed my coat and ran toward the Tetons.

"Hello? Who is this?" Joel was awoken in the middle of the night. "Zelda? Yes, she is here. Hold on, let me check."

"Gavin! Is Zelda with you?" He called down a level.

"No, Dad. She wanted to be alone tonight."

"She's not in the house?" Gavin tore up the steps. "The cars are still here. Who's on the phone?"

"Ben, Zelda's guaridan." They both were listening to Ben's rant. "Okay. Send us the coordinates. We'll call you back."

"Guardian? I don't understand." The men geared up for a trek near the mountain.

"Ben said her vitals were off. Her core temperature is below normal, and her pulse is slowing. She must be outside. Hopefully lost."

"Hopefully? What the fuck? He thinks she is trying to commit suicide again?" Gavin spat.

"Here. He sent us a map with her current location. She's not far." Within the next half hour, I was returned to the great house.

"You get her in the tub to bring up her temperature. Keep adding hot water. She has stage two hypothermia. I'll heat the weighted blankets." Joel was barking orders at Gavin, misplacing his anger and worry.

At three in the morning, I was seated by the fireplace with a whiskey in my hands. No one said a word. The fire danced behind the glass wall, mocking my future in hell.

"Zelda?" Joel knelt in front of me, offering his support. "Ben wants to talk with you." He took the whiskey from my shaking hands and replaced it with the phone. Gavin was seated on the floor against the wall. He looked emotionally exhausted.

"Ben."

"Zelda." I could feel Ben's rage three thousand miles away. I stared at the fire, wishing I didn't have to wait for it to consume me. He stayed silent.

"Ben, I got lost." Exasperation dripped from my disdain.

"Did you."

"Yes, Ben, I did. I needed serotonin, and I was fresh out of coke. So I went on a run." Adolescence crept in.

"Zelda."

"Fuck you, Ben. Luca got married. I have feelings. I'm allowed to have feelings! I wasn't good enough to marry him and certainly not good enough to marry you."

"I'll marry you." Gavin's voice rang loud and clear.

"Whose that?" Ben's anger switched focus.

"Gavin, Joel's son. He has seen my brilliance and only a glimpse of my shit show." Ben chuckled.

"Do I have competition?"

"No."

"I love you, Zelda."

"I know. I'm living half a life. The bad overtakes me so quickly."

"Luca was important to you. You two had a bond. A destructive bond. You understand why you couldn't be together." Ben was being magnanimous talking about Luca with me.

"When I'm in this place, I crave him. He was a kindred spirit. We satisfied each other's pain."

"Zelda, that hurts me to hear since I found you almost dead. I have PTSD every time the alarm goes off."

"What alarm?" Ben didn't respond. "Ben, what alarm?"

"Rowan called to see how you were. So I checked in."

"Ben, your voice inflection indicated deception."

"How do you like Wyoming?" I succumbed to his distraction.

"I love Wyoming. The mountains give me strength, and the air is so clean and crisp. I love this house and being here with Joel and Gavin." I looked at my hosts, who had not moved. Hearing our conversation, they had tears in their eyes.

"You finished the job?"

"Yes." I talked with Ben about my adventure here until the morning light came through the windows. Joel's low battery ended our call.

A new pain ceased me. I fell into Joel's waiting arms. He held me tight and rocked me as I sobbed. For a few moments, I felt my father's presence. Joel rubbed my back in circles, much like my dad used to. He even mumbled 'princess' softly into my hair.

"Gavin will start the fireplace in your room. You need sleep." Joel released me to Gavin, who scooped me up, keeping all the blankets tight around me. He started the fireplace and engaged the black-out curtains before turning to me.

"Stay with me." I was using Gavin to provide the support I needed. He wanted what I couldn't give him. He settled himself next to me, drawing me against him.

"I would marry you, Zelda."

"I know. Thank you, Gavin."

I wished I could love Gavin and stay in this house, creating a new life for myself. My demons would lure me to my destruction here, too, and Gavin would suffer. For tonight, I cherished his hold on me while his body heat lulled me to sleep.

We slept entwined until later in the afternoon. Gavin was masculine comfort, but he didn't satisfy my soul. Eventually, hunger drove me out of bed. I met Joel at the breakfast table.

"Well, good afternoon. Maria made a little bit of everything for us." He padded the seat beside him, placing ham, potatoes, and scrambled eggs on my plate.

"Joel, I'm sorry for the drama last night. I needed to go for a run, and I quickly got turned around. I loved Luca. I was mourning his loss and in a dark place."

"You said some harsh things about yourself. I think you are an extraordinary woman. Your parents would be proud."

"I don't think so. My destructive episodes are narcissistic and deprave. I'm on my second guardian already."

"Who is Ben? How does he have guardianship of you?"

"Uncle Theo's health didn't permit him to keep rescuing me from one of my episodes. I had ingested a bad batch of cocaine laced with fentanyl. The dose was lethal. Theo's friend Ben stepped in." Joel's eyes welled with tears.

"You love Ben."

"Ben is not mine to love."

"Ben is absolutely yours, my dear." He refilled my orange juice. "Ben and I talked this morning. He would like you to stay here until the end of March. I would like you to stay, too."

"I want you to stay forever." Gavin strode in and settled across from me. Gavin was a good distraction, but he was not Ben.

"I would love to stay. Thank you." The number of people who tolerated me increased by two.

CHAPTER TWENTY-TWO

Chasing Zelda

My empathy for Theo Alexander soared. Keeping tabs on Zelda was overwhelming. The Magic Compass showed me her current location and constantly gathered information on her body systems. An alarm would sound as soon as any threshold was compromised. My Pavlovian response to the alarm was panic, especially since Vegas. The health data collected could send a person into madness if monitored too often. I knew when she should eat or drink. I knew when she was overtired or overactive. My imagination went wild, speculating her activities. I had to convince myself she was an avid runner, sprinting often. None of this information could be shared with Zelda, or our surveillance of her would be compromised. Theo was adamant about keeping the existence of the Magic Compass between us.

Throughout the year, I enlisted my best friends to help keep watch over her. A debt I could never repay. They donated their time to keep me sane. A feat that was getting harder and harder to do. We planned for me to appear dedicated to the Roberts Group while beginning to extradite myself from their hold. Callum manipulated my marriage to Jillian. We were both pawns in securing my devotion to the company. She was compliant. I was duped.

Working at the Roberts Group was a dream come true for a poor boy without connections. The lure to power and wealth allowed my blindness to the stronghold Callum had. Keeping Zelda off his radar was difficult. I had to limit my contact to Zelda both digitally and personally. My transparent friendship with Theo allowed me to orbit her life.

Zelda's relationship with Luca had to be severed. Rowan became a great ally in accomplishing that goal. We had met in the hospital after

Zelda and Luca nearly died at the Bellagio. The two idiots never knew they were on the same floor. Rowan told Luca I had taken Zelda back to New York City. Luca wasn't required to stay in rehab. This was his first hospital stay from an overdose, and he didn't have a record. Rowan was convinced that since the product was laced with lethal doses of Fentanyl, it was a hit on Luca or Zelda. Luca was sent to Reno under the premise of setting up a new casino. With Zelda at Land's End for the holidays, neither knew where the other was.

Jealousy consumed me on her last trip to Vegas. Zelda was drawn to Luca. They had a connection I could never understand. Their relationship looked co-dependent and toxic to those of us on the outside. Rowan explained that they were both orphans that blamed themselves for their parent's deaths. They were both guarded, intelligent, and passionate. Finding a similar spirit unleashed their desire for one another. Rowan feared their desire was rooted deeply in debauchery and darkness. Even without drugs, their time together was perverse. I wasn't sure how to heal Zelda from debasement.

The birthday gift was meant as a distraction to give me a reprieve from her exploits. James's idea worked perfectly, getting me access to her even if it was virtually. My days were spent learning how to satisfy her at night. I learned how to push her boundaries, giving her what she needed sexually. My beautiful, sexy Zelda challenged me daily, opening a part of me I didn't know existed. The dominance I showed her at night transferred to my confidence during the day. My resolve to undermine my father-in-law needed a strength I never had before. A reason I was an easy pawn to manipulate.

Playing Legends of Zelda with Zelda was hypnagogic. A boy obsessed with the game could never have imagined he could save his own princess. Zelda didn't enjoy it as much as I did. She found her namesake character weak and powerless. Even in the end, she didn't fully understand the true nature between Zelda and Link. The damsel in distress trope blinded her to the teamwork required to defeat evil. The Magic Compass buried in her black diamond earrings allowed Theo and I to rescue her when her life was in peril. Luckily, she didn't understand the parallel story between the character and herself.

Theo and I talked every week. He could access her schedule and explain why she was in Chicago or Wyoming. Her vitals went haywire one night in Chicago, but the alarm didn't sound. I was still tempted to board a plane. My obsession with watching her vitals grew into mania. Most nights, I worried and couldn't sleep until her heart rate was below fifty. One night, I was rewarded with my infatuation by saving her from the cold while she was on a run in Wyoming. Joel had been the perfect substitute for her recovery. I was able to talk with her for hours using Joel's phone. My lunacy subsided, knowing she was in a safe place. He was treating her like a surrogate father. My heart was happy for her.

* * *

Zelda was a distraction to my plan. Extraditing myself from the Robert's group was not going to be an easy feat. I knew my father-in-law constantly monitored me, both digitally and personally. He trusted no one and had enormous resources at his disposal.

My wife Jillian and I hadn't seen each other in years. As soon as the honeymoon ended, she packed up and moved to Denver. I was initially crushed as it was a massive blow to my pride. My work was my only salvation, and Callum profited from it. James tried to warn me from the start, but my ego was so inflated having a girl like Jillian interested in me, I dismissed all the signs. She was New York high society while I was New Jersey poor. I wanted a life that was not mine and paid the price for my arrogance.

James had set up bank accounts for me in his name. For months, I began siphoning off money masked in expenses. He created a fake charity, and I transferred my stock and additional contributions. Callum routinely asked about my financial choices, which told me he was monitoring me closely.

James and I would meet weekly to discuss our progress. Each week, we had benchmark activities and goals. He kept me active at the gym, helping me to deal with Zelda's absence. I hated keeping my plan secret. I needed to keep her in the dark so she would never let slip our feelings for each other. Cruel, but the only way to keep her safe. I wouldn't underestimate Callum and his tenacity for control.

Once I had enough start-up money, I could begin my own company —a company I was proud of and that fed my passions. This is what Zelda said I was missing from my life, and she was correct. Before I met her, my life was not well lived.

The next phase would include my divorce. Once I served Jillian the papers, I still would have ninety days until it was final. Those days would be the most tenuous. Callum's wrath could be limitless. I didn't fear for Jillian. She met his expectations. I was unsure what he would do to me. He wasn't accustomed to being thwarted.

My divorce would likely coincide with my resignation or firing.

Either way, I had to have my end completely set up by then. James was invaluable as the company's frontman, at least for now.

Even when I was detached from my daily life, Zelda was a constant influence. She made me want to pursue my dream and be a better man. I worked to be worthy of her. My company's vision was philanthropic, making a positive contribution to the world.

* * *

Zelda was my obsession. My heart ached for her constantly. My goals and dreams became one-sided. I could hide nothing from James.

"What if Zelda doesn't want you and the end of all this?" James wasn't always convinced Zelda was right for me.

"That's not an option. I know Zelda. We are meant to be together."

"You seem to be making all the changes. Working day and night for her. What is she doing for you?"

"Knowing she exists in the world is enough right now."

"You have an unbalanced relationship. You have idealized her. What does she offer you?" My heart had no doubts, but James planted a seed in my brain. "You know she's not loyal to you. She seems to move from one man to another."

"You see that as a bad thing. Zelda won't commit to anyone because her heart belongs to me."

"How can you forgive her nature?"

"Zelda knows I'm married, yet subtly, she has faith and hopes we will be together one day. She gave up Luca. A feat I didn't think would happen. She doesn't give her love easily. I know I have it. The other men are inconsequential."

"You are a better man than I. I couldn't be devoted to a woman knowing she is with other men." James wasn't done with his objections. "Zelda is brilliant and passionate, but you know she has limitations. She won't be the doting wife and mother to the children of your dreams. I fear once you have her, she will be a dependent rather than a partner."

"Zelda's not like other women. I need a mind to match my own and a passion to challenge me. Regular women have always bored me. Her limitations are my strengths. I know in my soul we were destined for one another."

"I worry for you, brother."

"I love you too, brother."

CHAPTER TWENTY-THREE

Wyomng Vacation

I needed a break by the last week of my promised time in Jackson Hole. Gavin wanted more. Joel wanted more for Gavin. There was no future for Gavin and me. I borrowed a car and set out for some alone time in one of the more rural mountain towns. My final report was almost done, and the reprieve would give me an outlet to balance my agitated state.

Luca's marriage was emotionally and spiritually draining. My love for him would never wane even though we were forbidden to see each other. He would forever be my dark night. The passion and deprivation we had shared I craved right now. Gavin was nice. I needed wildfire.

I meandered north on a highway parallel to Jackson Lake without an agenda. Hunger motivated my itinerary. The Skinned Buffalo resembled an ole-time Western saloon and held the promise of authentic BBQ. The whitewashed bar looked run down but still had charm. The parking lot was still packed even though it was after the lunchtime rush. Mixing business with pleasure, I brought my laptop to work while I ate.

The bar was sparsely decorated but had sturdy tables and chairs. I chose a round booth against the wall to settle in. Lunch was delicious. As long as I didn't make eye contact, I was left alone while I ate.

The rest of the afternoon, I sipped on a tumble of whiskey, completing the report for the Rocky Mountain Mining Company. The after-work crowd began filtering in, and inquiring men constantly interrupted my solitude. Most of the time, I could sense their approach and exclaim 'go away' before they spoke.

My server needed me to pay my check since her shift was over. She was introducing me to her replacement when the back of my neck began to burn. Someone was directing a lot of energy my way. My eyes drifted around the room and settled on a group of bikers lined up at the bar. The largest brooding man was locked onto me. He was speaking to the group but never looked away. My first impression was danger. Corded muscles wrapped in tattoos poked out from his tight t-shirt on his massive body. The scowl on his face was more inquisitive rather than malicious.

My hands flew over the keys of my laptop as I tried to articulate the events of the last month. A chair was swung around from the next table. As I looked up, the biker sat himself down uninvited.

"How did you end up here, beautiful?" His gravelly voice and manly scent made my spine tingle. For that, I give him a moment of my attention. Long, thick black hair flopped into his face as he spoke, making him push it back with his fingers. The sides and back hair were shaved in an undercut, leaving the top long.

"A biker that drives a truck. Isn't that illegal in your club?" I stared into his dark chocolate eyes.

"Did you see me pull in?"

"No." I continue my assessment. "Living alone out in the woods is detrimental to processing the guilt you carry. You also need a new mattress and a full-length mirror in your cabin." I pointed to the stains on his tan-colored denim pants. He was very professional looking for a biker in a rural town. "At least try turning your current mattress over." I went back to working on my laptop. His rugged good looks were making me second guess my disdain.

"Can I buy you a drink?" I chose to ignore his question, unsure if I could deny him. Eventually, he double-tapped the table with the tops of his fingers and returned to his friends.

My skin prickled as I continued to feel his glare.

"Zelda Alexander!" Two men appear in front of my table. Interruptions were getting irritating, making me want to abandon the establishment.

"She's on vacation. Alone. Go Away." A gun trigger clicked into place, garnishing my attention.

"I have a message for you." Mateo's warning analyzed the situation. My money was on retaliation from George. *Fuck.*

A shadow appeared behind them. Two large hands grabbed the hands with guns and squeezed. My assailants screamed as their bones were crushed against the gun's metal. The weapons were released and fell to the floor, sliding underneath my table. My avenger nodded for me to move as he began rapid blows to each perp, rendering them immobile. His friends stood behind him, ready to assist.

"We are leaving now!" My avenger barked. I threw my items into a bag and followed him out the back door. He nodded to the bartender, who was already on the phone with the police. A lot was said with that one nod.

His massive body covered mine as if waiting for a second attack. "You need to grab your stuff. You're staying with me." The biker was moving me towards his truck.

"I'm not staying in a smoke-filled cabin isolated in the woods with a stranger, no matter how grateful I am for your assistance." He chuckled.

"Do you know me?"

"I just called you a stranger."

"Beck."

"Zelda."

"Ahhh...."

"Don't say Princess Zelda and lick your lips or some other dumb shit, or our friendship ends now."

"I was going to say Zelda Fitzerald. I can see the resemblance of genius."

"And the madness?"

"We have only just met." The biker gentleman was a scholar.

"I seem to know a lot of particulars about you." I stopped at Joel's car and took out my bag. The sirens in the distance made my decision easier.

"The police know you are with me. You can submit a statement tomorrow. I need to get you out of the area in case there are others." I followed Beck to his truck. No deception was indicated.

We headed in the opposite direction of the oncoming sirens. "So what was that about?"

"Could be several things," Beck growled. He was not in the mood for vagueness. "Balance of probability is a VP doesn't like the report I'm writing. Or the fact I reversed his sting. Murder seems illogical to add to his list of charges. Well, attempted murder. Thank you."

We both fell silent as Beck flew over the winding roads to his cabin.

"What do you do?"

"I'm a profiler. I audit companies for mismanagement and deception among their employees."

"Someone's not happy with what you discovered?"

"Bingo."

"Are you threatened often?"

"The last time my mafia lover caught me at my drug dealer lover's house. That didn't end well."

"Who lost?"

"The drug dealer."

"How many lovers do you have?"

"Presently, none. One of the reasons I took this trip. My last lover wanted more. I had to end it."

"What was wrong with him that you didn't want more?"

"It's not him. It's me. A future with me would lead to one's ruin. Madness."

"Honest or dramatic."

"Honest." We drove down his long driveway, eventually coming to a clearing where his cabin stood. "I pictured a more rundown cabin. This is lovely."

Beck said nothing as he took my bag inside. I followed, taking my time while looking at the amazing craftsmanship of the log home. The one-story structure had a prominent vaulted peak in the center with floor-to-ceiling tinted windows. A large stone fireplace chimney took up almost one side of a wall marking which side of the house was the great room. The outside had no unnatural landscaping making the cabin fit seamlessly into the environment. A wrap-around porch peaked from the other side of the cabin extending around the back.

Beck closed the door, allowing me a moment to absorb the surroundings. I could feel his gaze intensify the longer I took. "I have not had a woman in here for a long time." The energy zipped between us once the gravity of his statement hit me. I was alone with a deliciously attractive mountain of a man. His lethal strength excited my mortality, and his scent taunted my libido.

He wouldn't have saved my life only to bring me here to finish the job. The prospect was thrilling, making me feel again. Beck's body turned to mine, pressing me against the door. My hands locked with his as he drew my arms above my head. "I've been hard for hours watching you dismiss suitors while you worked. I thought I had a shot."

"You did. You claimed a moment of my attention." His whole body was now touching mine, making me feel his desire.

"You dismissed me." His mouth hovered over mine.

"Or avoided committing." I licked his lips, inviting him in. Beck's mouth crashed on top of mine as our bodies rubbed against each other in search of a release. He tasted like cherries and whiskey with a hint of mint.

"Tell me about this madness." His lips descended to my jawline and neck. One of his hands unbuttoned my blouse so he could palm a breast inside.

"No."

"Do you want me to stop touching you?"

"No."

"The madness." Beck pitched my nipple, demanding information.

"I dwell too long in the darkness. It calls to me. I need depravity to be satisfied mentally and physically."

Beck grinned like the devil. "I've been waiting for you, Zelda."

* * *

Beck was my equal in sexual needs and desires. The marks he left were not permanent but felt similar to Luca's. My soul was being serviced as my heart grieved. He worked my body with his dominance and strength. He was pulling me apart to make me whole again.

Sexual exhaustion finally came just after noon. "We need to stop in at the station, and I have a game tonight. We'll grab some dinner in between."

"What game?" I knew the answer before he confirmed it.

"The last Friday of the month, we have a standing poker game in the back of the Buffalo."

"Where are we going to dinner?" If he said the Buffalo, he wanted me to stick around.

"Depending on how long your statement takes, we can do pizza or BBQ."

"You don't want me to go to your game night?"

"I didn't say that." A raised eyebrow is all it took for a confession. "The guys are a little rough, and the barflies are worse. I get the sense that although you are a hellion in bed, you are used to a certain class."

"I can take care of myself. Can I play?"

"What do you know about poker?"

"My dad taught me."

"Fine with me. You got cash?"

"I always have cash."

The investigator took us to separate rooms and recorded all our information. Nothing said was new except for my theory. Since I was a visitor, I didn't think much effort would be put into the case. I sent a text to Joel warning him of possible retaliation against the company. My intuition was the assassination attempt was about something else.

We ended up eating at the Buffalo, which was fine with me. There were lots of classic dishes to try. By eight o'clock, Beck's friends were assembled in the back room. Most of the group I recognized from last night. "Where is Jace?" Beck asked.

"He's going to be late." Ron, one of the bigger biker guys that backed up Beck last night, answered.

"Good. That fucker always wins. Zelda will play." Beck made the announcement instead of asking for permission. They all nodded to Beck while locking eyes in surprise with each other. My usual order of play was poker, alcohol, drugs, and sex. The lack of drugs was making me a little anxious.

"How was work today?" one of the guys asked as he opened a cash box and a suitcase containing the chips.

"Didn't go. Had company." He failed to make eye contact with any of the men. We each put in a thousand dollars to get our chips. Beck got us both a whiskey and sat me across from him.

"You carry around that kind of cash, missy?" Ron asked.

"Of course, I was a boy scout. Always be prepared." The man thought I was lying. "You think Beck gave me the money? Like a hooker? I should be paying him for his stud services last night. Fucking epic." I winked at Beck, and he smiled.

"And all morning, doll face." Beck winked back. Man, he was handsome. Visions of him working my body flooded my brain. 'Later,' he mouthed, reading my mind.

"Are we going to talk about how Beck finally got laid or play poker?"

"Beck got laid." Most of the men said in unison.

"Marry this woman. I haven't seen a fucking smile on your face for over a year. She must be special if you bring her around us." Another man commented. There was brotherly love among these men. I was jealous.

"She insisted." Everyone took their place at the table. I loved feeling out new prey.

Candy. Baby. I tried not to destroy them too early, but I'm competitive. Beck caught on early to what I was doing. He had a well-educated, intelligent mind. I made an assumption too early based on his physique, tattoos, and leather. Jace came in a couple of hours into the game with two girls on either side of him.

"Where the fuck have you been?" Ron yelled at him.

"Hoes before bros, boys." He took a beer from the cooler and sat by the table. "Well, well, well. Who is this?"

"Beck got laid."

"Jace, this is Zelda. You want in?" Jace took a long look at me as Beck introduced us. He was into poker.

"Fuck no. No fucking way. You all are stupid assholes." He raised his beer to me in salute.

"What the hell, Jace." Beck snapped at him, defending my honor.

"You don't know who this is?" He walked around the table, evaluating everyone's pile. "Taking it slow tonight, Zelda?"

"The boys keep buying me drinks." I batted my eyelashes at him.

Jace rolled his eyes at the stupidity of his friends. "You're wasting your time. This woman can win tournaments with two grams of blow up her nose."

"Jace, fuck off. What is your problem with Zelda?"

"You all are the ones with the problem. Zelda Alexander is a World Series Poker Champion and one of the highest gross bankrolls for a woman. And you fuckers are her prey. Just give her all your money, and let's party."

"Zelda?" Shock, then anger, flitted over Beck's face.

"Yeah, I have skills. The highest bankroll?" I looked at Jace, and he nodded. "Were we ever opponents?"

"Yeah." Jace looked sheepish. "I watched you—a lot. So did a lot of other men. Luca Moretti made us give you at least a ten-foot radius. You were off limits. Those who ignored his warning were banged up and tossed out of the casino." At the mention of Luca, my heart ached.

"I'm sorry. I didn't know that. One of the reasons I liked staying at the Horseshoe was because people left me alone." The game was over. Jace had ruined the momentum with his revelation. Most of the men were still seated, staring at me with new appreciation. "Drinks are on me, boys." I pointed to the huge pile of chips and winked.

"Zelda, can I see you in the other room?" Beck was untucking my chair from the table as he spoke. He led me through the great room to a bathroom by the offices near the back.

Locking the door, Beck turned me toward the mirror and stood behind me. "Hands on the sink, Zelda." The gravelly voice made my juices leak. He reached under my dress and tore my thong off. "I asked you if you played poker." His hand pushed my lower back down, raising my ass into the air.

"My dad taught me." Smack. The palm of his hand snapped at my flesh. "He taught me well." Smack. The sting felt good.

"You were playing me?"Smack, smack. He spread my legs further apart.

"Nope, just having fun." Smack.

"You just happen to fail to mention you are a professional poker player." Smack, smack.

Breathlessly, I tried to answer. "No, not a professional. I have a business. I play for fun." His hits were harder each time.

"This is fun, huh, Zelda." He pulled my hands behind my back. Beck was pissed and fucked me hard. I pretended he was Luca.

We joined the group after a few rounds. Beck was still mad but high off of the punishing sex. A drink was placed in front of me the moment I gingerly sat down. "What is your problem, Beck?"

"You didn't tell me who you were?"

"Who the fuck am I? I don't know what you do for a living." What the hell? "My high bankroll is pissing you off. You would rather me be a damsel in distress. You're like all the others. You want me to be Princess Zelda. Men love rescuing the princess." Beck stayed stoic, knowing I was right. Fucking egos. "I don't give a shit about the money. I have no idea what is even in there. I never touch it."

"Twenty-five million dollars," Jace yelled from a few seats down. Beck and a few others gasped.

"How do you know this, and I don't?"

"Public record. The gaming commission keeps the top players' totals on their website." I was lost in thought, trying to understand where this money was.

"Zelda? You really had no idea, did you?"

"I never paid attention to the winnings. I just liked the competition. My Uncle must be in charge of it, or Ben?"

"Ben?"

"My guardian."

"Guardian?"

"I told you I live in the darkness. I have episodes. Depravity is the focus." Beck's eyes were dilating again. "Ben took over for my Uncle when he got tired of pulling me out of shady situations and overdoses. Ben is a friend of my Uncle's."

"Do you trust him?"

"Implicitly." Beck began snaking his finger under my dress. "Time to go home, Zelda."

* * *

The rest of the weekend, Beck and I stayed in the cabin. We ate a lot, fucked constantly, and got to know one another in between the other two events. This was the vacation I desperately needed. The shadow of Luca's marriage was beginning to dissipate. Beck helped me process the elements to balance me out. He gave me hope that living without my black knight was possible.

The cabin was a place of peace. Nature folded around us, cocooning us in. Beck held my attention, giving me a reprieve from my demons. Ben nobly thought if I owned them out loud, they would magically disappear. My parents were still dead because of the choices I made. Love was an illusion I was not worthy of.

"Babe, I have to go to work tomorrow. You'll be here when I come home?" Beck's question was more of a plea.

"Maybe I should go in with you and get my car." His body tensed immediately. Beck thought I would leave. Truthfully, I was living by the hour and had no plans beyond the day.

"I can have Ron and Jace follow me home with it."

"That's fine. I could use a day to recuperate." Beck's body visibly relaxed. My mountain man wasn't ready to let me go. Escaping life is what vacations were about. Beck curled my body into his tightly. His protection seeped down to my bones. I slept so soundly I didn't even hear him leave in the morning.

Soaking in a tub and lounging on the deck took up most of my day. By late afternoon, I was constantly checking the clock and the driveway for Beck's return. As twilight began to settle over the trees, I vibrated with need. Overindulgence with sex gave me the same withdrawals I had with drugs. I was pacing the length of the back porch as my car and two trucks finally pulled in.

"Zelda." Beck seemed surprised and anxious to see me. I had only bothered to wear one of his button-down flannel shirts all day. He tried blocking his friends from coming in.

"Get out of our way, Beck. You said we could eat here if we did this favor for you." Jace pushed past his friend, grabbing the bags of food from his hands. Ron was forced to stay behind him since he was too portly to get by. "Whoa." Jace froze when he saw me. His eyes traveled too slowly up and down my body. Beck grabbed him by the back of the neck and pushed him past me toward the kitchen.

"So fucking eat." He tossed all the containers on the island and took out plates and forks. Ron came into the kitchen, setting down a couple of six packs. Beck failed to meet my eyes again.

"So Zelda, you are shacking up with Mr. Perfect now?" Jace wanted to start trouble. "You know his dick is crooked."

"Lucky for us, so is my vagina." I tried to put snark in my comment but was too mesmerized by his eating. He shoved steak tips in his mouth, barely chewing before swallowing them.

"Let me give you my number when you are ready for ..." Before he could finish or swallow, Beck's hand was around his neck again, moving the choking man out the door. His patience was too thin. Ron didn't say a word as he took a container of food and beer, following Jace out the door.

"She's going to break your heart," Jace yelled as he got in Ron's truck.

"Babe, are you going to break my heart?"

"Yes."

"You need to be punished."

"Yes."

Beck stripped off his clothes as he walked to the bedroom. The man was feeling lust, love, and loss. All fueling an extraordinary night together.

Soft, swollen lips gently placed a kiss on my forehead as I pretended to sleep. Beck left for work. His actions dictated how tentative he was if he would see me again. My plans were undetermined.

The threat didn't return. Beck's friends and the police determined the two men were acting alone. On whose orders, no one knew. The men claimed it was a random robbery which no one believed. Joel's car was at the Skinned Buffalo Bar for four days as a lure, but no one else took the bait.

A growing part of me wanted to stay with Beck. I tried to imagine a life here with him, at least for a while. Few men held my attention, and fewer I looked at with equanimity. Beck was an anomaly, choosing to live in isolation in a rural midwestern town. All morning, I debated my options, finally deciding to make him dinner to see how it made me feel.

With a plan in motion, I drove to the small shopping center of the nearest town. Taking my time, I chose my items carefully. Risotto, short ribs, and roasted vegetables. I had all day to learn how to cook, taking the helpful butcher's suggestions. A small old bookstore caught my eye on the way out, and I was lost for the rest of the afternoon hunting treasures.

My demise came quickly as I tried to head back to Beck's cabin. No address. No phone number. I was lost on how to find his place. Nor did I know where he worked. My vacation was lowering my IQ by the hour. My only hope was to find his friends at the bar.

"Zelda, you still around?" The bartender from Thursday night had more info on me than I had on him.

"I'm staying with Beck but cannot find my way back. I don't have his number." I took a seat at the bar while the Bartender evaluated my statement.

"Beck's been without a woman for a long time."

"What did she do to him?"

"That's not my story to tell, but let's say he also no longer has a best friend either. What can I get you?"

"Whiskey, neat."

"I'll call Beck."

"No need." I could feel his presence before he even came through the door.

"Babe, what's going on?" He looked more hurt than angry.

"I wanted to surprise you with a homemade dinner. I don't know where you live or have your number." The smile that engulfed his face made the whole ordeal worth it. See, I could make another human happy. He climbed up next to me and shot down the rest of my drink.

"I thought you left." We stayed quiet for a few minutes as he processed his emotions. I knew what was coming next. "I want you to stay here. Stay with me. Forever."

"Beck, we have only known each other for a few days. You see only what you want to see in me."

"I see everything, Zelda. I see the darkness where your demons take you. I see the genius that sits behind your eyes. I see the caring, beautiful woman you are. You live in my heart and are everything to me." A sickness spread through my body at his words. "I can keep you safe. I can satisfy your needs. I can make you whole again."

Doubt crept in. I was in the wrong place in time again. I had done nothing to deserve Beck's love and devotion. Gavin saw me as a fantasy, and I feared Beck did too. They didn't know the real me. Convinced of my resolve, I escaped the next day.

* * *

Zelda was magnificent. She was witty, interesting, and exceedingly intelligent. I loved watching her observe everyone around her. She needed to talk very little. I never thought I would meet my equal in the bedroom. She was wildfire riding the line between pain and pleasure. She was what I desired in a partner, but my fantasy scared her.

She was right. I wanted Princess Zelda. The damsel in distress, my nature was a protector. My gut seared with pain when I came home to find her gone. Deep down, I knew she would leave. She was a force I couldn't keep.

Weeks later, a box was set down in front of me at the bar. "The usual?" I could only nod my head. The package was from Zelda. Of course, she would have had to send it here. I never gave her any of my personal information. I would have to process that another time.

Opening the package, a black velvet box sat surrounded by several uncut and polished black diamonds. In the velvet box was a Rolex black diamond watch adorned with gunmetal accents, a black leather strap, and a note.

A diamond in the rough, just like you.

Congratulations on your promotion.

I'm sure it is well deserved.

I will always cherish our time together.

Thank you for making me feel I was enough for you.

Zelda.

The watch was exquisite and worth probably more than I made in a year. Zelda Alexander was an enigma—a beautiful light that filled your heart, settling there if you were lucky enough to encounter her. How did she know I had an interview the week she was here? We never talked about my work. More importantly, how did she know I got the job?

* * *

The drive back to Jackson Hole was pensive. My choices always led me back to Ben. My purgatory wasn't being able to have the man I truly loved with all my heart and soul. I would encounter men like Gavin or Beck for the rest of my life, making me feel incomplete. My selfishness was beginning to take its toll.

Joel was happy to have me back in his clutches after the assassination attempt. He was sure George didn't have the means to order a hit. The cost outweighed the satisfaction he would have gained. According to the police, the men were paid a million dollars each to complete the task. This amount could have even been a deposit. I agreed. George wasn't a viable suspect.

"Zelda darling, I want you to consider moving here." The love in Joel's eyes reminded me of my father. "A place to recharge after a consulting job will benefit you."

"What do you get out of this move?" My tone was teasing, but Joel's face fell.

"Darling, I'll not pretend I don't feel guilt for not seeking you out sooner. Your father was one of my best friends, and I failed you both. I enjoy you here as if you were my own."

No deception crossed Joel's face. He was earnest in his request. "I love being here. Thank you. I'll think about it."

We sat in silence for the rest of dinner. "I don't think Gavin will see me as a sister."

Joel laughed. "No, I suppose not. But I would love to see you as a daughter."

Over the next few days, I met with the police again, giving them my account of what happened at the Buffalo Bar. Joel had been very active in getting the two police departments to work together. Charges were filed, and all parties accepted their plea deals. My time in Jackson Hole was done.

Joel took me to the train station the following weekend to start my journey back to New York City. "Zelda darling, please consider my offer. At the very least, I would like you to be a frequent guest." Joel embraced me, squeezing me tight. We didn't want to let each other go. I felt my father's presence again, making my heart feel his love.

With every high comes the low. During the five-hour journey back to Salt Lake City, the bad dismissed all the good. I convinced myself Joel was acting out of guilt as my father's best friend. I agreed he enjoyed my company and valued my services, but thankfulness does not equate to love. Gavin saw me as a fantasy. We were attracted to one another, and he liked solving the case together. Appreciation does not equate to love. Beck was good at being who I needed him to be. The protector and the dominant feeding my emotional needs. Beck had never given me his address or phone number. How committed to me was he really?

CHAPTER TWENTY-FOUR

Stranger in the Night

Wyoming rejuvenated my soul and helped heal my heart. The beauty of the land reminded me to look beyond myself rather than stay entrenched in darkness. The craving for Luca receded, but there was still a dull ache pressing on me. The men of Jackson did impact me, even though I was quick to discredit their sincerity. Joel gave me moments where I felt my father. A feeling of peace and love, if even for a moment, was to be cherished. Gavin gave me his submission, always considering my needs. My selfish being took from him without much thought. I enjoyed working with Gavin, but I'm sure I never told him so.

Without realizing it, Beck had given me hope. My rhythm of despair and unworthiness was interrupted. I was enough for him. In vain, I tried to accept what he offered, but my heart wanted Ben.

My foolish soul was devoted to a man that could never be mine. He was good and earnest, whereas I was a burden full of arrogance and disdain. These past months were full of distractions, but my life felt empty at its core.

Ben had another life I never let myself dwell in imagining. I never permitted myself to think about the person he married. The wife he made a vow to must have been spectacular to earn his love. My intuition told me the union was one-sided since she was absent from his life. Theo believed most Fortune 100 companies courted Ben's genius and skills. Roberts had his daughter seduce him to ensure the deal. I was doubtful Ben was that easily fooled. But love is blind or sees what it wants to see. Pot. Kettle. Black.

My days at home were pensive and full of reflection. I made an effort to connect with Theo, promising to visit. He was almost fully recovered from his heart attack after Thanksgiving. The heart attack that coincidently happened the same day Luca and I almost died. Transgressions and debts were piled so high in my mind. I owned them all, perishing from the guilt. My road to perdition was already well paved.

My thoughts often drifted to the idea of starting a new career, identity, and life far from the madness I created for those who care about me. A place that keeps my demons at bay and gives me peace in the solitude I seek. A glimmer inside me played with the idea of contributing to the welfare of the greater good. Nothing ever manifested past the brief thought. I didn't feel the charitable philanthropy my parents were well known for. I added another disappointment to the list.

* *. *

March 31 fell on a Wednesday this year. A date that would be forever remembered as the night my world turned upside down. Winter was lingering longer than usual. A cold rain storm was pelting small hail against my windows. A cloud-filled sky blocked out any light as night began.

A pounding on the door scared me. No one comes unannounced to a woman's door. "Zelda? Are you home?"

I pulled open the door to see my poor Ben looking like a drowned rat. "Ben, are you okay?" Something egregious must have happened. Ben stepped through the door and paused. "Here, take that off. I'll get you a towel and dry clothes." Ben obeyed but solemnly. He said nothing as I took his wet clothes from him as he changed.

"I'll hang them in the laundry and put the rest in the dryer." Ben's eyes looked vacant. He was starting to scare me. I came back, and he was still standing by the door. Gently I pulled him towards the couch and sat him down.

My arms engulfed him. One kiss into his hair unleashed his tears. "Zelda, I have nothing. No one. Everything has been taken from me. People are so cruel I had no idea." Ben sobbed into my neck as I listened, trying to understand what had happened.

"Shhh. I'm here, Ben." He continued to cry into my chest as I rubbed his back. "I'm here, Ben."

"God, Zelda. I love you."

"I love you too, Ben." His head popped up at my admission.

"Do you really, Zelda?"

"Of course, my handsome prince. We're meant for one another."

"You believe that, don't you?"

"Yes, Ben. Even though I don't always show it."

"You've never said it."

"You were never mine to say it to."

"What has changed?"

"You needed to hear it."

My finger lifted his jaw toward me so I could lean down and show him my love for him. A gentle kiss turned passionate as I touched and tasted him. "Ben, it has been so long since I have touched you."

"112 days." He mumbled into my mouth.

"Fuck, Ben. Please." Ben scooped me up with renewed energy and brought me to bed. He stripped off his clothes showing off an even stronger, more muscular body than before. "Ben?" My jaw was on the floor as his sculpted muscles flexed, lifting his shirt above his head.

"James had me working out more. He said I was still grumpy." My hands flew to his chest, feeling the improved planes of his carved physique. I licked the crevasse between muscle groups excitedly. "James said you would appreciate the definition." I looked up at Ben's darkened face as he watched me. He leaned over me to pull off my nightshirt. A growl escaped his throat in appreciation.

Ben stalked over me like he was assessing his prey. Chills zipped through my body in anticipation. "I need you, Zelda."

"I'm always yours."

As if it was a dream, Ben was gone before I woke.

* * *

James' visit caught me off guard. Ben and I had an intense single night, and he left before the sun rose. In the brief time, he had taken a part of me with him. My feelings were always locked up in solitary confinement. I gave them to Ben without regard to the consequences. He left with the knowledge of my love and devotion to him. I felt like a fool.

I was compliant in an emotional rape. My body stayed in a coma of depression for several days until James knocked on my door.

"Zelda." James' face was full of forlorn. "This is from your guardian." He handed me a package wrapped in brown paper tied with a string. I unwrapped the gift tentatively.

A vintage four-volume set of the first edition of Edith Wharton's *Old New York* book series. Each book was housed in a beautiful slipcase of multicolored embossed flora on tan cloth. I had never read the *Old New York* Book Series. The series contained central themes of her work, most notably the meaning of marriage, the bonds between parent and child, and her insight into the turbulent lives of men and women caught up in a rapidly changing society. This was a message sent loud and clear. James was ready to embrace me as I burst into tears.

"Please understand he is keeping you safe until."

"This doesn't make sense."

"You have to believe in him. Give him time." His hands were comforting, rubbing my back. "We are always with you, wherever you are. You are not out of sight or out of mind. He knows you are waiting, and we acknowledge your plight."

James stayed and made me tea. We sat on the couch and talked about nothing. He left as sullen as when he came. I wish I knew what was happening to Ben. He never considered I could help. I thought Link and Zelda needed to be a team.

CHAPTER TWENTY-FIVE
Triforce Gala

Since I was a teenager, Theo conjured up important jobs only I could complete at his company. This didn't change even as an adult. A month after Ben's visit, I was still untethered. Working was the best distraction, so I gave in to Theo's ruse.

Most days, I worked on tasks from an office in Theo's building. Some were interesting, others mundane. Even financial wizards had pockets of fraud and deceit. On mental breaks, I began looking into Ben's life. I read articles on his climb to success within the Roberts group. He was a genius in his area, although his career was inconsistent with his passion. His educational journey began at a university and ended in graduate school. Beyond finance, he studied global economy and STEM coursework. His graduate thesis was focused on using microbes to clean polluted rivers. No wonder he looked spiritually bankrupt the first time we met.

Callum Roberts was a titan on paper and a tyrant in the media. Beyond being a CEO of a profitable company, he didn't appear to have a life well lived. He was estranged from his three ex-wives and only daughter. Even foreclosing on his childhood home when his parent's medical bills exceeded their income. His company was never involved in charities, and he had a vendetta against most other companies in the financial district.

Theo eventually allowed me to audit his whole company. Once submerged, I didn't think often about Ben Walker or Callum Roberts. Theo had people to fire and secretaries to interrogate. I ended up making more work for him, but his company would run more smoothly, and his balance would increase. I began working on my final report gathering all the evidence and laying out a viable plan.

* * *

I usually stayed late at Theo's office on Friday nights to get my reports done from the week. A large box with a red bow was at my door one night when I came home from work. Anxiety flooded my system, warning of repeat events. The door to my apartment opened, startling me. "There you are, Zelda. Why are you so late? Come in." Theo opened the door wide to allow the package and me to go through. "I couldn't open the door and carry the box in. Go put it in your room. Marilyn is already in there."

"Uncle, what's going on?" He was dressed in an elegant tux, looking back to his usual vibrant self.

"Oh, it's a surprise, dear. But get a move on. We're going to be late."

"Uncle, I don't do so well with surprises."

Marilyn interrupted me before I could protest further. "Zelda darling. Come in here. You shower. I will lay out the dress."

"Dress?" Marilyn's stare meant she meant business. "Fine." I jumped in the shower and quickly did my routine.

Marilyn handed me a towel and then a bathrobe. She sat me down on a chair in the bathroom to do my hair and make-up. I watched her float around with the dryer, putting long waves in my hair. "What?" She snapped.

"My mother was the last person to do my hair for me."

"Oh, Zelda darling." She stopped the hair dryer and hugged me. I allowed it.

"No hugging. Drying!" Theo commanded through the doorway.

"We were having a moment. You've been so grumpy lately." Marilyn's remark made me chuckle.

"I know the cure for that." The comment made me sad as I spoke. I missed Ben.

Marilyn continued with my hair and then my makeup. She was very good at it. My dress was a smokey gray minidress with a paper-thin, soft fringe layered throughout. The lingerie and shoes matched the dress. The night was warm. We didn't need a coat. Uncle had hired a car to take us to the event.

We eventually crossed the Queensboro bridge, heading along the water to Astoria. The car slowed near a giant blue building housing *Triforce Solutions, Inc.* "Uncle?" My body began to shake nervously. "Uncle, I don't believe in coincidences." The car stopped in front of the building, and a valet opened the door. Marilyn exited first and waited patiently. She was a proper woman.

"Zelda?"

"I can't, uncle. I'm not prepared."

"We'll be right there with you." Theo gave me a push, and the valet pulled me out the rest of the way. Marilyn took one hand and Theo the other, propelling me forward.

"I feel a huge tantrum coming on." Theo laughed nervously. He knew I was serious. The doors to the building were opened for us. The ground floor looked like a museum. I was too disorientated to understand the displays. In the center of the lobby, a giant escalator carried people to the next floor. Theo steadied me as I tried to absorb the scene before me.

The architectural design was all clean lines and bold colors. The space was enormous. My heart started pounding in anticipation of seeing Ben. This was all Ben. As we rounded the top of the escalator to the next floor, my heart stopped. My handsome prince stood waiting for me in his elegant tuxedo. His hair was a little longer, and a 5 o'clock shadow darkened his face. His eyes were bright with excitement as he waited not so patiently, rocking on his toes with his hands in his pocket.

We started processing one another as my assent grew closer to him. I barely stepped on the top step before I leaped into his arms. Our lips crashed together in a long, pressing kiss. "You're here." He breathed into my hair, tipping his nose to smell my neck. "You're beautiful and radiant. Ninety days is a long time."

He continued to kiss me until it was blatantly untoward. "Thank you, Theo, Marilyn." He took my hand and gripped it tightly. "The festivities are this way."

A simple but stylish party was in full swing. Tastefully dominated by black, silver, and gold decorations, glittery balloons and hanging stars sparkled in the light. A DJ was set up next to an open bar. Servers floated around, passing out appetizers, while tables were dedicated to different kinds of food.

Ben wrapped his arm around my waist as lots of people came to greet us. "He gallantly introduced me to a plethora of people. All I could do was nod and stare. Brilliant smiles were genuine on everyone's faces, giving me a complex. I felt like a rare specimen in a zoo.

James cleared his throat into a mic on a meg-shift stage erected in the middle of the space. Ben handed me off to Theo as he walked toward James.

"If I can have your attention, please. As you know, this is a special night for many reasons. Our fearless leader, Benjamin Walker, has moved this company into a thriving global company in a record ninety days." Claps and cheers deafened the room. "Today also marks the triumphant day where he is officially extradited from the Roberts group. Their lawyers have conceded." More cheers erupted. "We hope to celebrate another huge milestone in the next ninety days, and I'm sure he will be less grumpy." James found me and winked. "I give you our founder and our CEO, Ben Walker."

My handsome prince took the stage, and his company went wild. "Thank you, thank you all. This journey could never have happened without the hard work and dedication of all of you. Let's give yourselves a round of applause." The room quieted after a few moments. "There's one person here who I have to thank most of all. About a year ago, I met the most beautiful, brilliant, mesmerizing woman and fell instantly in love. Unfortunately for me, she didn't feel the same way. My charms didn't sway her even though I admitted to rearranging the place cards so I could sit next to her at dinner. In our first conversation, she called me a coward for my, at the time, current superficial life choice. She said I was bored, unchallenged, and ignoring my passion in search of power and money. All of that was true. I was an empty shell of a man. My Zelda inspired me to live my dream no matter the cost. To be true to myself and work on what I was passionate about. She is the reason *Triforce Solutions* exists. I had to become the person worthy of her…"

Ben continued his speech, but the thundering sound in my ears drowned him out. My vision got blurry, and I started to sweat. James discovered my distress just in time. I heard his voice, so I assumed he caught me before I hit the floor. I felt my body being whisked through the air but could not get my bearings. "Zelda, it's James. I got you." I nodded. "Too much for you, huh, princess." James kissed my head.

"James, you are married."

Two people laughed as we entered a large lift. "My wife is right by my side, princess." James gestured to his right. "Zelda, this is Audrey."

"I like that you keep him on his toes, Zelda. It's a pleasure to formally meet you." I nodded to her in understanding. She had shifts to watch over me at times.

"Where are we going?"

"Penthouse." Just as he said it, the doors to the lift opened. A large, spacious apartment unfolded.

"I think I'm going to be sick." James got me to the bathroom just before the first round hit. My body gave out as the adrenaline was purged from my system. Audrey placed a cold cloth on the back of my neck while James held back my hair, hovering me over the toilet.

"You ready to stand up?" I agreed prematurely. James held me upright as a large bang sounded through the apartment. "Fuck. Go, Aubrey." She left to intercept a shouting Ben.

Ben opened the bathroom door just as another round hit. James put me back into my position. Ben growled. "What's wrong with her?" He snapped as if it was James' fault.

"Aubrey and I told you this would be too much for her. This is just too much adrenaline and panic in her system. Here, switch places. My back is killing me." Ben removed his jacket and rolled up his sleeves as he controlled his worry.

"Here's a hair tie." Aubrey handed Ben the tie, and he expertly piled and secured my hair on top of my head.

"You have to suspend her, or her knees will hurt." Ben placed a folded towel at the toilet's base for my knees to rest on. James stepped away as Ben secured his hold.

"Thank you, my friends." Ben kissed my head as I unloaded bile. Aubrey returned with a fresh, cold cloth that Ben placed back on my neck.

"I'm sorry, Ben." Tears dripped into the toilet. "I feel I ruined your night."

"Shhh. My princess. You're here. You made my night." He rubbed soothing circles with his palm on my back.

"I think I'm done." I flushed the toilet again while Ben braced my body against his. He led me to the great room where James and Audrey were waiting. "I need to sit for a few minutes."

"Why don't I stay with Zelda while you two wrap up the evening."

"I'm not leaving her." Ben snapped.

"Ben, I'll be fine with Audrey. I promise I won't move. Until you return." Ben hesitated, but James stepped in.

"All part of the CEO package, my friend."

"Fine. Don't move." I crossed my heart and blew him a kiss. He relaxed enough to get out the door.

* * *

Aubrey made tea, and we sat on the couch, getting to know one another. "It's hard to say no to Ben. Especially when he worked so hard and was so proud to show you all this tonight."

"Why ninety days? He said he couldn't contact me for ninety days."

"The night he came to you, Callum had him thrown out of his apartment when he heard Jillian signed divorce papers. He's a vindictive man, and Ben was locked out of all his accounts. Ninety days is the time it takes for a divorce to become final. Knowing of his ruthlessness, he didn't want you on Callum's radar. Today is the ninety-first day. He's legally a free man and has acquired his own wealth."

"He did all this in ninety days?"

"No, not really. This started the day you rejected him for being married and not living his dream. He worked tirelessly to be worthy of you."

"Worthy of me?" I shrieked. "He's the white knight. I could never be worthy of him."

"That he is. I'm sorry for the loss of your parents. James knew your father. He was a great man."

"I didn't know that. James never said. Yes, he was. Thank you."

"I don't think you and James ever had a normal conversation."

"Audrey, did you and James pick me up near the Plaza Hotel one night?"

"We didn't think you woke up."

"I didn't. I didn't smell Ben afterward. I usually smell Ben's cologne on me. My face was washed." I looked to Audrey for confirmation.

"I hate waking up with makeup on."

"Audrey, thank you. I have no excuse for my bad behavior over the last year. I haven't been myself since my parents died. I didn't know I was such an imposition on you all."

"Ben was inconsolable after he found you at the Bellagio. James and I tried to hate you. We tried to convince him to leave you alone. He said you were his destiny, his soulmate, his one true love that brought out the best in him."

"I think he has a misguided perception of me."

"I thought so, too. Then I followed you. You are kind to strangers when no one is looking, you observe everything around you and see what no one else does, and you make Ben happy just by being in the world. I'm not sure what hold the mafia has on you, but they even look at you with awe." Audrey took my hand in hers. "It became an honor keeping you safe."

"You were keeping me safe from myself."

"In part. Callum will spare no expense now to ruin Ben. We were afraid he would come after you. Ben didn't want you to know."

"You and James are extraordinary friends. Ben is lucky to have you in his life."

"Zelda, you have us too."

"I drive everyone away."

"Maybe you can try not to do that." Aubrey was funny.

"Sounds so pragmatic I can give it a try." I laughed.

At about midnight, James and Ben came back to the apartment. I was nibbling on crackers while Audrey entertained me with the group's past exploits. "Lies. All lies. My wife must be drunk." James came in and gave Audrey a loving kiss. Ben stood in the doorway watching me.

"I'm fine, Ben. You knew I have a hard time with surprises."

"I thought this was a good surprise."

"The quality of the surprise is not the issue. The unpreparedness for the event is the issue." I stood and moved to Ben, wrapping my arms tight around his torso. "I'm so proud of you." He wrapped his arms around me, resting his chin on my head.

"Thank you, princess. Having you here seems unreal."

"Well, that's our cue to leave. Things are about to get real." James wiggled his eyebrows up and down. Aubrey rolled her eyes in an apology and dragged James out the door.

"We'll talk soon, Zelda." I waved as they left, still clinging to Ben.

"I don't ever want to move." I planted my face in his chest and breathed in his scent. "I missed your scent so much."

"Just my scent?"

"Well, maybe your strong arms too. And your wit. And your intelligence. Maybe your great taste in video games. Knowledge about Edith Wharton. Stalker-like tendencies…"

"Nothing else?"

"I missed how the light behind your eyes dances when you look at me. The devotion in your soul. The love in your heart and the way you say my name when you come."

"I love you, princess. Stay with me always."

"Okay." Ben scooped me up and brought me to his room. A large California king dominated the room with his and hers matching dressers lining opposite walls. An ensuite bathroom was adjacent to a huge walk-in closet already filled with female things.

"Um, Ben? Whose are those?" I pointed to all the feminine aspects of the room.

"You want me to dignify a dumb question with an answer?"

"This doesn't make sense."

"When I would miss you, I felt better if I bought you things. Made a home for you."

"You were nesting?"

"Yes, but in a manly way. Like a bowerbird. But I was trying to attract a specific female."

"I can't wait to see your hunting and courtship skills."

"How about my sexual prowess?"

"That I already have experience with."

* * *

Ben took me to the lobby the next morning to explain his vision. You can imagine the inspiration. He lectured as we walked through the different scenes on display.

"Triforce Solutions was a perfect way to meld the three areas I'm most passionate about. The imagery of the Zelda artifact just fueled my philanthropy. My skills in finance came from my father. He was insistent on getting a degree that would pay the bills. James and I like to invent things. Even as kids, when my mother was still around, she inspired us to create."

As we walked the first floor, Ben continued, "The triforce from the Legend games has three parts: Power, Courage, and Wisdom. I applied those principles to the ideas that have been festering in the back of my mind since childhood. In college, I created a prototype for the portable solar tile we sell, **Power.**

The new technology is an ultrathin lightweight solar cell that can adhere to any surface. The super-collector can turn any surface into a powerful solar power source. Clothing, cars, and objects can be activated in remote locations in emergencies. Our next step is to manufacture the tile into sheets that can be applied to a boat sail, tarps, or drones. Solar power while out at sea or in disaster areas can be utilized instantly. Drones that can fly indefinitely. The military has already contacted us."

"James has headed our research and development team in **Courage**. They have created an artificial intelligence filtering device that cleans polluted water. Once deployed, the AI device interacts with the environment adjusting the mechanism to filter out unbalanced or toxic levels. The design is ingenious and modeled after the aerodynamic sailfish. Improving water quality will expand around the globe to reuse water and decrease pollution. This technology can be adapted for use in wastewater treatment plants creating safe reuse of treated water. Courage monitors the world's water systems."

"The third aspect of the company is **Wisdom**. To create products that cleverly reverse the effects of pollution by the population. One of our products is a probiotic cleanser. A soap that doesn't pollute rivers it leeches into. It helps clean them organically. The soap in any form contains microorganisms that can remove pollution by feeding on the pollution in the water. Nitrates and ammonia cause a more alkaline pH that causes toxicity to animals and plants. Nitrates bond to the hemoglobin in fish's blood, which prevents the red blood cell from carrying oxygen. The fish suffocate internally. Ammonia will irritate and damage gill tissue, for example. Countries that still have the tradition of washing their clothes at the riverbanks already are piloting this product."

My brilliant prince. His passion and genius were on display. I was so proud of him.

* * *

Zelda and I were inseparable the following weeks after the Gala. Adjusting to a real relationship was more difficult than I imagined. Denial of our love for one another took a toll, and our union still felt forbidden. My role as guardian was to protect her and keep her safe, or alive if I was to be honest with myself. Zelda was not a traditional woman. My expectation of achieving a traditional relationship was unrealistic. The past year my goal had been to win Zelda. The obstacles I had to overcome were overwhelming at times. Now I had to keep Zelda. A fear brewed in me that I wouldn't be enough for her. My first wife abandoned me. I didn't want the pattern to continue.

At first, we ignored everyone and concentrated on each other staying in the Triforce apartment. Cohabitation was heaven with Zelda. We were insatiable sexually. Our intimacy evolved quickly. I couldn't stay away from her long, even with a thriving business to run. James took over in my absence. My team gladly gave me the space I needed.

Theo and Marilyn orbited around our new relationship. They were admirably vested in encouraging Zelda and helping her adjust to life with another person. Her superior mind was at times held hostage by normalcy or routine behaviors. The curse of her high intelligence was blind to societal norms and expectations. She knew they existed but didn't think they applied to her.

As a high-functioning genius savant, Zelda still struggled with meaningful social connections. She focused on a goal, finding other people a distraction. She had extraordinary abilities and feats of mental skill but was not able to cook and reason through difficult emotions. She was a risk taker, rejected routines, and was constantly distracted processing huge amounts of information. Profiling other people took the focus off of herself. When alone with her thoughts, negative emotions were more common.

Zelda was happiest when winning. She needed goals to direct her life and keep restlessness at bay. She didn't mind being different and embraced her eccentricities regardless of the consequences. We were always fearful she would ruminate on emotions she couldn't process effectively, triggering the physical stress response. These internal struggles were the curse of a genius.

Zelda tolerated Theo, James, and me the most. She determined we were equals and, therefore, treated us differently than most others. I tried to foster a female relationship for Zelda with Aubrey.

"What did I forget? Why is my wife here?" James looked around in a panic.

"She and Zelda have plans."

"That sounds like it will cost us a lot of money, bro."

"I hope so. Zelda needs to learn to have fun."

"Fun for Zelda is usually at someone else's expense. Is she going back to the World Series this year? I would like to see her play."

"No. Theo and I are hoping she doesn't mention it. Living here with me has been a big change for her. We are wary that her happiness may be a trigger."

"You think she'll relapse because she's happy?"

"Zelda has to love and forgive herself before her demons are put to rest. I know that hasn't happened yet."

My goal was to incorporate her life into mine and make a plan for the future. Zelda was still not letting me into her hidden places. I could see turmoil reflected in her eyes.

CHAPTER TWENTY-SIX

Vegas Job

Ben was out of town meeting with a group of Japanese investors who wanted to take his company global. The potential was there to be extraordinary. My prince was brilliant.

James was running things with Ben gone, so I decided to visit Rowan. The World Series had just concluded, so the hotel wouldn't be as busy. Time away from NYC would be good for me. My life had changed so much in the last month that I needed time to process and a job.

A huge smile engulfed Rowan's face as he saw me approach. He quickly dismissed his managers to make room for me. Rowan made me feel special. He rose to greet me.

"Zelda, darling. You never warn me when you're coming." He kissed my cheek and gave me a tight hug.

"What would be the fun in that?" I sat across from him as he called to a server.

"Are you hungry?"

"I'm always hungry. You know that." Rowan ordered enough food to feed ten.

"What can I get you to drink?"

"I'll have an iced tea. I don't drink on the job."

"You're here for work. Good. I thought you were here to wipe me out of my hard-earned series money." Rowan was thoughtful for a moment. "We missed seeing you, Zelda."

"I know. I thought about it but didn't want to make it difficult for Luca."

"He got married in the spring." Although the thought was painful, it wasn't unbearable. "He's content."

"I'm glad. Really Rowan. He deserves to have a happy life." I could never lie to Rowan. "I just miss my dark knight. We were kindred spirits."

"He still loves you. It was thoughtful of you not to come." A false grim masked his sadness. "So tell me about this job you have?"

"Well, there's this handsome gentleman who runs a casino inefficiently. He should be making twice as much in profit. Usually, he's good about flushing out fraud or waste. He must be losing his touch."

"Oh, my dear, I would love your help. How did you know?"

"I didn't—a good guess. I just wanted to spend some time with you. Every business should have an audit every so often. My services are expensive, though." I winked.

"How about a 48-carat Harry Winston black diamond necklace? I hear it's worth one million dollars."

"How do you have it?" Tears filled my face. "I thought it was lost. My punishment for…"

"I saw it on the floor when the EMTs extracted Luca from your room. It was covered in blood." Tears filled Rowan's face as well. "That was a hard day."

I placed my hands over his. "I'm sorry, Rowan. Truly. My demons surfaced so quickly and powerfully that I gave in."

"Ben is a good man. He's the right man for you." I smiled, almost believing him.

"So about that necklace."

"You'll get paid when the job is done." The twinkle in his eyes gave me so much.

* * *

On the third day of working with Rowan, I found it odd Ben hadn't checked in. Courting investors was time-consuming, especially in the Asian time zone. Still, something was nagging me.

Instead of an office, Rowan had set me up in the lounge. He commandeered a long table so I could work fluidly within the casino or hotel. We would have a morning meeting and a dinner meeting daily. Rowan kept excellent records, which made my job easier.

As we stood in line at the steak house waiting for our table, Rowan suddenly leaned in to whisper in my ear. "I believe our dinner is about to be canceled. We'll have to reschedule." A huge mischievous smile formed on his face.

"Rowan, what's going on?"

"That's what I want to know." Ben stood over us with his arms crossed over his expansive chest. Drool leaked from my mouth, and Rowan laughed. Ben's expression was still stern. "What are you doing here, Zelda?"

My brain short-circuited by Ben's sudden presence. "I.." I couldn't think why I was here. I just wanted to climb my man like a tree.

"If I may interject. Zelda is doing an audit on the Horseshoe and …" Ben quieted the most revered mob boss in Las Vegas with a stare. "Well, I'll let you two sort this out." He kissed my cheek and hurried away.

"Ben.."

"Zelda.." Ben continued to stare at me as I started back with equanimity. "Fine." He bent down and threw me over his shoulder.

"Ben!" He whacked me on the ass every time I protested. "Ben. What are you doing?"

"You've misbehaved. You need to be punished." My body responded, gearing up for dark pleasure. We passed through the lobby, and I could hear Rowan chuckle. I would be embarrassed if I weren't so turned on.

"Room 1112."

He whacked my ass again. "I know the room. I have a key."

"I'll have to put the security is lacking in my report." I got whacked again upon entering the elevator. An older couple laughed at my current predicament.

"Are you two married?" The woman asked, smiling up at us.

"Um. No. But I feel like I am." Ben whacked my ass again. The couple laughed again.

"My girl here thinks it's fine to leave our home in NYC and come to Vegas on a whim." The couple gasped in mock shock and alarm. "She needs to be punished when she steps out of line."

"That a boy." The man slapped Ben on his shoulder. "Never spare the rod and spoil the wife."

"You one-dimensional fool. That's not what he's doing. *Compliance is easy.* He wants to keep life interesting." His wife corrected him.

"Edith Warton said that."

"Ohhh, a man who knows the classics. Marry him, my dear. And keep misbehaving. I think he likes it." The elevator door opened, and we exited. "Have fun." She called out before the doors closed.

Ben had the right room and a key. He deposited me on the couch while he took off his shirt, belt, and shoes. My drooling returned. "Take off your dress, Zelda."

I stood and obeyed his domineering tone. "Ben, I don't understand why you are so mad. You were …" His lips silenced my rant. He devoured me like a starved man. "Zelda, you are such a bad girl. How can I keep you safe if you flee from me."

My handsome prince was feeling insecure. "You're right, my love. I should be punished."

"Turn around, Zelda." Ben propped my hands on the back of the couch while his long fingers separated my legs. "Why are you being punished, Zelda?"

"I left without telling you." Slap. His palm burned my ass. "I came to Vegas." Slap. "You thought I was coming to see Luca." Slap. Slap. Slap. Slap. *Fuck.* Very insecure. "You thought I would do drugs." Slap. Slap. "You forgot how much I love you."

He bent me back up and turned me around, crashing his lips to mine. My prince wasn't ready to be away from me. Men were so delicate and emotional. "I missed you too." We continued kissing as I pushed him towards the bed. "I need you, Ben."

We stayed united most of the night and into the morning. Dosing periodically as our libido rested. We slept entwined around each other, untangling only when necessary. "I'm hungry," I whispered into his hair as I kissed it.

"Let's go have breakfast. We can come back and have a nap. I'm still your guardian, you know."

* * *

Ben stayed for a few days until he felt secure, leaving me with Rowan to finish the job. He was afraid I'd leave him. Our unconventional courtship implied our commitment to one another. I felt Ben had expectations I wasn't meeting. Relationships were not my forte. Besides Luca, I never allowed a status to develop beyond sex. I tolerated few people.

Rowan was delighted at my audit. We updated his banking systems and employee scheduling. Liquor and food orders were now streamlined to keep appropriate stock in inventory. We set up event revenue in separate accounts to track profitability more accurately. Security was also an issue that needed to be continually updated.

By the end of the week, a 48-carat Harry Winston black diamond necklace was placed around my neck. Tears sprung as the memory of my time with Luca surfaced. I loved Ben. I would also always love

Luca. I missed playing with the devil. A part of my soul was his.

CHAPTER TWENTY-SEVEN

Monsters

Callam Roberts was not a nice man. Theo's theory was correct. His only daughter was used as a pawn to capture the talented Benjamin Walker. After he was secured and tied to the company, she escaped to Colorado, never living with her new husband.

Ben was misled by more than his wife's affections. Callam made it perfectly clear that he would ruin him if he thought about leaving his position. Ben was a made man with money and connections in the financial industry. He would never have had an opportunity without Roberts's ministrations. Or so he was told.

Although Ben and James had a careful plan to extradite him from Roberts' clutches, Ben's loss to his company was great. My little investigating painted a grievous picture of a ruthless and power-hungry man. Ben walked away with only the clothes on his back. Roberts was able to commandeer his bank accounts, apartment, and personal possessions by a legal clause buried way down in his contract. Once Ben served his wife with divorce papers, which she signed gratefully, Ben was a target. With the marriage dissolved, Ben wasn't trusted with any knowledge of the company. Callam couldn't control Ben anymore in his position as CFO. I wished Ben trusted me enough to tell me all this himself.

The man I had been investigating confronted me on the sidewalk outside Theo's office building. Deception, malice, and greed were displayed on his face.

"I see you have been poking around my company, young lady." His bodyguard appeared flush against my back. "What are you looking for?" His face was full of pure malevolence. Finally, a man I was afraid of. His coal-black eyes were reminiscent of an ancient evil reborn. He was the being at the end of my road to perdition. The monster I was waiting for.

"Let's go for a ride. We can talk, and then I can extract compensation for my losses." Strong hands grabbed my arms from behind me to prevent my escape. He knew with my training. I could escape him easily.

"Get in the car, or I'll turn and shoot every person within a 100-yard radius. I don't think your life is worth that much. Right, Zelda?" *Fuck.* I was on their radar for a while. Ben thought he was keeping me safe all this time. Evil was lying in wait.

"Right." I stepped past the men and got into the waiting town car. My fate accepted made the journey sufferable.

"Zelda Alexander. You've cost me more than the few million I spent hiring thugs to extinguish you like the annoying insect you turned out to be. In the end, I'm satisfied it has come to this."

The bossman kept growling nonsense at me while his dickhead accomplice panted at the threat of violence. As we traveled down a long dusty road somewhere on the city's outskirts, zip ties were used to secure my wrists. We stopped, and dickhead pulled me out of the car and led me into a warehouse in a row of identical warehouses.

Inside, an arsenal of weapons was placed on a side table. A couple of chairs were in front of a giant hook suspended from the ceiling by a chain. *Fuck. Fuck.* A quick punch to my face made me see stars and knocked me off balance, tumbling me to the ground. Dickhead pulled me up by my hair, only to slap me down again. A couple of well-placed kicks snapped a few of my ribs instantly. I had no skills against the muscle beating me.

"Not too fast," Bossman commanded his servant as he sat in a chair, ready to watch the show. Dickhead placed my zip ties through the hook and engaged a wheel crank that raised me so I was dangling in the air. Blood was pooling in my mouth, draining from a sinus in my broken nose; spitting it out required access to muscles that were compromised. My only option was to let it drool out of my mouth.

"Phase two, princess." Both men were disturbingly excited and hard and seemed proud of it. I wondered how many people had been subjected to the same fate as me. This event seemed well rehearsed. They knew to keep the pace quick, so I couldn't process anything.

Dickhead began to use a long razor creating little slits, making me bleed. "You like that, don't you, Zelda? My man isn't some handsome mob boss, but you can use your imagination." I was getting pissed my death was being dictated by sadistic assholes. My vision for my death was always so beautiful. Peaceful. I tried to embrace the pain like an old friend, but the monsters had control. Torture was previously missing from my recipe for redemption. I wasn't sure where this would land me, heaven or hell.

I looked at Callum. He was a father. At some point in his life- a lover and a friend. Immoralality turned his soul black. Power and money led to cruelty and deprivation. He was seeking a control that was once lost. All killers do.

My brain unlocked unused training from Quantiaco. To take control, I had to get inside his head. This was the end battle of a war. To be victorious, Link had to use all the weapons and artifacts he had collected throughout the adventure. Timing and skill would finish the monster. But I wasn't Link.

"You realize as the devil you're hard to vanquish but not impossible." The details of the scene formed in my head.

"Oh, and Princess Zelda has the power to vanquish the devil. You're right. I am the devil reigning here on Earth. Those who wrong me pay with their lives." Callum Roberts saw himself as infallible and prideful.

"That's the code of the Mafia. Except they have elegant rules. You're just a thug in a nice suit."

Bossman nodded to Dickhead, and I felt pain. Pain radiating through an impact in my shoulder. Throwing up in this position was too difficult. I panted through the nausea. They stood admiring their work. I avoided playing with the minds of killers. The trail forward was never equitable.

* *. *

"Zelda, you are quite beautiful. A shame you lured Ben away from my Jillian."

"Who will mourn the loss of you from this world?" Talking was harder than breathing.

"Haha, Zelda, are you going to kill me? You're in no position to make threats."

"Threats? That was a question. You're intelligent enough to have thought about the repercussions of your ways. Even psychopaths know the eventual consequences of their actions."

"I'm invincible. As you saw, my company is unable to be breached. The victims will never be found."

"I didn't investigate your company. I investigated you. Beaten by your tyrant father and unloved by your socialite mother, power and success were the only ways to get their attention. Emotionally bankrupt. All your wives cheated on you with people you trusted. Your evil ways are not unfounded."

"Shut up. You know nothing. You're just a whore ruining one man at a time, beginning with your father. The world won't mourn the loss of you."

"You seek the power and control that was taken from you as a child. Blackmail and intimidation are the only ways you know how to interact with others. I'm sorry for the loss of the love from your daughter." Callum's face flickered in sadness. For a moment, I had empathy for this man.

"Quantico taught you to survive torture. That isn't on the traditional curriculum, Zelda. Let's see what more they taught you to endure." Bossman nodded to his servant. Pain followed.

* * *

My face stung, and my breathing labored. Something was lodged in my back that I couldn't identify. The next item on their agenda looked like a TAZER. My skills seemed to be only getting me hurt more. The zip ties had cut so deep into my wrists that blood was streaming down my arms.

This wasn't an elegant way to die. Torture, pain, and anguish. "Phase three, princess."

"How many more phases are there? This is a question, not a complaint."

"I'm surprised we haven't put a bullet in you yet. Your stamina is surprising."

Dickhead shot the TAZER dart into my back and pulled the trigger. *Holy Fuck.* My body gyrated like a fish hanging on a hook. Pain shot down every nerve ending. The cycle lasted five seconds, but it was a long five seconds. My muscles cramped in mid-air as soon as the electro-current stopped.

"We're experimenting on you. We need to be ready when it's Ben's turn." Bossman's face came into view. His smile was not of a man but a deranged beast. "We're going to leave you hanging, rotting in this warehouse. We'll send him pictures and videos until he goes mad. I'll take over his company and burn it to the ground. Hopefully, with all those do-gooders in there. Make a note of that, Brent. Another good idea."

Instead of responding, Dickhead rereleased the TAZER. The pain was excruciating. Bossman was getting off again on my suffering. He was a sick fuck. "How do you think Ben would feel if he knew I fucked you?"

"He would kill you," I whispered through a gravely breath.

"I don't think so, princess. Ben was easy to manipulate. A sweet girl made him feel special, and his balls were mine. My mistake was not making sure he got laid regularly. He was so weak I forgot he was a man." He adjusted himself in the chair but made no move toward me. My breathing was limited to pants. "I'm going to string pretty boy right next to your lifeless body and see how long he'll last. I'll give him a play-by-play of everything I did to you."

Fucking psychopaths. Rage filled my veins as I visualized everything Callum said. The snickering of Dickhead behind me made me see red. My life was not my own anymore. Princess Zelda was going to save Link. Link could fight battle after battle, but he could never defeat Ganon on his own. Zelda had the power to destroy Ganon. Faith.

"Unless necrophilia is your fetish, I need a break." Dickhead deployed the TAZER again as a response. More blood and drool came out of my mouth as I found it impossible to swallow anymore. *Wisdom* was my only weapon left. I have to be smarter than my captors. Think Zelda.

"You'll need condoms. I have syphilis." A bored defeated statement gurgled out of my mouth.

"You do not."

"Of course I do. My brain has already started deteriorating. Can't you see the signs?"

"We'll just fuck you in the ass."

"Transmitted there too."

"Google it."

"She's right, boss."

The two men stared at me, assessing their risk-reward ratio—prideful idiots.

"Go to the store. Get me something to drink too." Dickhead went to leave, "For fuck sake, leave the gun. They'll think you are robbing the store." Dickhead placed his gun on the table. "Lower her a little. My dick can't reach that high."

Dickhead cranked the wheel, loosening the chain that lowered the hook so I barely touched the floor. "Good. Go. I'm fucking hard."

Bossman just stayed in his chair, barking orders.

"Why would you warn me, Zelda? You better not be lying to me."

"Dementia has already set in. I'm sure you are aware."

"Your mother was a nice piece of ass. She saved it for your douchebag of a father. I tried to have her for years. How do you think she would feel knowing I was about to fuck you? This revenge gets sweeter and sweeter." He grinned at me like the true devil.

The fire in my eyes just simmered as he taunted me. I never wanted to live so badly as, at this moment, only to kill another person.

"I need to take a piss." Bossman got up and stepped outside. The darkness in me felt like light. Righteous light. I thought of Luca's rage if he knew my predicament. Rowan's revenge would be long and horrific. Theo and Marilyn. James and Audrey. Joel and Gavin. Beck. I thought of the life my parents would have wanted for me. And my beloved Ben. Just picturing Ben filled me with light, energy, and power.

Kill them, Zelda. My mother's voice rang in my head as clearly as if she was standing next to me.

I pulled down on the zip ties causing them to cut deeper into my skin, allowing my toes to touch the ground. Pushing up with all my might, I cleared the zip ties off the hook. I was still tied but free.

The gun was within reach just as Callum Roberts came back in. "No!" He yelled, but I was faster. Without hesitation, I grabbed the gun, aimed, and pulled the trigger, putting a kill shot into his forehead. He dropped to the ground instantly.

A car door slammed a few moments later. Dickhead was back. I stayed in position, gun at the ready. He came through the door, only having a moment to come to the realization that he was dead. I pulled the trigger, landing another bullet straight through a man's skull.

Condemnation did not come. Regret was absent. Pride seeped in. Princess Zelda won, triumphing over evil. Heinous crimes against me settled my morality. The tires of many cars were approaching fast. Princess Zelda now had to save herself. I wiped my prints off the gun and bent down to Callulm's body. After pressing his fingers onto the trigger and the handle, I tucked the gun next to his left hand.

Back on the hook, I reattached the zip ties and dangled. The TAZER prong was still logged into my back, and so was whatever was poking into my deltoid. My body burned in agony. Tears leaked from my eyes, having to endure the pain. I embraced the light inside me, desiring me to live. Focusing on the light, I sent myself adrift.

* * *

My sleep was disturbed by the beeping monitors. The overhead light was thankfully turned off. "Zelda?" Ben's deep voice settled deep inside me. He was safe.

The scene was reminiscent of the last time I woke in a hospital room. Except this time. I wanted to live. "Ben." My handsome prince was disheveled and exhausted.

"You've been out for days." Tears leaked out of his eyes. He gently kissed the back of my hand.

"Three by the deep purple around your eyes."

"Zelda? How did you endure what they did to you?" His thumb made small circles at the place he just had kissed.

"You had created enough light in me. I could defeat the ancient evil." My hand cupped his handsome face. He was so full of love and anguish.

"Zelda?" Ben knew. I expected nothing less. He was my equal.

"Ben, does anyone know?" Ben shook his head, but his eyes locked with mine.

"The current theory is that there was another person present. You'll be questioned."

"He was going to kill you next. After you saw my lifeless body."

"You should have never …I.."

"You gave me the power. Ben. We did this together. Zelda had the power to destroy Ganon, not Link." Ben stared at me, trying to put all the pieces together. "My mother gave me permission and an order to kill them."

"Your mother told me to save you." Ben was crying in earnest. "Ben, you healed me. I wanted to live. That's how you saved me." His head lay on the back of my hand. I suspect that is the only place I wasn't injured. "Zelda and Link had to work together to beat Ganon. They were a team, each with their own role. Zelda possessed the power in the end."

The detectives assigned to the case interrupted our reunion. "Ms. Alexander, we need to ask you a few questions." I nodded, but Ben threw a fit.

"Are you fucking serious? She just woke from a three-day coma from being tortured and left for dead. You're vultures. Fucking vultures."

"Mr. Walker, we appreciate your concern, but the best information is collected before the brain's natural editing takes over." I nodded at the investigators to continue.

"Ms. Alexander. Who were your abductors?"

"I called them Bossman and Dickhead. We weren't formally introduced. I deducted one was Ben's former boss Callum Roberts."

"Why were you taken?"

"They blamed me for Ben's departure from the family and the business. They wanted Ben to see my lifeless, tortured body dangling next to his when he was eventually tortured and killed."

"How many people were in the warehouse?"

"Just Bossman and Dickhead."

"What did they do to you?"

"Really? Can't you just look at the log of my injuries? I was hanging in space. There was a table of torture devices. You make the deductions."

"Were you sexually assaulted?"

"That was step three or four. I can't remember. Yes, that was their plan. I passed out, so I'm not sure if they did?" I looked at Ben pacing in the back of the room, holding back tears.

"I think I have had enough." I think Ben has had enough.

"How were you rescued, Ms. Alexander?"

"I'm not sure. The last thing I remember was being slightly lowered. I was too high for their dicks to reach. My feet still didn't touch the ground. I gave up."

"How did your assailants die, Ms. Alexander?" Clever questioning.

"I assumed you had them in custody. I didn't know they were dead." I leaned into the pillow. "I'm actually relieved." Tears sprung to my eyes. Confirmation of their death made it real.

"We are sorry for your trauma. We wish you well in your recovery. Please let us know if you can remember anything else." The detective gave his card to Ben.

"Ben." He was dutifully by my side in an instant. "Did you find me?"

"Yes. Well, me, Theo, and an army of policemen."

"Oh, God. Poor you. Poor Theo. Is he okay?" His haunted eyes glazed over. "Ben, I'm sorry you had to see me half-dead again."

The doctor brought a bag of Demerol to drip into my IV. "Zelda, you gave us quite a scare being out for so long. Let me check your wounds; this will let you rest easier." I saw Ben eye the bag, wondering if the painkillers would cause me to relapse. The doctor looked satisfied at my bandages and set the drip. He gave Ben some instructions as I perseverated on a thought in my head.

"Ben, something inside me changed. I don't feel my demons pressing on me anymore."

"Maybe you are still in shock?"

"No, I feel different. And not because I killed two men."

"You forgave yourself. You love yourself enough now to choose life."

"And I love you, Ben."

CHAPTER TWENTY-EIGHT

Foreshadowing

Six years ago

"This wedding is beautiful but a sham. Does everyone not see it?"

"Rose darling, Jillian Roberts and Benjamin Walker are a fine match. What do you see?"

"She hasn't touched him once. This is a grand show of pomp and circumstance. He looks happy enough, but I bet Callum Roberts sent her to secure Ben for his company. He's brilliant, top in his field, and well thought of by all."

"Grayson, don't you think he would be perfect for our Zelda?" Rose mused, looking at the groom.

"Zelda is only twenty. I'm not marrying her off any time soon. Especially to someone who is already taken."

"Ben is so handsome and tall. He has a light in his eyes, similar to Zelda's. The man has a passion simmering just below the surface and enough gallantry to keep it there. He's her equal. Theo don't you agree?"

"Well, I do."

"Thank you, Alice. Women are always superior at observing such things."

"You two are full of nonsense. How is Zelda?"

"Let's check." Grayson took out his phone, activating an App.

"Grayson gave Zelda her 21st birthday present early."

"Black diamond earrings? They are beautiful. What am I missing?" Theo knew his brother well.

"Harry Winston black diamond earrings set in platinum," Grayson explained.

"Grayson found some hot shot new tech inventor. A tracking device in the earrings is hooked up to an app. The device also monitors her vitals."

"That is intrusive. I can't imagine Zelda in favor of this."

"When you have a daughter knowing where she is and that she is well will occupy your thoughts constantly. It's all I think about."

"Zelda has a good head on her shoulders. She would never give you cause for concern."

"Zelda is currently in Quantico, Virginia. She's doing an internship with the FBI in the Behavioral Science Unit. Her vitals are perfect." Grayson showed the group Zelda's data.

"The FBI BSU doesn't have internships? You apply to the academy after your undergraduate is completed."

"Sounds like you looked into this, Uncle Theo."

"I keep tabs on my goddaughter contrary to popular belief. I thought it would be a great next step for her."

"The FBI made an exception for Zelda. She'll graduate early and they are courting her with this opportunity. She'll enter the academy in the fall."

"What does she want to do after graduation?"

"Grayson is first taking her to Vegas for the Poker World Series in June. They have their eye on a bracelet. Now that she will be 21, she can legally enter the tournament."

"What is the significance of this bracelet? Poker is an odd way to bond with your daughter. I never understood your passion for it."

"Zelda loves the challenge. She said it keeps her skills sharp. I get her all to myself for an extended time. What's not to love about that."

* * *

Zelda was slow to heal over the next couple of months. Even though much of her inner turmoil was resolved, she still had trauma from the event. Haunting dreams filled her nights, and painful physical therapy filled her days. She began to prefer the solitude of Land's End to the activity around the TriForce apartment. The three-hour drive back and forth was taking a toll on me. I was torn between nurturing my new company and nurturing Zelda.

"Another piece of Zelda was taken that day. I don't know what to do for her." Theo was as concerned as I was. "The light is not back in her eyes."

"She needs time, Ben."

"I think the opposite. We are leaving her alone too much. Idleness and solitude are not good for her."

"Take her on a vacation. You two have not had proper time together."

"I have a company to run and ..."

"Power and money. Isn't that what you gave up to secure Zelda?"

"This is my passion. I am responsible ..."

"For Zelda. You hired good people with the same vision. Your best friend heads research and development. Your company is second. Your future wife and mother of your children are first."

"Are you trying to tell me you approve of my asking Zelda to marry me?"

"You know her mother foretold your union to Zelda when she met you at your wedding to Jillian. Such an odd thing for her to say at the time. Now I can not imagine you two not together. So yes, you have her mother, and I's blessing to ask Zelda to marry you."

After making several stops, I was en route to Land's End. The three-hour drive was ample time to convince me that my theory was correct. Zelda was trying to live in the light. Maybe that is who she was before her parent's death, but trauma changes a person. She didn't do so well living in the darkness either. Zelda needed balance.

Zelda was a warrior. She took on every situation as a battle. A battle to find a company's weakness. A battle to be the best in poker. A battle to survive a social event. A battle to survive herself. Killing Callum was like the final battle in the Legend games we played. Zelda defeated Ganon. The story was done, and the heroes lived happily ever after- in fantasy.

A warrior cannot ignore their passion. I had been pretending Zelda would be content being taken care of and assimilating into my passion, my life. Zelda was avoiding her darker elements.

Twilight reflecting off the water lit the outside of the house. The inside was dark, but I knew she was there. The key scraped the lock loud enough to announce my arrival. Zelda was in the great room, standing at a floor-length window looking out to the ocean. She knew I was there but made no movement.

"The endlessly changing moods of the misty Atlantic." She whispered Edith Wharton's quote about Land's End. My Zelda was dipping into madness. The last of the sun's rays bathed her body in light as if causing her mania.

"You've been a bad girl, Zelda," I stated in my most menacing voice. "You need to be punished." Her face turned toward me. A fire lit in her eyes. She focused on the leather collar I was flipping between my hands, and her eyes went dark. My warrior needed to feel all parts of her soul.

* * *

After a full night of dominance and submission, my Zelda was satiated. The darkness she was oppressing surfaced, sparking a carnal wildfire in her. All that desire focused on me was the most erotic, intense experience of my life. The plaster covering one-hundred-year-old oak planks had the impression of a headboard forever indented in the wall. The destruction of my room was little consequence as the beautiful love of my life rested peacefully.

Zelda was full of love and passion. Her zest for life was untoward and broke norms, but that was what enamored me from the beginning. My beautiful girl was a rare gift that had to be nurtured and tended to like the delicate gardens that surrounded Land's End.

My exhaustion was ignored, and I rose to set the stage in the morning sun. Zelda wouldn't sleep long if I were not by her side. Pride flooded through me at the thought—my Zelda.

As if on cue, she staggered out on the patio dressed in only a thin silk robe. She looked like she had been fucked hard all night long. The bite marks on her neck were darkening in the light of the sun. Light wrist and collar burns made her look dangerous. I was already hard again.

"Ben?"

"Come here, Zelda." Her eyebrows rose in defiance. Her warrior tamed, obedience was not an option."Please, Zelda." I gestured to one of the patio chairs.

The morning light wrapped around her setting her aglow like the goddess she was. Kneeling in front of her …. "My beautiful, brilliant Princess Zelda, I've been enamored since before we met. Your courage, strength, and nature bring out the best in me. I love your darkness equally as I love your light. You're the most important thing in the world to me, and I'll endeavor to be worthy of you… will you marry me?"

Zelda stayed alarmingly quiet as I showed her the four-carat emerald-cut black diamond Harry Winston engagement ring set in platinum. I took her hand and slipped the ring on her finger. She stared at the ring and then at me. I was unsure if shock or hesitation was flooding her thoughts.

"Zelda?" I kissed her hand, trying to bring her back to me.

"Ben, how can you love me so? I'm broken, unworthy of you. This doesn't make sense to me."

"Zelda, I will follow you into hell and bring you back into the light every time. I will feed your darker desires. I will champion your battles and your dreams. We were meant for each other. You know it in your heart and soul. We belong together, forever." She stroked the large black diamond of the ring, listening to my declaration. Her eyes welled with tears as love filled her face.

"Yes, Ben. I will marry you." My mouth crashed to hers, igniting our desire once again. This woman was making me insatiable. Her legs wrapped around my waist, and I pulled her onto the grass. I couldn't get inside her again fast enough. We fucked like we were starved for each other. The climax tore through our bodies as a violent possession. We stayed united, slowly making love in the warm sun on the grass of the beloved Land's End.

CHAPTER TWENTY-NINE

Epilogue

After proposing, I created a space to house Zelda's business. Her services were in demand, and I liked she had a place dedicated to work near me. On our first attempt, my office was too close to hers. Now that we were committed, all the feelings and desires we had held back were unleashed. We were constantly drawn to one another, undeterred by obligations or workplace norms. James one day moved her to a different floor. Zelda agreed where I pitched a fit. James threatened to move her across the river next.

Zelda would embrace the light during the day and play in the darkness at night. We evolved to a place where darkness didn't have to be destructive. The pain she desired was slowly replaced with playfulness. Limits were still pushed as her mind and body were satisfied. She gave me the deep love and commitment I had always yearned for. My Zelda was extraordinary and a privilege to love. She still overwhelmed me most of the time, keeping life exciting.

Theo and Marilyn took us out one evening to celebrate our engagement. They rented one of the small back rooms of Zelda's favorite seafood restaurant in Greenwich Village. We ate heartily, ordering several appetizers and entrees to share. I loved Zelda's appetite. It was a sign to me that she was healthy. Marilyn was pulsating with ideas for the event. Zelda gladly gave her control with a few conditions. Theo stayed quiet, keeping his eyes on Zelda throughout dinner.

"Zelda, darling." Theo finally spoke. "Marilyn and I have a wedding present for you and Ben." He nodded to Marilyn to give us the news, but she declined and held his hand instead.

"Marilyn and I would like you to gift you Land's End. The house is an important part of your story. You'll continue to make incredible memories in a place you love so much." Tears streamed down Zelda's face. She instantly climbed onto Theo's lap. He embraced her as if consoling a child. Some things would never change. Marilyn produced a box with a beautiful red velvet ribbon handing it to Zelda.

"Here, darling. These have been in my possession and are long overdue to belong with you." In the box were framed photographs of the Alexanders. Several photos of Grayson and Rose were taken during their marriage. Pictures from Zelda's childhood and family photos were placed in an album.

The tears continued as Theo and Zelda flipped through the album together. "How did you get these? I thought they were lost."

"That's a story for another time. It's safe to say I felt the strength of my best friend, Rose. I knew she would want you to have them. And the books." Tears leaked from her eyes as well. I moved over to console her and heard a faint growl radiate from Zelda. My Zelda. How juvenal that her growling filled me with pride.

"Thank you, Marilyn. I'll cherish them and Land's End." She finally looked at me. The sentiment was overwhelming her. "We both will." She left Theo's side and cuddled with me. The enormity of the events this year hit me as I wrapped my arms around her.

I had to forgo the overwhelming amount of guilt I had from Zelda's involvement with Callum. Her mental and physical rehabilitation took precedence. Although she claimed that her training at the academy prepared her for the event, Zelda was still human and went through a terrible ordeal. No amount of operational skills or gun training can prepare you to take two lives. I knew she killed to save me. She lived to make sure I did as well.

In saving me, Zelda saved herself. Together we were whole again. Theo and Marilyn said their goodbyes. The waitstaff cleared the table. Zelda and I stayed entwined the rest of the night.

* * *

Since Zelda tolerated few people, a wedding at Land's End was perfect. Our future summer home, where we met and fell in love, made the journey come full circle. Our haven, protected by the ghost of Edith Wharton, made our love bloom. Trials tested our continence. The devil tested our mortality. Our hearts and souls were eventually united.

James and Aubrey were our attendants while Theo gave her away. Marilyn was the consummate hostess making sure everything was special. Joel and Rowan were the only other guests allowed.

The bride wore an exquisite short off-white silk and antique lace dress. The dress hugged her figure showing off her curves and black diamond necklace. The diamond trifecta made her luminous. The three most important men in her life adorned a claim on her body. Different aspects of love and devotion manifested in each piece. The black diamond earrings were given to her by her father and entrusted to Theo. Security and custody were procured at all times. *Wisdom.* The necklace was secured for her by Luca. His love and passion for her can not be denied. *Power.* The black diamond engagement ring secured our devotion and united our hearts. *Courage.* The coincidence of the triforce elements couldn't be reasoned away.

Green eyes danced in anticipation of the day. Red velvet lips enhanced porcelain skin. Zelda's long auburn hair snaked down her torso in its thick signature waves. The moment we stood together, the whole world fell away. The pinnacle of my life events was set in this garden. The sentiment was overwhelming.

Marilyn's gardener had created a trellis adorned with climbing white roses. We spoke our vows in the garden while the wind took them out to sea. My bride was enchanting.

Two years of torment and hardship were required to get to this point. I would forever follow Zelda into hell to bring her back to the light. She lived in my soul. She made me a better person, and I felt whole and complete.

Vintage Dom Perignon was used to celebrate. Congratulations were said by all. Everyone was beaming at Zelda, overcome by her beauty and their devotion by those who loved her.

The joyous occasion was suddenly paralyzing. My body was drawn to her, vibrating at her nearness. I needed to claim this woman. Zelda read my thoughts instantly.

The light in her eyes turned to fire as our gaze connected across the room. She moved from the room, and I followed. I would follow her anywhere. She wound her way upstairs to a bathroom towards the back of the house. "We invited too many people today," Zelda whispered as her tongue licked my lips. "I need my husband inside me." Husband. Zelda was mine. Husband and wife. Forever.

I took her from behind as we watched our lovemaking in the mirror. Our passion burned in the reflection. We were the stars of an epic love story. Zelda and I, together forever.

* * *

Marriage to Ben was a dream come true. His devotion to me this past year was astounding. He loved me in darkness and light. My prince. My savior. My husband. He made me want to be a better woman. Worthy of his love and dedication.

My mother and father lived inside me again. They helped me defeat the devil and save my one true love. My demons were defeated but not completely absent. I don't think I could ever let them go. They were now a part of me—a part of my journey. Complete redemption wasn't possible. Faith, love, and hope were hard to find in me. Alone made me weak. Ben made me strong.

My mask would always be firmly in place, protecting my mind from intrusion from the outside world. My norms were defined by me. Breachable only by Ben, my biased blind spot was hidden. Profiling others was more comfortable than recognizing my own flaws—one of the many curses of mind.

Everyone always underestimated me, never truly seeing all my abilities, including my parents. I was trained at Quantico, in the behavioral unit, at the academy, and in special forces. I discovered the tracking device shortly after my father gave me my birthday present. He was transparent, and the pattern was easily detected. The secret kept me safe, and my father kept me safe. I was the black diamond—brilliant but dark. Deep down, maybe I always wanted to be found.

Note from Margaret Savoy:

Thank you for reading the story of Zelda and Ben.
I hope you enjoyed it as much as I did researching and
writing it.
Please consider leaving a short review on Amazon or
your favorite book site.

If you or someone you love needs assistance with
issues described in the book,
please consider the following resources.

Substance Abuse and Mental Health Services
Administration
National Helpline: 1 (800) 662-HELP (4357)
(TDD) for the hearing impaired: 1 (800) 487-4889

Love gives hope to your darkest days. Margaret Savoy lives in New England, where she teaches forensic science. Reading romance became a way of self-preservation, and she now creates stories to balance the study of the worst of humanity with that of the best. A common trope in all of her writings is the quirky woman who becomes her own empowered heroine. Hard rock and metal music influence most of the scenes where the characters come from dreams. Three amazing kids, and one grumpy dog, fill her days while creating stories fills the nights.

www.ingramcontent.com/pod-product-compliance
Lightning Source LLC
Chambersburg PA
CBHW060326260626
47160CB00007B/2689